WITHDRAWN

Sicilian Tragedee

Farrar, Straus and Giroux
NEW YORK

Sicilian Tragedee

Ottavio Cappellani

TRANSLATED FROM THE ITALIAN BY FREDERIKA RANDALL

FARRAR, STRAUS AND GIROUX
18 West 18th Street, New York 10011

Library of Congress Cataloging-in-Publication Data
Cappellani, Ottavio, 1969–
    [Sicilian tragedi. English]
    Sicilian tragedee : a novel / Ottavio Cappellani ; translated from the Italian
by Frederika Randall.
        p.   cm.
    ISBN-13: 978-0-374-53104-1 (hardcover : alk. paper)
    ISBN-10: 0-374-53104-8 (hardcover : alk. paper)
    1. Sicily (Italy)—Fiction.   I. Randall, Frederika.   II. Title.

PQ4903.A55S53513 2008
853'.92—dc22

                                                                    2008009124

Designed by Gretchen Achilles

www.fsgbooks.com

1   3   5   7   9   10   8   6   4   2

Contents

CONTENTS

ACT TWO

Celebrity as Will and Idea

CONTENTS

ACT THREE
The End of Tragedy

EPILOGUE

PROLOGUE

Two Months Later

Two months later.

"Fifteen euros?"

"Twenty."

"Deal, twenty."

The two shake hands.

"Hey, wait," says one, "only if it happens when he grabs his dick."

"Right, okay . . . right when he grabs his dick . . . Romeo goes for his crotch and . . . pow!"

"Perfect."

A third party is listening in on the conversation. The two young men must be lawyers, only lawyers would be dressed like that, like TV presenters. It seems incredible that someone could be betting on what's happening, but they are. Isn't there always something strange about the interval between the acts, whether it's at a play or an opera, isn't there always a distance, a gap, between what's happening on the stage and in the foyer? Can it be that these people are really improved by going to the theater? What's the problem? *Is* there a problem?

These thoughts are interrupted by the second bell. The performance is about to resume.

Avvocato Coco, urban beautification consultant for the city of Frigentini, suddenly feels faint and sinks down onto the red carpet that adorns the stairs.

This is Noto, capital of the Sicilian Baroque, inside the Teatro Vittorio Emanuele II, a nineteenth century jewel, a precise, smaller-scale replica of the majestic Teatro Massimo Bellini in Catania. *Jewel* and *majestic*: there you have two terms that *La Voce della Sicilia*, the daily newspaper of eastern Sicily, is especially partial to.

The police hustle over in tight formation, hands on their guns. Several arrogant-looking youths in designer tuxes with pointy, shiny black shoes also hurry to Coco's side, with reassuring words to the police. "It's okay, it's nothing. We're friends, isn't that right, Avvocato?"

Coco, flat on his back, nods yes.

The young tuxes help him up and show him to the men's room under the wary gaze of the police. It had been a false alarm but that didn't mean the state of emergency was over.

"Move along, move along, everything's under control."

After a few minutes, Coco, very pale, comes out of the men's. "Nothing, fine," he says to the police. "I feel much better . . . much better."

In the pit and in the boxes, the usual cheerful chatter has been replaced by a low hum, broken now and then by slightly hysterical laughter.

Avvocato Coco, paler than ever, takes his seat in the rows reserved for the local notables: mayors, commissioners, consultants, all of them nervous and tense, glancing back at their families lodged in the seats behind. Some bite their fingernails, some lie back in the red velvet seats as if awaiting takeoff on a charter flight of some Balkan airline. This is Sicily, and no matter how ready the police are, if something is supposed to happen it is very likely that it will.

The lights go down.

The chorus comes on, peering out curiously into the dimness of the pit. They begin chanting, without much conviction; it's obvious their minds are elsewhere:

CHORUS Now old desire doth in his deathbed lie,
    And young affection gapes to be his heir.

The theater is totally silent.

Rarely has Shakespeare enjoyed such concentration.

Then someone in the audience begins to recite the text in a low voice, as if he knew it by memory or was trying to read it in the dark.

"Where are we now?" the voice says, not so low now.

"Shhh . . ."

Everyone wants to pay the closest attention at the point where the tragedy will reach its climax: Act Two, Scene Four. Whatever the author's intentions, it has become, as some of the ladies wearing their best jewelry would say, the *high point* of the evening.

BENVOLIO Here comes Romeo, here comes Romeo.

The audience quivers.

Mercutio, played by Cosimo Cosentino, fifty-eight years old, looks around.

Both he and Romeo, played by sixty-year-old Jano Caporeale, are genuine stage animals. A lifetime spent pounding the boards of the dialect theaters, up against real audiences, not intellectuals.

Nobody's laughing tonight at their skimpy costumes, at their tights.

Both pause now here to emphasize what everyone is asking him- or herself: Will it happen again tonight?

MERCUTIO (*Looking toward the public, half squatting, with a screwing motion thrusts up his arm and then follows through with his whole body, rising off the stage in a little hop*) Nay, I am the very *pink* of courtesy.

ROMEO (*Covering his crotch with both hands, then spreading them out slowly as if something were swelling in his undershorts*)

Pink in the sense of something that flowers? That explodes with the joy of springtime? Or pink like something that pricks? That swells and stands up? Stands up like a turret? Pointed like a mountaintop? (*He joins the five fingers of his right hand and thrusts it upward.*) Or are you not speaking of an uphill struggle through nettlesome bushes?

Pause.

Cosentino-Mercutio has to admit, not without some annoyance, that Caporeale-Romeo is in superb form tonight.

A voice in the audience whispers, "Holy shit, he's over the top. In the English text here, it just says 'pink for flower.' "

"Shhh . . ."

MERCUTIO (*Bouncing on his knees while he moves his arm back and forward like a pendulum, a pendulum that culminates in a finger pointing toward Romeo*)

Thou hast most kindly hit it.

ROMEO (*Brief pause while he seems, though no one can be sure, to wink at the audience, then he moves his arms in a circle and positions his hands once again on his crotch, which he clutches meaningfully*)

You want to hear my reply? It's this great, big, pointed, sweet-smelling, flowering explosion of my great, big, hotheaded, crazy dick!

It is in that moment that Chartered Accountant Intelisano begins to fly.

At first, and from that point of view (Intelisano's, that is), it is the stage which appears to descend below the horizon line of his bifocals. Then, for about a tenth of a second, he feels his head is spinning. Finally, objective reason gives no further room for doubt: Intelisano has gone into orbit.

There is a boom like a giant rocket taking off, the same noise you can hear during the feast of St. Agatha in Catania, if you push through the crowd and get right up near where they're setting off the fireworks.

And from behind the scenes, the unmistakable voice of Rosanna Lambertini (that night as in every preceding hot-blooded night the body and soul of Juliet), with an angry, almost offended howl, pronounces the following words, "Fuck, no—not again!" while Intelisano takes flight toward the richly decorated ceiling with its plaster angels and friezes and frescoes of freshly minted gold.

After a few minutes the lights come up on the confusion.

The next day the *Mirror* of London will carry a little item.

Under a photo of an ancient map of Sicily kept in the Vatican Museum, the one with the island upside down as if seen directly by the eye of God, the headline is unequivocal:

A SICILIAN TRAGEDY

The Birth of Comedy

CHAPTER ONE

Two Months Earlier

Two months earlier.

An explosion of loud yellow and red.

Pinwheels and whirligigs.

The scene widens between flashes of intarsia. A man is lying flat on his back in a piazza: *a crime in a public place*, as befits the seriousness of the offense.

A red stain is spreading over his white shirt.

Another man, dressed like the first (white shirt, black trousers, white stockings up to the knee with red pom-poms, red sash knotted around the waist, black beret), holds up an enormous knife in victory.

Eyes widening in a furious grin.

A woman runs from the piazza, clad head to foot in black, a shawl over her hair, a hand on her breast. You can tell she's running by her skirt, the way her speed lifts it up and makes it stick to her legs.

The woman is screaming.

Her hair's a mess.

Her features are blurry but they give force to her expression, they spell out passion and murder just as we imagine them to be.

Jano Caporeale and Cosimo Cosentino, two pillars of the Catania dialect theater, are looking, perplexed, at the scene. It's painted, as tradition would have it, on the side of a Sicilian cart. The death of *cumpare* Turiddu in *Cavalleria rusticana*.

Both are wearing heavy wool jackets (Caporeale's in brown, Cosentino's in a blue and orange check) and threadbare gray flannel trousers. They wear no neckties and under their shirt collars the raveled edges of flesh-colored underwear can be seen.

Caporeale straightens his jacket with one clumsy hand, then looks around.

The waiters, in worn-out white cotton jackets, black trousers shiny with age, and well-scuffed shoes, are hastening from one room to another of Palazzo Biscari, getting the tables ready for lunch. Chairs squealing as they are pushed over the floor, the clink of heels, flatware, and glasses echoes in the reception room empty of all decor. Memories of old-fashioned grandeur just good enough for catered events these days.

Caporeale looks at Cosentino.

Cosentino looks at Caporeale.

"What time is it?" asks Caporeale.

Cosentino doesn't move a muscle. He continues to allow Caporeale to stare at him. "Why? You don't have a watch?"

Caporeale raises his eyebrows. "If I ask you what time it is, it means I don't have one."

"At the pawnshop?"

"I asked you what time it is."

Cosentino turns to look at the Sicilian cart once again. "I hocked mine too."

Caporeale nods, also turning to stare at the cart.

"I'd say it's past noon," says Cosentino.

"And at past noon the only thing here that's ready to eat is this fucking fruit painted on the cart?"

"What, you think they're all retirees like us who eat at the stroke of noon? Me, seeing as how they invited us for lunch, I even ate a light meal last night."

"Light, huh?"

"Light."

Outside on the sidewalk, a North African selling pirate CDs and DVDs pushes the play button on a huge radio, out of which comes "No Roots" by Faithless.

This is the Civita quarter of Catania, in Via Archi della Marina. Traffic here flows slowly, dammed up between the arches of volcanic rock in the shape of an ancient aqueduct over which the train tracks pass, and Palazzo Biscari.

Until the end of the nineteenth century, the arches nuzzled up against the sea, Via Archi della Marina didn't exist and Palazzo Biscari didn't open onto a street draped with sidewalk salesmen and upholsterers' workshops, but directly onto the water. Beside the main door there were still iron rings once used to tie up the boats.

The arches of the marina are the principal subject, à la Magritte, of the oil paintings that adorn the many *trattorie* serving fish in the quarter. What you usually notice in these paintings is a certain disproportion of dimension: Mt. Etna in the background is always too big or too small compared with the mullet laid out on the fishmongers' slabs.

Later, tons of landfill were thrown into the sea to build the port, and the arches were swallowed up by the city. Now, under the vaults, tiny parking lots, improvised and illegal, alternate with the carcasses of automobiles that have been stolen and dismantled, garbage bins, street peoples' homes of cardboard and plastic, fruit and vegetable stands, flower-sellers, vendors of Chinese and African merchandise, a kiosk selling beer and seltzer with lemon and salt.

Across the way, on the other side of the street and the noonday traffic, is the Baroque Palazzo Biscari, and behind that, the Duomo of Catania.

It's a beautiful day and Etna looms over the landscape.

Mister Alfio Turrisi, at the wheel of his Aston Martin—wheel on the right—is stuck in traffic. He looks in the mirror to see if his Brylcreem is holding everything in place (hair that was once thin, curly, and white, but which now, thanks to the admirable services of a barber in Ognina, is straight and black). Mister Turrisi would have liked to wear it thick and combed back, but the barber (who was totally bald) told him he had yet to master miracles, and so he had to content himself with a style that swept rightward from a left parting, covering the necessary.

He wets the tip of his little finger, with its diminutive signet ring, and smooths the tips of his pencil mustache and his eyebrows, watching two punk kids as they cut in front of him carrying a swordfish a couple of yards long.

The crushed ice man (ice for the crates of fresh fish at the fishmonger's next to Porta Uzeda, where Via Etnea, Catania's main street, begins) is sitting thoughtfully on a straw-backed chair smoking a cigarette while he watches a block of ice melt in the July sun.

Turrisi turns the air-conditioning up to the max: he hates sweating but it's a habit he's unable to break. One time he had problems with the hair dye and it began to drip down his forehead. He looks at his watch. Turrisi has a lot of business in England and he likes to be on time.

On the sidewalk, organized by size from the smallest, about four inches high, to the largest, about five feet, stands a row of wooden elephants. They all have their trunks pointing to the sky. Turrisi cranes his neck to see the elephants better.

Behind him, someone honks.

Turrisi, annoyed, shifts into first.

All around him is the midday crowd, old guys who are wending their way home from a morning spent on a park bench in the sun at Villa Pacini, getting a good look at the asses of the female students waiting for the bus in front of the Bar Etoile.

Turrisi notes that the old folks and the young girls are dressed identically. In London they call it *vintage*.

"Sicily certainly is full of whores," says Caporeale, to pass the time while they wait for lunch.

"Huh?"

Caporeale, his hands joined behind his back, points with his chin toward the wooden cart. "Lola, shit, what a slut. She gets *cumpare* Turiddu killed." Caporeale nods to himself. "And now that I think of it, his wife is a great big bitch too, spying on *cumpare* Alfio."

"Me, I really like the carts where they show the puppet theater, with the plume of colored feathers on the helmet that makes a fashion statement with the plume of feathers that they put on the horse's head."

Caporeale looks at him. "What do they do?"

"Make a fashion statement," says Cosentino, putting a hand up over his forehead like a plume of feathers and reciting, "Sing to me, O Goddess, of Achilles son of Peleus."

"What the fuck does the goddess have to do with it?"

"It's a theater lunch, isn't it? There are always goddesses."

It's a commemorative lunch in honor of the 350th anniversary of the birth of Francesco Procopio dei Coltelli. Born in Sicily, founder, in 1686, of the famous Café Procope in Paris, across the street from which the Comédie Française was installed. Obviously no one knew when the fuck Francesco Procopio dei Coltelli was born, and nobody knew where he was born either—some said Palermo, some said Messina, some said Acicastello in the province of Catania. But in order that the commemorative lunch, the pet project of the commissioner for culture of the Sicilian regional government (a regional government proudly autonomous from the rest of Italy), not end in strife, the commissioners for culture of all the Sicilian provinces came to an agreement to mutually forgo any parochial claims to his birthplace, and so on the invitation it was just written *Sicilian*. The celebration had also had the official blessing of the national minister of culture, thanks to a deputy minister from the nearby town of Avola, who, when he learned that French theater had been invented by an Italian, was emboldened to give national visibility to the event, commenting, "Let the French try to bust our balls with their wine."

"Apropos of goddesses," said Caporeale, "that queen of bitches Lambertini, who's usually the first one to arrive because God knows she doesn't want to miss any compliments, isn't even here yet."

Rosanna Lambertini had put on her Giorgio Armani suit that curved around her ass like a mandolin, and with that mandolin she was playing a serenade to Via Etnea that would have stopped all the traffic if the street weren't pedestrians only at this hour. She was wearing high heels too, obviously, which on the basalt pavement were keeping up a percussion beat with her ass like a mandolin, while the whistles of the boys completed the music—violas, violins, and contrabassoons, depending on age and style of whistling.

Every so often she would stop and look in the windows of the shops, but the show, the real show, was when she leaned over to check the price tags, and the construction workers up on the scaffolding restoring the Baroque facades of the palazzi would fake passing out and plunging to the pavement.

With her Farrah Fawcett blond hair and those Dolce & Gabbana shades she looked like Paris Hilton's mother, God bless the whole family.

CHAPTER TWO

The Director
Tino Cagnotto Is
Descending a Plexiglas
and Neon Staircase

The director Tino Cagnotto is descending a Plexiglas and neon staircase. Left, right, left, right, without missing a beat.

In front of him the pop, pop, pop of photographers' flashes.

He can't see the crowd, blinded as he is by the lights, but he knows they are there, all there for him.

He feels relaxed and easy: it's the first time he has worn an evening dress that shows off his legs. He had even argued with his tailor in the dressing room, where instead of his usual tuxedo he had found this sequined number and a pair of very high heels.

"But I didn't even get a wax job," Cagnotto had shouted in the dressing room.

"Sure you did, last night," the tailor had replied.

"Last night?" Cagnotto couldn't remember.

What had he done last night?

It seems to be true, he has had a body wax, and in fact he feels extremely elegant inside the dress as he descends toward an embrace with his fans.

He spreads his arms to express his genuine amazement, his all-embracing love, his infinite thanks, and discovers he is wearing a pair of gloves above the elbows, and on top of the gloves all kinds of rings and bracelets that sparkle under the artificial light.

Where had he gotten the jewelry?

When had he put it on?

His thoughts grow confused; he begins to feel agitated. Was it really a good idea to let himself be convinced to dress up like this? What if somebody is fucking him around? He hears a laugh. Is that joyous laughter or is it contempt? Doubt makes him wobble. Right left right right . . .

The bodice is beginning to bother him; he looks down at his cleavage and sees that his chest hairs are tangled up in the sequins, so that every step is agony. Chest hairs? He has never been very hairy. Just the necessary . . .

Gasping for breath, he realizes only now that the dress is too tight.

A terrible thought assails him.

He lowers his eyes again, aiming below the neckline, below the gut. Oh, God.

His stomach is huge.

Then finally he gets his eye on it. Oh, horrible. It's there, monstrously in evidence. No way you could not notice what is politely called his *member*, glistening with spangles.

The bull's-eye toward which all the lights and flashbulbs are aiming.

The more he moves, the more the dress seems to shrink. It seems to be climbing up his legs. Cagnotto can't remember what kind of stockings he has on, body hose or a garter belt?

The dress is riding up his thighs, the sequins are scratching his skin. He feels something around his head, pressing on his brow. Oh, God, is he also wearing a wig?

Left right left . . . Cagnotto falls.

He shrieks.

Drenched in sweat, he wakes up in his bed, the black silk sheet twisted around his arms and legs, his head pressed under a sweaty pillow, the chain with the huge pendant on it, which obviously he had not taken off last night, clawing into his chest.

Still gasping, Cagnotto nevertheless feels better.

It was only a dream, a horrible nightmare. Rita Hayworth isn't his ideal of elegance. That tailor, who was that? And those disgusting gloves. He's an avant-garde director, he would never dress like that on Oscar night. And anyway, what do the Oscars have to do with it? He's a theater director.

Shaking off the sheet, he stretches out noisily. His body is beginning to hum, his mind is taking charge of his limbs, he feels a pleasurable frisson that makes him think of waking up on a Sunday morning, when there's no school. He ought to take a nice bath, a nice, relaxing, and invigorating bath. *Okay.* This new-generation antidepressant is starting to take effect—and what an effect. Damn, these new-generation antidepressants are magnificent.

With a beatific smile on his face he turns to look at the alarm clock. Noon. It's *great* to wake up at noon after a full night of deep sleep, nightmares apart. Damn that satin sheet. Silk in bed can be hazardous to your health. Certainly, he thinks, smiling, all that alcohol he'd drunk last night didn't hurt. The doctor had said not to mix alcohol and antidepressants. He wouldn't do it again. With this antidepressant he wouldn't need alcohol. And he'd lose weight too. That's what he would do today, sign up at the gym, at the pool. Get moving . . .

Cagnotto stretches once again, full of new energy.

Then it seems to him that something doesn't quite square in the perfect architecture of the new day that is beginning. It must be the antidepressant that hasn't yet taken hold. What had the doctor said? Three weeks before it kicks in, and there were still a few days to go. Some anxiety on waking was normal. And no alcohol, no alcohol, as we said . . . He could use a coffee, a magnificent coffee.

A smile creeps over Cagnotto's face.

He remembers that he has just—thanks to a TV sales pitch— bought the ultimate in automatic machines for espresso, cappuccino, and all that. Cagnotto buys a lot of stuff from TV salesmen. The doctor said it was due to the depression; he was a compulsive shopper. Cagnotto still buys stuff from TV salesmen and now the doctor says it could be an effect of the antidepressant. Cagnotto asked him what the difference was. The doctor said that now he was only buying things he really needed.

It's true!

The espresso machine is shining on the countertop of the kitchen that is his pride and joy. He thinks of the coffeepots you used once upon a time, the ones you had to screw together. Certainly technological progress is amazing. Art . . . shouldn't we also treat technology as an art? The creation of a machine to make coffee, wasn't that also art? He might write something about coffee . . . about coffee . . .

Now Cagnotto remembers the lunch to celebrate Café Procope.

He looks at the clock.

It would be foolish to scream, although that is what he wants to do. He limits himself to shaking and moaning.

As reality dawns on him he goes for the closet like a fury, hoping there will be something clean and pressed.

Sad, solitary, and abandoned, a blue suit hangs, depressed, from a hanger. Cagnotto stares at it with pity, for himself and for the suit. The only reason that the suit has been spared his busy social life is that Cagnotto bought it last year, when he was firmly determined to lose weight. In the past year, however, he has done nothing but eat.

Loneliness was to blame, that and the absence of love, the only true incentive for the artist and the theater.

The suit makes him look grossly fat, even if it is by Ferré. But for an occasion like the Café Procope lunch you need to look as if you already have money if you want to ask for more. It's better to wear an expensive suit that makes you look overweight than another expensive suit that's wrinkled, has no creases in the trousers, probably has spots in inexplicable places—and can only signify that you don't have a large wardrobe.

He looks at the clock again and sees that there is no time even to take a shower.

Sniffing his armpits, he lunges toward the bureau, where there's a huge bottle of 4711 cologne. He pours it on liberally, smells his armpits again, looks at himself in the mirror, satisfied, smiles . . . frowns, and now, yes, begins to scream.

CHAPTER THREE

Like the Ballroom Scene in *The Leopard*, but More Now

"Like the ballroom scene in *The Leopard*, but more *now*." The commissioner for culture of the Sicilian regional assembly, Murabito, had been categorical. The celebrations for Francesco Procopio dei Coltelli must be memorable. These continual accusations that the Sicilian region didn't promote culture were intolerable. The region promoted culture, absolutely.

The ancestors on the walls are watching the guests arrive but there is none of that distance, that difference, that distinguished the Prince from plebeian Don Calogero Sedàra in *The Leopard*. Here the ancestors look like the guests, and vice versa.

"There you go, I knew they would come dressed like hacks," hisses Murabito to his little tribe of assistants as he glares at Caporeale and Cosentino without acknowledging their presence. "I told you we should have specified 'black tie,' I told you."

"But Commissioner, we couldn't write 'black tie' on a brunch invitation," says an assistant who is following him around.

"Well, we should have written 'tie,' then . . ."

"Um . . ."

"How do you do, Principessa?" Commissioner Murabito bends to kiss the hand of the Principessa Cerasuolo while he watches the door out of the corner of his eye.

"Do forgive me, please come in. Thank you for honoring us with your presence." Murabito grabs his assistant by the arm, drags him into a corner under the portrait of the wife of a prince, a baron, or whatever, and shouts at him, "What the hell is 'brunch' supposed to imply? You invited them to come at dawn? You had people arriving here at sunrise when the palazzo was all shut up?"

"No, Commissioner, 'brunch' means lunch."

The commissioner stares, irritated, at the portrait of the noble-woman, frowning with disgust. The prince or the baron or whoever he was had definitely married a certifiably ugly woman.

"Oh, really, and what the hell does 'lunch' mean, afternoon tea?"

"No, Commissioner, on the invitation we specified 'buffet at twelve-thirty' so it would be clear to everyone."

The commissioner glares at his assistant. "Peasant," he says. He glances at the portrait of the aristocrat who was married to the hag and discovers he was even more hideous than his wife.

The crowds that are filling the reception rooms take the edge off the commissioner's anxiety, for there are ladies in long dresses, ladies who take care of themselves, you can see they've been to the hairdresser this morning. More than just "see," Caporeale is study-ing, with great interest, the arrival of some big shots.

"What's so fascinating?" Cosentino asks him.

"Look at that. One year hair is long, the next year it's short. And this year it's *big*."

Big hair is what Tino Cagnotto has, whatever hair he has left is stick-ing straight up as he sits immobile in traffic at the wheel of his BMW

X5 SUV. It seems he has remembered everything except to comb his hair.

Moving just his eyes, he looks to the left, to the right, and down.

With his left hand he drums his fingers on the wheel, while with his right it's unclear what he's up to.

He moves his eyes again—right, left—and when it's clear no one is looking he grabs a greasepaint stick and with lightning speed swipes it over his face, his neck, and his chest.

Under his good blue suit he's wearing a bright-colored shirt unbuttoned partway down his chest.

Tilting the rearview mirror, he takes a quick look and sees he has forgotten about the hair.

The horror of it makes him jump back while the BMW X5 leaps forward and smashes into a Peugeot full of Afro-Sicilians.

At this very moment Rosanna Lambertini and her mandolin are making their triumphant approach to Palazzo Biscari, her gaze taking in the large entrance hall decorated, for no apparent reason, with a grand piano. The mandolin sways enthusiastically in appreciation of the eighteenth century murals depicting the Biscari estate with its several industries, including wine and silkworms. Yes, this is a stage worthy of an artist, an intellectual! From the entrance hall she moves into the picture gallery with its polychrome majolica tile floors laid in 1711 by craftsmen from Vietri, then into the Rose Room, with its portraits of the Biscari family, and on into the ballroom, a rococo delirium of plaster and painting on three levels, right up to the dome of the music gallery, with Vulcan presiding over the Council of the Gods, to which the musicians could ascend via a staircase shaped like a cloud.

Anyone who doesn't know her might think that Lambertini is feeling dizzy, but actually this is her interpretation of a "poor but clever young woman who, after having spent her youth cooped up in a humble but spotless chamber, meets by chance a prince who marries her and takes her home to his castle."

Caporeale and Cosentino, who on the other hand have known her since she took her first steps onstage, exchange a meaningful glance, and you can bet that they are thinking, veteran dialect actors that they are, that Lambertini is in high gear as "poor but clever young woman who, after having spent her youth cooped up in a humble but spotless chamber, meets by chance a prince who marries her and takes her home to his castle."

Lambertini in turn takes from her bag a pair of tiny glasses, puts them on, looks at a picture with a superior air, takes off the glasses, puts them back in the bag, and sends Caporeale and Cosentino a look that says, *I appreciate.*

"She *understands*," says Caporeale.

"Yes, sir, she's a connoisseur," says Cosentino.

"It's obvious that she's seen a few."

"A real collector."

"The reputation of a polite but inflexible art expert which was to accompany her quite unwarrantably throughout her long life," adds Caporeale, hitching up his trousers.

"Huh?"

"I quote from *The Leopard.*"

"Shit, you read that stuff?"

Caporeale makes his *sure, who the fuck did you think I was?* face.

The palazzo's reception rooms resound with the clack of heels as two provincial culture commissioners, Giarre and Militello, hustle over toward Lambertini exchanging glances of competitive dislike.

"Here come the rats escorting the flaming rose."

"*The Leopard* again?" asks Cosentino.

"Certainly. Angelica, she was another real bitch. But if we start counting the rats trailing Lambertini we'll have to call Iancelo the exterminator."

• • •

Cagnotto is desperate.

He stares straight ahead without moving a muscle.

The Afro-Sicilians have gotten out of the car and are circling around the BMW X5, studying it with curiosity. They're jiving to the beat of *"Vitti 'na crozza"** in a rap-dance-remix version that is swelling out onto the street from the subwoofers installed in the front doors of the Peugeot, flung open for the no-fault accident report.

One of the Afro-Sicilians sticks his face right up against the window of the driver's side.

Cagnotto can't pretend not to see him.

He whips around.

He sees those two black, burning eyes, and his soul paints an expression on his face.

The black, burning eyes see the expression that Cagnotto's soul has painted on his face.

It frightens the Afro-Sicilian.

He says something to his friends and they jump back into the car.

Cagnotto gives the wheel a jerk. He looks at his watch, the watchband speckled with glittering colored stones.

He jerks the wheel again.

These Afro-Sicilians always blocking traffic. Cagnotto leans on the horn.

The Afro-Sicilian at the wheel sticks his Rasta head out the window.

Cagnotto gives him a chilling grin.

Turi Pirrotta's liver is on fire—*his* liver, not the goose liver on offer at the buffet—if only he could handle that, he'd gladly eat Wanda's

*"I Saw a Skull," Sicilian folk song.

liver too, that goose he had married when he was a kid, and who thank God seemed to have found herself a boyfriend recently because she was busting his balls much less than usual.

At home, that is.

Because on official occasions, ball-buster that she is, she loves to show up with her dear husband at her side, revered, adored, respected, and admired.

Only that just now the mayor of Siracusa had pretended not to see him and the president of the fucking province of Siracusa had chatted with him for a millisecond and then headed off with some excuse, and the commissioner for public works of Pozzallo had given him the smart-ass treatment, and Bad Luck Wanda had that look on her face that said she was about to start torturing him right here in public.

Her eyes were burning with the acid question that her lips were posing: *Isn't there something you should be telling me?*

There's absolutely fuck-all I should be telling you, Turi Pirrotta's fixed smile continued to reply.

But the fact is that word has been spreading, this is the kind of news you can't keep secret. His business rival, Alfio Turrisi, privately known as Alfio Dickhead Turrisi, that moron who has people calling him "Mister" Turrisi, has been gobbling up all the real estate between Rosolini and Ispica, where it is pretty clear by now that drillers have struck oil.

An American company had gotten the natural gas rights but the documents spoke of "liquid extraction rights" and down at the regional assembly environmentalists, engineers, and commissioners, all of whom were intent on their own interests, were squabbling over whether those "liquids" included petroleum.

Meanwhile, however, it was to be expected that someone would grab the titles to those properties, and Turrisi, with his alluring liquidity, his favorable pound-euro exchange rate (for he was well introduced among London banks), and his perfect dick of a face . . . well, everyone knows that the guy with the dick-face always manages to screw his neighbor.

London!

Hey, Turi Pirrotta himself could have gone into business in London if it hadn't been for that disaster of a wife of his who in his younger days had kept him on a leash shorter than a pit bull's. And if it hadn't been for that double disaster of a daughter of his, Betty, who for all the paternal goodwill in the world had turned out to be a supreme ball-breaker, with a cherry so well chiseled that even the artisans who carved the putti in the houses designed by Vaccarini couldn't compete.

Under these conditions, the last thing you want to do is be seen on some public occasion. You want to be seen staying home and plotting—what's it called?—*strategy*, vendettas, war, and all that shit. You don't go to the big lunch where the mayor of Siracusa comes up to you, stares at you with that cocksucker face of his that says it all, pauses a moment to see if you have anything to tell him, you who have nothing to tell him because all the land is being sold to Turrisi, and then moves on, with an excuse, to somebody else.

And then they complain when they get blown away.

What is Pirrotta supposed to do? Go out and gun down the brokers, the real estate agents, threaten the property owners, blow things up? He's too old for that kind of stuff. And meanwhile Turrisi is young and energetic.

Turrisi is young, energetic, and, as we said, a dick-face.

And he doesn't have his nerves shredded by someone like Wanda who if you didn't take her to the big lunch with stars of stage and screen would have raised such a firestorm at home that Pirrotta would have had to forget about slipping out to see Rosina, a girl so fine—young, pretty, sweet-smelling, and not even that much of a bitch—that Pirrotta can't figure out why the Good Lord has given her to him.

. . .

Mister Turrisi is fiddling with his hair with the mother-of-pearl comb he keeps in the glove compartment of the Aston Martin.

He has found a place for the car in Piazza Duca di Genova because he knows the guy who runs the illegal parking operation there, and now, climbing the double-ramp staircase of Mt. Etna basalt, he walks though the reception rooms, laid out for the party but deserted.

Turrisi's Brylcreemed head pokes out onto the terrace, where he sees that the party is well under way. Good. Someone of Mister Turrisi's status should arrive after things have gotten warmed up.

With the nice weather the guests have all migrated to the south terrace, where, admiring the black basalt walls with their flowers, putti, and muscular columns sculpted of Siracusa limestone, they are broiling under the sun because in houses like this it is cooler inside than out.

But how could they live without that magnificent view of the traffic and the upholsterers, the street salesmen looking up with humility and admiration on that glorious festive crowd sporting here and there even a hat or two? How to resist that terrace that if only by a few meters stood above everyday plebeian mundanity? Who could forgo that ineffable caress that only a glance of envy can deliver?

The recent, but solid, success of Turrisi is quickly confirmed by the Baronessa Faillaci, who throws herself on him shrieking so all can hear. "Mister Turrisi!"

Turrisi, flashing a measured smile, inwardly exults. He has been recognized by the aristocracy at last! He can hardly wait to invite some of them to his home in Pembridge Square, Notting Hill, and show his English partners, who still appreciate that sort of thing, God save the Queen, that he has real aristocratic connections.

"My dear Baronessa." Turrisi is in a bit of a bind, he wants to

kiss her hand but she has already clamped herself to his arm. Someone had once explained to him that true distinction lies in not betray-
ing emotion, so all he manages is a stiff half bow.

Pirrotta wishes they would all go screw themselves: actors, comedi-
ans, showgirls, aspiring directors, aspiring choreographers, aspiring scriptwriters, aspiring whatevers, commissioners, counselors,
mayors, wives, lovers, girlfriends, bitches, sluts, tarts, cognoscenti
and other smart-asses, businessmen, tradesmen, financiers and fi-
nancees, vote-getters and vote-buyers, mentors, protectors, PR man-
agers and spin doctors, decorators, drug dealers, doctors, dentists,
plastic surgeons, pharmacists, theater directors, bank directors,
lawyers, judges, and associates.

News, as we know, is born in the world of business, moves from
there to the world of politics, then to society, and from there to sleaze.
The moment a piece of news gets down to the sleaze level, it means
it's in the public domain. The baroness who's hanging on Turrisi's
arm is an eloquent signal: everyone knows how matters stand, everyone at that instant knows that the Pirrotta family is on the way out.

Cagnotto cannot be late.

He owes his reputation to a couple of artistic seasons financed
once by one commissioner, then by another, hoping to showcase, as a
brochure put it, their "leading role in the context of cultural activities to relaunch Sicily as a Mediterranean nexus and crossroads for
exchange among peoples" assisted by the purchase of expensive advertising supplements in *La Voce della Sicilia*, which guarantees the
favor of local critics for the commissioners' initiatives and also by de-
fault for Cagnotto's experimental productions, staged, once again in
the words of the brochure, "in urban spaces that are prime examples
of industrial architecture," i.e., lofts.

All of this naturally had the patronage and benediction of Sicilian Regional Commissioner Murabito.

Cagnotto had recently redone his kitchen, and, after having read in *Amica* that minimalism was out not only on the fashion runways but also in interiors, had tried to correct his course halfway through the project. Even he, even before *Amica* said so, had begun to tire of those receptions where guests studied a single halogen lamp lighting up a bare white wall while they toyed with a celery stalk doused in vodka. In place of the "open space look," he had installed five "settings": the solid "Victorian look"; flaming zebra-striped kitsch; the seventies "orange look"; the "musician look" complete with a Petrof baby grand piano; and finally, his favorite, the "bed corner," with three white sofas surrounding an orgy futon in place of a coffee table. He had also bought up three whole collections (balls, elephants, and cigarette cases) and scattered them around. Then he had dumped a whole truckload of fine gravel on the floor of the guest room and built a fake waterfall, no expense spared for the engine that pumped the water. And finally he had brightened up the home theater corner with a leopard skin complete with sparkling eyes and a great big grinning mouthful of teeth.

It was definitely time someone signed him up for a new theater season.

It has been at least two weeks since he has given even a simple dinner for twelve and the fancy food shops still won't extend him zero-interest credit with no down payment. And what's more, he doesn't have the slightest theatrical inspiration, and, having run through all the avant-gardes that there are, envies authors of a classical persuasion who can make do with a love story, a couple of homicides, and some bourgeois family drama.

Cagnotto parks the BMW X5 on the sidewalk of Via Archi della Marina, next to a Chinese guy selling cheap junk. He ignores the Chinese curses coming at him and, dodging between the cars, aims for the reception.

Seventy-year-old Contessa Salieri, the historic queen of Catania bitchdom and now the undisputed light of the city's intellectual life, signals it is time to go inside, whispering in the ear of her companion, thirtysomething Arturo Paino, the up-and-coming commissioner for culture of San Giovanni la Punta, "We'd better get off the terrace; it's too hot and I left the number of the ambulance service in my other bag."

Paino debates whether he should laugh admiringly at the Contessa's irony and youthful spirit, but, watching her clutch the stonework as she presses into the grand *salone*, he decides not to.

And so, as the grateful crowds begin to stream off the terrace, the Contessa and Commissioner Paino are the first people to cross Cagnotto's path as he hastens over the polychrome majolica tile floor of 1711.

"Contessa! My deep and most sincere admiration," shouts Cagnotto, breathing heavily and trying to kiss her hand, the loose skin of her forearm lasciviously bound up in the bushels of bracelets she's wearing.

The Contessa's mouth opens on the biggest set of dentures Cagnotto has ever seen apart from the teeth on the leopard flattened on the floor of his house—or maybe it's that the Contessa is shrinking around that Godzilla set of teeth. From the makeup she is wearing it looks as if she has fallen face down in a plate of *ripiddu nivicatu*, the Catania gastronomic specialty inspired by Mt. Etna: rice tinted black with cuttlefish ink and piled up like a volcano with a splash of red sauce for the lava spilling out and a dollop of cream on top for snow.

"Hey, great to see you," yells Cagnotto, pretending to notice Arturo Paino just at that moment.

"Ah, Cagnotto, I have big plans for you," says Paino, automatically looking away. "I just spoke with my fellow . . . uh . . . party member, you know who I mean, yes?" he adds, looking the other way.

"Padovani?" asks Cagnotto, his voice going wobbly.

Paino nods, gazing at the Contessa with loathing.

"Dear Arturo," says the Contessa, "he always has a nice thought for everyone, don't you agree, Cagnotto?"

Cagnotto makes a *you could have fooled me* gesture with a rapid shake of his head, adding, "What would we do without him? Oh, by the way, Commissioner, I called to make an appointment with you last week . . ."

"And I preceded you! I've already spoken to the mayor and we agreed that San Giovanni la Punta can't go another year without one of your productions. We'd like of course to do a whole season, but for that we'll have to join forces with some other town, budgets being what they are."

"But nobody . . . I haven't heard from anyone."

"Dear Arturo, he's so *sensitive* about letters, about the spirit," says the Contessa, gazing at him fondly.

"Nobody?" says Paino, staring at Cagnotto.

Nobody, nobody, signals Cagnotto with a swipe of his head.

"Mister Turrisi, allow me to present Signor Timpanaro," chirps young Baronessa Faillaci, who has only just come out and can't wait to present someone to someone else. As the last to be introduced, she's eager to introduce someone and be the penultimate.

"Mister Turrisi, very pleased to meet you." Timpanaro is emaciated and has dandruff, along with a suit that hangs on him, not that you could find a suit narrow enough to fit Timpanaro.

Turrisi shakes his hand. He has no problems about the proportions between his belly and his sleeve length, he doesn't give a fuck about odd sizes, he has a London tailor—two, actually: Turnbull & Asser at 23 Bury Street.

"I'm told you have interests in the London theater."

Turrisi, rather than nod, makes a little bow, like a very genteel nod. "Well, yes indeed, I'm thinking about it. I do love to walk through the streets of Soho in the evening, and between us, I might add, I've been taken by a certain . . . ah . . . appetite for the stage."

Timpanaro smiles at the Baronessa, who is gazing with a certain admiring wonder at Turrisi and his interesting diction. "Soho! Marvelous! All those movie stars pounding the boards! But wait, couldn't we organize something in Soho? Some auditions . . . a Sicilian production in London, maybe a translation of Nino Martoglio . . ."

What business does he think I'm in? Turrisi wonders to himself. I like Soho because it's full of *models* and the *model* business is in the hands of the Afro-Brits—and I have some deals going with the Afro-Brits. But as for the theater, I don't have any, ah . . . introductions, those English bastards are real snobs, but just wait till I make some aristocratic friends here and bring them back to London where, God save the Queen, these things still count, and then we'll see about those shitheads who come to the bank for loans and then play the snob. So let me organize something in London for this Timpanaro and we'll see.

"Excellent idea, Signor Timpanaro, call me . . . call me in the office."

In Turrisi's mind, lines of credit are already piling up, letters of introduction, stage shows bombing out that could be used to launder truckloads of money. And to think that in the early days he used to go and launder money in the currency exchange at the airport.

Cagnotto, what with the heat, the rush, the stress, the disappointment, and the bills to pay, is feeling light-headed. So he decides to grab something at the buffet, which thanks to the region's largesse is abundant: eggplant parmigiana and caponata oozing with olive oil, cauliflower buried under anchovies and olives and sautéed with cheese, fried zucchini flowers, *risotto alla pescatora* made with frozen mussels, *involtini* of eggplant and spaghetti (many thanks to the region they have not provided plastic forks, which as the Prince, a

mathematics buff, would have said are incommensurable with eggplant and spaghetti *involtini*), *ripiddu nivicatu*, black spaghetti with
cuttlefish in which the pieces of cuttlefish are big enough to destroy
your dental work, veal cutlets, skewers of pork, mixed fry of small
fish, mixed grill of large fish, mixed salad of midsized fish, shrimps
and giant prawns.

Cagnotto decides to go for a giant prawn. He takes one and
places it in the middle of his plate, puts a knife and fork next to it,
and realizes that in all of Palazzo Biscari there is not one level sur-
face on which to place the plate and behead the prawn. Okay, there
are the mantelpieces of the two fireplaces but apart from the fact that
they're lit (they're *lit*?) the fireplaces are as big as two garages and so
the mantelpieces are too high.

Now his gaze falls, tumbles, collapses on Bobo: extremely tight
white jeans (how long has it been since he has seen white jeans? not
since the days of *Charlie's Angels*, TV version), a shirt with very fine
multicolored stripes open to his navel, a nicely modeled chest free of
hair and adorned with a plain red chain that clings to his Adam's apple, from which hangs a pendant in the shape of a . . . car jack? No,
it's a Fascist, uh, bundle of sheaves, that is, the fasces . . . The
fasces? No, maybe it's a bunch of little daisies tied together with a
blade of grass. Maybe.

"You . . . I must say . . . as usual . . . there's no place to put the
plate down," Cagnotto says to him.

Bobo turns. Bobo has hair in fake casual disarray as you can only
do when you have a lot of hair, a square jaw, nice cheekbones, and
bored lips. Bobo looks with distaste at Cagnotto's too-tight suit while
Cagnotto tries to suck in his stomach. Bobo turns to look with greater
interest at a casserole of baked rice.

Bobo smells of vanilla.

Cagnotto lowers his head over the giant prawn. In any case he
doesn't have the money to invite him to dinner. He feels as if he

might burst into tears. When was this damn antidepressant going to kick in? He's about to walk away, and then he remembers his grandmother's famous saying, "Nobody gets anything for free." (Actually, his grandmother used to say that to his sister, encouraging her to dress up like a tart so that she didn't give away the men's admiring glances to the competition, but he had been listening.)

Cagnotto sucks in his cheeks, making a molar that is loose because of periodontitis wobble. Sure, we all have a deep desire for intimate candor, for simple sincerity, moments in which we would like to capture our prey with just a nude, unarmed glance. But these are archaic dreams of a bucolic state, thinks Cagnotto. Adrift in the great, globalized metropolis, love has become war, a hunt where reciprocal diffidence, fear, and terror make appearances more important than sentiment. And if appearances are a weapon, they are a weapon Cagnotto can use, if it will get him that scent of vanilla!

Cagnotto turns on his heel. He comes to a halt next to Bobo. "I'm Cagnotto, Tino Cagnotto. Maybe you've heard of me."

Bobo, temporary salesclerk and aspiring actor, has heard of Tino Cagnotto. Yes indeed.

Cagnotto sets down the plate with the prawn. The faint feeling is gone and anyway he's on a diet.

Betty Pirrotta bumps into a waiter bearing a tray of titties of St. Agatha, the little *cassatelle* in the shape of breasts that were invented in honor of the martyrdom of Agatha, Catania's protectress.

How to describe the harmony of the spheres that suddenly descends on the numbered accounts and letters of credit, on the short-term loans, on the bank lending rates and capital transfers?

Turrisi, fatal move, turns to look while the titties fly through the air, locking eyes for a second, sealing his fate and future punishment, with the blue orbs of that unknown young lady, blonder than all the babes of Chelsea.

Without thinking, Turrisi looks around for Pirronello, the photographer for *La Voce della Sicilia*, finds him, walks slowly over to him, leans over his ear, and, practically biting it off, murmurs something.

Pirronello slips—gracefully, due to his slight stature—back and forth among the guests, snapping a photo of Betty, who smiles and doesn't get it.

"They were the most moving sight there, two young people in love dancing together, blind to each other's defects, deaf to the warnings of fate, deluding themselves that the whole course of their lives would be as smooth as the ballroom floor, unknowing actors made to play the parts of Juliet and Romeo by a director who had concealed the fact that tomb and poison were already in the script," says Caporeale.

"Screw Tomasi di Lampedusa and his *Leopard*; he was pretty fond of that aristocratic *di*, wasn't he? However, it doesn't seem to me that the guy in the zoot suit and the little blond blow-job artist are actually dancing together."

"Who?"

Cosentino points with his chin.

"No, no, I was referring to Cagnotto and his new conquest." Cosentino turns to look. "They're not dancing either."

"Wrong, those two are *ball*room dancing, with the accent on ball."

Goethe, in his *Italian Journey*, wrote of Palazzo Biscari:

CATANIA, MAY 3, 1787

We were about to take our leave when [the Prince] took us to his mother's suite to see the rest of his smaller works of art. Then we were introduced to a distinguished-looking lady, who received us

*with the words, "Look around, you will find everything just as my
dear husband arranged it. This I owe to the filial devotion of my
son, who not only allows me to live in his best rooms but also will
not allow a single object in his father's collection to be removed
or displaced. In consequence I enjoy the double advantage of
living in the fashion I have been accustomed to for so long, and
of making the acquaintance of eminent foreigners, who, as in
former times, come here from far-off countries to look at our
treasures . . ."*

*We were sorry to have to leave her and she was sorry to see
us go.*

On this occasion there is no sorrow in Palazzo Biscari when it
comes time to bid the guests farewell. Nor are the guests sorry to
leave the palazzo. Tight shoes, pinching bodices, sweaty crowd, melting makeup, and fried eggplant: all are grateful to see the end of the
celebration in honor of Francesco Procopio dei Coltelli.

Outside, on the terrace, the white putti lit up by the sun look as
if they need to take a piss.

CHAPTER FOUR

Car Theater Elegance

"Car Theater Elegance. E-Class Mercedes. Two 5.8-inch moni-tors in 16:9 format installed in the front headrests?" asks Turi Pir-rotta, in the kitchen, reading aloud from a dealer's brochure.

Betty's face is sodden with tears and mascara is running down her cheeks. (When the fuck had she put on that mascara, when it was still practically dawn?) "Yeah, that's right, the Mercedes with the TV," says Betty, all pragmatism.

Last night Turi Pirrotta, feeling fucked over as always in recent months, needless to say because of that slimeball Turrisi and his petrochemical investments in the Ispica countryside, had to take two Ambien to go to sleep.

And a quarter of an hour ago he had been shaken out of bed by the shrieks of Betty, who was howling as if somebody were dissolving her body in quicklime.

Accustomed by now to his daughter's hysterics, Pirrotta was only moderately concerned, and rose from his bed swearing, took a look at his wife (that other bitch who slept like a baby, with an eye mask on her face that looked like she was riding on a jumbo jet and two

earplugs with cords like Tampax), put on his dressing gown, threaded his toes into his slippers, went flying as he tripped over the African footstool, got up somewhat rattled, ran to Betty's room, and found her on her knees in the bathroom with her head inside the toilet bowl, while she vomited ranting nasally (the screams echoing off the porcelain of the toilet bowl), "That bitch Anna! They did an article about her in the paper. For that *hopeless* party of hers in Taormina. That ass-kissing-bitch-of-a-goddamned-whore!"

Her pale white arm pointing, Betty indicated *La Voce della Sicilia*, crumpled up and tossed in the sink.

Pirrotta took the newspaper, sat on the rim of the bathtub, put on his glasses which he took from the pocket of his dressing gown, crossed his legs (with a bit of difficulty), and read the article about the party hosted by his daughter's best friend.

A party at the Panasia Beach in Taormina, with even a guy who was famous on television among the guests, it seemed. There was a half-page photo of Anna Pizzone, there was a photo of a watermelon cut like a starfish, and there was not even *one* little photo of Betty.

A catastrophe, to say the least.

"Frigging fucking water heaters," Betty screamed again, in reference to the company selling and installing boilers owned by Anna Pizzone's father, a company that, by buying regular advertising space in *La Voce della Sicilia*, guaranteed the daughter a suitable social profile.

Pirrotta nodded, folding the newspaper carefully (he had yet to read it and look at the shape it was in), took off his glasses, and speaking to no one in particular said, "What was that car that you liked?"

Betty raised her head from the toilet, shoved it back inside, coughed up for good measure the last stream of vomit, got up coolly, flushed the toilet while she wiped her mouth with her forearm, and said, "Wait, I have the brochure."

They went to the kitchen and while the Filipina maid prepared their coffee Turi Pirrotta read the dealer's brochure.

"Yeah, that's right, the Mercedes with the TV," says Betty.

Pirrotta recalls that when she was little, after the fainting fits (Betty, pubescent, used to pass out when she wanted something), his daughter would look at him with big eyes all red from crying and afford him that paternal joy that at least repays some of the sacrifices you make for a family. Now Betty has become more pragmatic, like her mother, and despite the rivulets of mascara has a shark's expression stamped on her face.

Pirrotta, who has also grown pragmatic, to get her to stop throwing her guts up, and above all to get her off his ass, goes into his study, makes a couple of calls, and gets an assurance that the Mercedes will be delivered right away. "I don't give a fuck about the papers, just tell the dealer to send it to me as is."

Brand-new, flaming red, shining, the Mercedes is parked this morning on the gravel in front of Villa Wanda's neoclassical entrance. In the center of the gravel is a full-scale reproduction of Liotru, the elephant that is Catania's symbol, the only difference being that here the water flows out of the trunk.

Betty Pirrotta stares at the car with a contempt alloyed with hatred.

It is not the expression her father would have expected in the face of such a present. But only Betty could know how much pain and suffering that automobile had cost her. It was inhuman to have had to suffer that much for a lump of steel; it was unjust to have had to spill so many tears, to have forgone the pleasures that life could offer for such a long time, just for that *thing* there.

With the heels of her Manolo Blahnik sandals sinking into the gravel (a pain in the ass, this gravel, how many broken heels had she left in the fucking gravel, which her mother had insisted upon because she'd seen it some-fucking-where), Betty advances determined and injured toward the Mercedes.

You can see she's had enough from the way her Prada bag is twitching, with the same hard, dry blows they use to beat fresh octopus to death against the volcanic rocks at Acitrezza.

"Not in front! Behind, behind!" Carmine, known as Mina among friends, yells at her. Carmine, Betty's "lady's companion" ("It's cool to have a gay guy as a lady's companion," says Betty, "they have them in America, don't you watch the sitcoms?") is racing down the white steps at the front of Villa Wanda.

Carmine is wearing an orange suit of raw silk with sinuous orange embroidery, pointy black shoes, and a shirt with a Chinese collar.

Betty halts with her hand on the car door.

She looks defiantly at Carmine.

What the hell's the matter with this faggot, wonders Betty, that he's so excited about this fuck of a car? He wasn't the one who cried all those tears.

"You have to ride in the rear, sweetheart," Carmine says to her, opening the back door.

Betty flashes an irritated smile. "The TV screens are in the front headrests, I read it in the brochure."

Carmine looks heavenward. "Sure, darling, that's why you have to ride in the rear. You want to go the whole way with your head screwed on backwards?"

Betty slams the door hard.

Turi Pirrotta gazes at her radiantly.

Enjoying the scene from the top of the stairs, he smiles at his wife Wanda and goes back in the house smiling and smoothing down his thin white hair which lately he has begun to wear a bit longer in the back.

. . .

Yesterday afternoon, in fact, because the Supreme Being is just and knows how to reward a good father, Turi Pirrotta had received a *pizzino*, a message of the sort mobsters send, written by hand on Alfio Turrisi's letterhead. (What a gas this Mister Turrisi is, what with his letterhead bearing a crest worthy of the Juventus soccer club.)

The guy Turrisi sent with the message was dressed identically with the late-model Elvis Presley, in white pants and a jacket with fringe, and white boots with metal studs, so that Fernando, who works as Pirrotta's doorman for Villa Wanda, got nervous that someone wanted to blow Pirrotta away and thought this was the killer in disguise.

Pirrotta, instead, had understood immediately that this guy was Pietro, the one who parked his sandwich truck, the "Pietroburger," in Piazza Europa and who every once in a while did some business for that cocksucker Turrisi.

The message said:

My dear and esteemed Signor Pirrotta,

My sincere apologies for interrupting you in your worthy domestic tranquillity blessed by the Lord and the Sacred Bonds of the Family. I trust I explain myself.

Let us hope this finds you in good health and prosperity.

With this note, I would like to convey that any unfinished business matters between us do not, not even for an instant, diminish the respect I feel for you as a man of experience, a man who knows the ways of the world in Sicily.

That caveat accepted, I would like, should you agree, to illustrate the following to you and to your Esteemed Wife, to whom I bow in honor.

Having caught a glimpse—in a public place, on the stage of

*Palazzo Biscari at an event in which you also deservedly took
part—of your distinguished offspring, I would very much like
(with your permission, of course) to pay tribute to her aesthetic
qualities (inherited, certainly from her Lady Mother) and above
all to her style, magnanimity, and farsightedness, biological
inheritance from her most worthy Father.*

*With all due respect I hope that it will be possible to meet (not
alone, of course, needless to say) Lady Elisabetta (never was a
name so apt) for lunch at a date to be established, with the
exclusive aim of exchanging views on some theatrical business in
which I am engaged, as you know, in London.*

*Considering the views of Lady Elisabetta in these matters to be
of the utmost value, she being an esteemed voice of youth culture,
I pray you, and the most honorable Lady Mother, to grant me
the privilege of this meeting, certain that dialogue between
generations and civilizations is the basic foundation on which all
reciprocal prosperity between peoples and Families is built.
I trust I explain myself.*

Hoping you will be so kind as to let me know,

*Bowing deeply once again to your Lady Wife, I remain
humbly and most cordially yours,*

Alfio Turrisi

Turi Pirrotta, bent over double with laughter, had handed the letter to his Lady Wife, not to say Lady Mother of the Lady Daughter,
and Wanda had snapped, "What the hell do you think you have to
laugh about, you animal, you peasant, you ape! This Turrisi, now,
there's a gentleman!"

Pirrotta had to step out into the garden to catch a breath of air
and settle his cough. Style, magnanimity, and even farsightedness,
shit, I can't believe it, thought Pirrotta, holding his side.

And now Betty—shit, how sweet it is—is getting into that fucking Mercedes to go on her date with Turrisi!

Want to bet I'm going to kill two birds with one stone? thinks Pirrotta. Not only will I get Turrisi to share the oil rights with me, but also (I can't believe this) I'll get Betty out of my house and into his. I can't believe it.

Carmine adjusts his lacy shirt cuffs, crosses his legs, and tunes the Mercedes' TV monitor to MTV.

Carmine, to tell the truth, likes Turrisi. He's seen him around, elegant and a little bit melancholy, with his English automobiles. He's hard to resist; he looks lost and homeless. And then he has that pencil mustache, that Brylcreem in his hair, that aura of power and respect.

He's not entirely sure whether Turrisi will make an equally good impression on Betty, who for her lunch has put on the sort of bright pink vinyl minidress that only a turbocharged blow-job expert would wear.

However, it's also true that girls like Betty can plow though half the men in town, then go on to marry someone like Turrisi. They seem to positively go for guys with wimp faces. And a wimp-face is what Turrisi has, shit if he doesn't. Carmine, to tell the truth, wouldn't mind at all saving him from that inferno populated by bitches like Betty!

Betty, getting into the backseat, slams the door in a fit of pique, flashes a smile that has fuck-all to do with it, and asks, "So what's this Turrisi like?"

Carmine, about to say something, changes his mind, looks out the window, and replies, "Mature."

Betty settles into her seat, her minidress riding up above her thong. "Mature. Good. A guy who can understand me."

Carmine, still looking out the window, replies, "Sweetheart, the fact that they nod when you talk doesn't mean they understand you."

Betty grabs her bag, opens it, looks at something inside, closes it, and jams it between herself and Carmine. "You're jealous because I can decide whether to ride in the front or the rear, and you can only go for the rear."

Then, addressing the driver, "And what the fuck are *you* waiting for?"

"What a drag of a life," murmurs Carmine, sighing. "Everybody waiting for a fuck."

CHAPTER FIVE

Each New Love Brings Great Tumult

Each new love brings great tumult and Cagnotto grows ever more desperate. How true it is that love hits you when you least expect it, and above all, when you're least looking for it. Cagnotto, sprawled on the sofa before an immense plasma-screen TV, broods.

His collection of balls on the low table looks unstable. He blames the antidepressant for this impression. He's bloated, with alcohol and anxiety, with poisons ingested and a dissolute existence, with ideas that won't come, with discontents. No, this isn't the moment to fall in love.

No.

The extra weight puts his elegance in question, strains his movements, his words, his assurance. His bank account has dried up and he doesn't have even half an idea for a new theater season. The culture commissioners speak of nothing but *proposals*. "Give me a proposal. We need a proposal. Have you worked up a proposal?"

Proposal. What fucking proposal?

Maybe if he had a proposal his fat wouldn't be such a problem.

Cagnotto thinks of Orson Welles: How did he manage to be so fascinating even as he was growing rotund? Cagnotto thinks he looks like Orson Welles, the young Orson Welles, when he was just a little bit overweight; can it be that Bobo doesn't see how much he looks like Orson Welles? Cagnotto reflects that Orson Welles had many, many proposals, his problem was that he had *too many* proposals. Cagnotto's problem, instead, is named Bobo.

Bobo is confused.

Yes, that's it, confused.

He's confused because of his youth, his impetuousness, his passion. Bobo is a young colt who's frightened of nothing: such is the torment and the delight of Cagnotto, who spends hours seeking the right words to maintain a delicate balance between veiled reproach and patient tolerance.

Oh, the thin line between courtship and hypnosis! thinks Cagnotto.

Bobo is like a lost puppy rescued from the street, torn between the appeal of a new owner and the mistrust that drives him toward a dangerous freedom. Only male puppies behave this way, the females jump up and slobber all over you as soon as they see there's a chance of finding a home, thinks Cagnotto, tormenting—and equally enjoying—himself.

Cagnotto feels the attraction and the rude ingenuousness of a creature hungry for art but still untutored in the ways of the avant-garde and its experiments.

He needs to be taken by the hand, Bobo, broken in, almost: seduced, co-opted, gently pushed into the meanders of experimentation. Oh, what a difference, Cagnotto observes to himself, between the unripe, green soul of Bobo, into which (Cagnotto even hears the imperceptible sound) the Wisdom that Cagnotto holds in his hand enters with difficulty, what a difference between that and his own soul, abused over the years by great big experimenters.

Bobo, all unaware, wounds him, flattens him. The mention of another director, of whom Bobo speaks with enthusiasm, wrings from Cagnotto a tight-lipped nod of approval, then many circumlocutions and verbal pirouettes to wrest Bobo's mind away from those extraneous claws trying to snatch him.

Cagnotto carves that unripe mind with the precision of a sculptor carving a block of rare and precious marble. One false move and the whole may end up in splinters.

Oh, how well Cagnotto knows the cynical world of the theater.

How to explain to Bobo what true inspiration is, loyalty to his art, seriousness of purpose, artistic humility, without planting in that well-disposed soul the suspicion that all of this is really just the basest of jealousy?

In this great confusion of worries and invocations, Cagnotto remembers that he must pass by and pick up Bobo.

He has invited him for lunch at Capomulini.

Bobo had sighed at the other end of the line, and oh, God, had said yes, not sounding very sure.

What should he wear?

Behind the wheel of the BMW X5, stuck in traffic in Capomulini, he takes a covert look at Bobo.

Bobo's too serious today.

Since he had gotten into the vehicle (Cagnotto had the imperceptible impression that Bobo had slammed the door), he hasn't said a word. The sculpted cheekbones that are pointed out the window, the sulky lips in sync with the radio, the strong jaw resting on his knuckles.

His attitude is unmistakable: something's wrong.

Cagnotto is sweating. He's sweating although he has turned up the air conditioner to the max.

He's sweating because in his weight-loss anxiety this morning he has taken a diuretic, has spent the whole morning pissing, and now he has low blood pressure.

When you have low blood pressure, cold sweats, and are stuck in traffic under the broiling sun, it's normal, thinks Cagnotto, to have a panic attack.

Cagnotto's having a panic attack.

He tries to distract himself by looking at the traffic.

Capomulini is a little town on the sea between Acitrezza and Acireale, made up entirely of one U-shaped street, one side of the U being the seafront, the other, the road out of town. On the seafront side is a row of a dozen piers looking out onto the water that serve as restaurants. The kitchens are across the street on the ground floor of the buildings opposite and the waiters cross over with platters of bass and bream, spicy sautéed mussels and raw sea urchins.

Everybody comes here at lunchtime to eat something and cop some sun.

Often, some shopkeeper of a driver, rushing to get back in time for afternoon business hours, smashes into a boned mackerel, a grouper, or a *fritto misto*, but since there's always traffic and it moves at a snail's pace, nobody ever gets hurt in the collisions, although it can happen that somebody gets hurt in the fistfights that follow.

Cagnotto likes Capomulini a lot, he likes to suck out those raw sea urchins with the sun in his face, the sea whipping under the chair, the smell of salt in the air.

The customers who have finished eating wouldn't dream of getting up and vacating their tables; they laugh, they stretch, they close their eyes and catnap, their faces turned toward the sun to catch the midday rays.

Has he said something wrong?

Has he made an irremediable error in his courtship?

Has he acted too possessive?

Is he just too fat?

And if he is just too fat, what's the use of all the talk about art?

Is Bobo using him?

Is he looking for a part as an actor in his next production?

What next production, if he doesn't even have a proposal yet?

Cagnotto feels fat, in love, and penniless, he has no idea what his next show will be, and in order to take Bobo out to lunch he had asked Sailesh, the Indian who comes to clean his house, to go down to the Monte dei Pegni to pawn two Rolexes, five rings, and two chains. (Sailesh had been arrested coming out of the pawnbroker's, the police alerted by an employee who had had a bad experience with an Indian, and Cagnotto, to his burning shame, had to go down to Via Sant' Eupilio at ten in the morning to try to explain to the carabinieri that he had given those objects to the Indian himself. "Of my own free will." "Of your what? Okay, so these watches are not yours?")

No! Bobo can't be. He can't be just the latest salesclerk aspiring actor who fakes an interest in a famous director to get a part. No, impossible. Cagnotto has gotten to know Bobo in these days and . . . yes, it is all too possible.

Cagnotto grabs a quick look at Bobo out of the corner of his eye. Bobo is staring with loathing at Capomulini.

Oh, fuck. This is not the attitude of a man in love, thinks Cagnotto.

When you're in love everything, even things that are old and worn, seems beautiful, fresh in the light of the new sentiment that transfigures the everyday, endowing it with poetry, or something like that.

Cagnotto swipes his middle fingertip across his forehead.

He looks at it.

Filthy and oozing with sweat.

He wishes he had a salt cube.

Salt cubes don't exist, he thinks.

In the very moment that he begins to pass out he finds a parking place, and revives.

Cagnotto has ordered boiled cod.

Bobo has an octopus salad, a shrimp salad, and one of *masculini*, as Capomulini's raw anchovies are called.

That's what he's doing to him, he's eating him alive, as alive and raw as a piece of sushi. Cagnotto looks at the sad, solitary codfish. To cheer himself up he calls the waiter, and seeing that his love is now certainly destined to remain unrequited, orders spaghetti with sea urchins, *sparacanaci*, minuscule fried mullet, and fried shrimp and calamari.

Bobo has done nothing but stare at the sea without participating in the conversation. Looking distracted and rather rude. Even a bit sour.

This, thinks Cagnotto, is the moment when I should exhale, raise my eyebrows, look at him with disdain, and spit out at him how dishonest it is to play around with the feelings of a poor theater director, especially when he's in obvious trouble.

But hey, you can't see that I'm in trouble, can you? Because you can't talk about work, can you? Because your secret aim is to make it in the theater world by grabbing on to my coattails, isn't it?

See, I've unmasked your game, Bobo.

Cagnotto thinks he should grab his napkin, toss it with rage on the table, and walk off without paying the bill.

Wait, who's crazy here?

The cold white wine, the fried calamari, and a gust of salt air, rotten wood, and wet rope stir his groin.

Look at the facts, thinks Cagnotto, calming down. I'm in Capomulini with a really nice piece, young and moody, and everybody's seen me. And I should let *feelings* spoil the party?

At this point *first* I lay him and *then* I leave him.

Okay.

He asked for it.

He wants to play social climber.

Okay.

Climb!

"Hey, Bobo, I wanted to talk to you about my next production."

"Okay," replies Bobo, continuing to stare at the sea.

Cool, he's not showing too much interest. "I was thinking about you for a couple of parts and I wanted to get your input, that is, I wanted *you* to decide, uh, which character struck you as the most congenial."

See, I want you, kiddo!

Because I'm the only opportunity you've got in your ignorant fucking life. I want you. Let's see if you keep staring at the water with that bored look . . . Cagnotto remembers that he has no clue about his next production, no plot, no characters, no nothing.

It doesn't matter, I'll invent something. I'm still Cagnotto and something will come to me.

You're fooling yourself, I'm going to screw you and then dump you, you'll see.

Bobo continues to stare at the sea. He grinds his teeth. You can see he's grinding his teeth because his jaw muscles begin to move up and down.

"Bobo?"

Up and down, up and down.

Cagnotto turns to look out to sea.

What can be so interesting?

Nothing.

"Bobo?"

Bobo snaps around, lowers his gaze, closes his eyelids to a slit, and bellows at him through clenched teeth, "Asshole!"

CHAPTER SIX

Mister Turrisi's Brylcreem Reflects the Sun of Piazza Lupo

Mister Turrisi's Brylcreem reflects the sun of Piazza Lupo. He's wearing an impeccable double-breasted pin-striped blue linen suit with generous lapels and pale blue, very fine stripes.

Turrisi's pinstripes get wider and more intense as the sun goes down: for breakfast he has a series of suits whose stripes can only be seen in a strong light; for evening, a set that resemble pedestrian crosswalks. He is also fond of stripes in all the colors of the rainbow.

Behind his Brylcreemed head the sign of the restaurant Trinacria in Bocca pokes out.

Female tourists go crazy for this restaurant because they like the double entendre: "a *mouthful* of Sicily."

Turrisi likes it because it's a place the British flock to.

The tables are set behind a bamboo fence, on the other side of which parked cars bake in the sun.

Turrisi looks at his watch.

He rocks on his heels.

He checks the time again.

He can't remember whether in England young ladies are permitted to break the rules of punctuality. He knows that in Sicily, it is the female who must wait while the male tarries, he knows that in Italy the opposite holds, but he isn't sure what the rule is in Great Britain.

A Mercedes car theater purrs silently down Via Ventimiglia, enters the piazza, and comes to a halt, double-parked.

Turrisi stares at the automobile, then at his watch.

The car theater sits immobile, the sun sparkling off the hood.

Turrisi stares at the rogue "parking attendant." The man, sitting sideways on a beaten-up scooter, stares back, with some curiosity.

Turrisi glances away.

He fiddles with the knot of his tie.

Shit, it's hot.

Betty Pirrotta is slumped on the floor in the space between the backseat and the front (on which is installed the TV monitor that's showing a duel from a western, probably a Sergio Leone).

"Sweetie, the windows are tinted, he can't see in," Carmine is telling her.

Betty Pirrotta, her little snout turned up like a ferret snug in its den, says, "They're not tinted. I can see that guy perfectly and I'm not getting out."

Carmine, staring at the ring he wears on his thumb, says in a level voice, "No? Fine."

Betty nods, swiftly and firmly, as if to say, *Of course it's fine; what's the alternative?*

"And what will we tell your father?"

Betty stares at him with distaste, her eyes squeezed tight. "What do I care? You get me out of this. I'm not going anywhere with that guy. Don't bust my balls."

Carmine looks for the remote control, finds it under his rear end, and begins to zap through the channels.

"Well?" says Betty, curled up in a ball down there on the floor.

"I'm thinking."

"Great, make it fast."

The "parking attendant" gets up lazily from the scooter, scratches his ass, stretches, and moves toward Turrisi.

Turrisi pretends not to see him.

The man stops next to him, stares at him, then stares at the Mercedes. "Fucking nice car. What's up, they need to park?"

Turrisi doesn't move.

"Okay, if they want to park, you, sir, you let me know. I'm over there," he says, pointing to the scooter.

Turrisi looks at his watch.

"So?" asks Betty.

"So, what? We can go and tell your father that Turrisi didn't show up."

"Fucking shit, he's *here*."

"I can see that, I can see that."

"You could go and tell him I'm not feeling well and would rather stay in the car."

Carmine looks at her as if she were a moron. Correction: not even "as if."

"No? Why? I came, and if I didn't feel well in the car it's not my fault."

"Your mother and father want you to be here."

"Wow, that's fucking brilliant. If they didn't want me to be here, what the fuck was I doing here now?"

Carmine reflects on the grammatical construction of Betty's sentences.

"He's wearing Brylcreem."

"Huh?" Carmine looks down at Betty and then takes a quick glance out the window. "Brylcreem's coming back."

"Yeah, in Giorgio Armani ads, on models. He's got a tiny little mustache."

"That's coming back too."

"Mustaches, not tiny little mustaches. On gay guys like you. He's old."

"In his forties."

"Ninety, he's at least ninety."

"Look, in the meantime, you need to get out of the car, go have lunch, and then afterwards we'll come up with something to keep your father happy."

Carmine watches Betty get up, smooth her minidress, take a tiny mirror out of her bag, look herself over, get rapidly out of the car, and walk, smiling, over toward Turrisi.

"Oh my God," says Carmine to himself in a whisper, and then he hurries out of the car, smiling and pleasant as he can be.

Mister Turrisi lights up.

CHAPTER SEVEN

I'm a Salesclerk,
Not an Object

"I'm a salesclerk, not an object," says Bobo, turning once again to stare at the sea.

The sun sparkles tremulously off the crests of the waves. The rubber rafts, bobbing on the water, are melting under the sun. Some teenagers have parked their motorbikes on the concrete breakwater and now they're competing to see who can make the biggest splashes with his cannonballs. One of them is doing cannonballs dressed and wearing a pair of trainers.

"Huh?" Cagnotto doesn't get it.

"You heard me." Bobo looks pleased with himself. He doesn't even bother to look at Cagnotto. Yeah, he's pleased with himself. *He told him.*

But wasn't it supposed to be me who told *him*? thinks Cagnotto.

What's going on?

What's happening, kiddo, is that you're really beginning to make me lose my cool.

How dare you talk to me like that?

This is what I get for treating you like an equal?

Hey, this is the way it goes with *climbers*; it's always a mistake to let them get too friendly. They get a kick out of mistreating their superiors, just because you let them get friendly and because you act like a civilized person.

"I heard what?" says Cagnotto with mounting rage.

"That's right," says Bobo, as if Cagnotto has finally understood.

Cagnotto raises his eyes to the heavens.

Bobo turns to look him in the face, his hands placed firmly on either side of his plate, his gaze decisive and firm, implacable. "You think I haven't understood that you just want to have sex, you pig; you think I don't get it that all this cultural blah-blah"—the word *cultural* comes out with a sarcastic snarl—"that I hear from you is only aimed at scoring a fuck? You think I don't understand because I'm only a salesclerk?"

"But . . ."

"You think I don't know about you famous directors, the way you think you have the whole world at your feet? The fuck you do. But there you go. There you go, there you go . . . I was waiting for it, you think I wasn't waiting for it, I was saying to myself, Hey, I wonder when he's going to offer me a part in one of his plays? You think I wasn't waiting for it . . . hey . . . because I'm just a salesclerk, no? A salesclerk aspiring actor, no? So you can treat me like shit, give me all this cultural blah-blah"—the sarcasm rises to the level of disgust—"because I'm, like"—he mimes the face of an ingenue—"here to gobble up all the nice blah-blah you put out, because you're a director and I'm a salesclerk and you don't get it, you don't get it, you don't get—" Bobo's voice cracks.

Bobo turns toward the sea, his chin pointed at the horizon.

But what's going on? He's crying?

Confirmation arrives with a delicate sniff.

Cagnotto is reduced to silence.

"Because of course you have forgotten"—Bobo is back with his hands at the sides of his plate, head down, staring at his octopus salad—"that once you were just a kid crazy about Art . . . sure, because success has destroyed you, it made you abandon your ideals, it made you into a monster without feelings who doesn't understand . . . doesn't understand . . . doesn't understand . . ."—Bobo raises his head, then lowers his eyes—"doesn't understand that even someone like me . . . someone like me . . . can have feelings . . . can . . . can . . ." Bobo stops.

He waits without lifting his gaze from the octopus.

He hears Cagnotto say, in a faint voice. "Can?"

"Be in love with you."

Bobo, gasping, starts to cry.

Cagnotto sits there with his head tilted to one side, his tongue lolling limply on his lower lip, his eyes looking as if the antidepressant has in that precise instant delivered all its punch.

On the highway back from Capomulini to Catania, Cagnotto still has the same expression on his face, while Bobo looks puzzled, if relieved by the outburst, which has calmed his nerves.

On the windshield the wipers are going back and forth, even though the sun outside is hot enough to fry an egg.

CHAPTER EIGHT

No, He Can't Stand Her When She's Like That

No, he can't stand her when she's like that. He just can't, Carmine thinks. Really, every molecule of indignation in him rebels.

Betty's got a dreamy-hypnotic-nutty look on her face as if she has just, who knows? . . . discovered a treasure, found out that the human race is not as evil as it seems, as if she has only realized just now, with surprise and joy tempered by a note of diffidence (revealing a strong character loyal to her own ideals) that the man sitting before her is not only worthy of her attention, capable of penetrating her critical awareness, but also actually capable of charming her and of (really!) teaching her something, taking her with the strong and masculine arms of experience, imparting useful knowledge gained in the years that separate them (not many, not as many as you might think), years that only reinforce the conviction that no one who doesn't have the experience, the history, and the intellect of Mister Turrisi could ever be an acceptable interlocutor with whom to share in that moment the friendship that Betty is always so reluctant to concede.

Give me a break, thinks Carmine.

What we have here is the pure archetype of a slut dressed up as ninety pounds of tits and sandals.

It can't be true that Betty is conversant with such depth and sensitivity. Where does she get this stuff?

It must be that Betty has a plan. Carmine is sure of it.

"Carmine, dear, could you make a note of this book that Mister Turrisi is recommending?"

Carmine, ever patient, takes his BlackBerry out of his inside jacket pocket and turns toward Turrisi.

Turrisi is laughing up his sleeve.

Carmine sees Turrisi, immobile, his Brylcreem, his little mustache, his expressionless face, and yet he knows Turrisi is laughing up his sleeve, he knows it from the voice Turrisi uses as he says, "*Gangs: The New Aristocracy.*"

"*Gangs: The New Aristocracy,*" he repeats, barely concealing his disgust as he relays the title of the book into the handheld's voice recorder.

Betty nods happily. A kind of luminescence lights up her face.

"As I was saying," continues Turrisi, polishing his mustache with the corner of his napkin, "this British historian draws interesting parallels between the family as we know it in the Mafia sense, and the nobility. Contracts, rituals, formality, even the state marriages that bind together highborn European families. It's a fascinating window on the upper classes through the centuries."

"It certainly sounds worthy of consideration," says Betty.

What kind of fucking language is this? And how would she know?

"Carmine, did you hear that?"

Wow, she's even talking to me, politely now, making me part of the discussion. It sure wasn't Wanda who taught her these table manners. And it sure wasn't her father, either.

"Yes, I did. Very interesting."

Turrisi nods, while, with no regard for Carmine's reply, Betty's attention is once again riveted on Turrisi as she asks, "Is there any truth to what I've heard that Soho can be dangerous?"

Is there any truth?

"Only after a certain hour of the night, and never if you're with me."

Betty smiles, lowering her eyes.

I can't stand this, I'm getting up, I'm going to drown myself in the lobster tank, and don't rescue me.

"Certainly, if it were possible, that would be nice . . . but I don't think my father . . ."

Your father would walk up Via di San Giuliano on his knees if it meant getting you off his ass.

Betty gives him a kick under the table. "Oh, yes, her father is, um . . . an old-fashioned guy."

There he goes again, laughing up his sleeve.

"But I know your respected father very well . . ."

Her respected father. Who? Turi Pirrotta, known in his youth as Riddu the Cement-Mixer because when he got off work at the building site he would drive down to the bar in his cement-mixer and could never find a place to park?

". . . and, I must say, I approve of his approach. I would of course never dream of asking you to come to London. I merely wanted to show how much pleasure the thought gives me. While manners and good form prevent us, as well they should, from behaving in inappropriate ways, there is nothing to stop the mind from pursuing beautiful thoughts, especially when they are based on good intentions."

All *right*. Not *bad*.

"You would never dream of it?"

There it was, that little pinch of maliciousness calculated to operate subliminally on the male gender.

"Ah . . ." Turrisi conveniently changes the subject, having achieved what seemed to him at that moment the maximum victory that decency, queen of the occasion, could concede.

Don't make me say something vulgar.

In the car, after lunch, Carmine, deflated, puzzled, outraged, and curious, asks, "So what are you up to?"

"Me? Nothing."

"Okay, explain."

"What?"

"The whole performance."

"Performance?"

CHAPTER NINE

O Sometimes Insufferable Pomposity!

O sometimes insufferable pomposity! thinks Cagnotto, whose soul has opened up and taken flight. The whirlpools of a thousand wishes stir in him: conversations, disagreements, ripostes, attractions, and repulsions. Contests, concerts, deceptions, subterfuges, mirages. Dictates, contradictions, hypotheses, theses, and antitheses (syntheses are a bit scarce). Plots, subplots, surprises, illusions, dismay. Oh, how he had misjudged the sincere love of a young man just taking his first steps on life's path.

Oh, how desire and will have been subverted by foul cynicism.

Wasn't Bobo perhaps right?

From the depths of his instinct, Bobo had understood and articulated all that Cagnotto had concealed from himself.

Were his instincts pure? No, sir.

Were his passions sincere? Nope.

Cagnotto thinks of Richard Gere. In *Pretty Woman*, overwhelmed by the uncomplicated affection of that ex-prostitute who is going around with his credit card insulting shop clerks, and repenting of his onetime arrogance, he tells his coworker, as he piles one glass upon another, "Hey, when I was a kid I liked blocks."

There you go, Cagnotto feels something like that.

Cagnotto curses Art even as he blesses Bobo's authentic feelings. He thinks of how he was as an adolescent, when the simplicity of a line of verse could work its way into his heart, keeping time with his hopes.

And then?

The anxiety to say something new has alienated him from that state of grace.

Ambitions, jealousy, backstabbing: the theater thrives on the opposite.

The more lofty the ideals onstage, the baser the sentiments behind the scenes.

To pan a work because it is by a rival, to praise someone else to win favors, to declare that congenital idiots are masters. To waste time on empty words. To bow once to the public, once to the critics, and once to the powers that be. Is this all that is left of the young Cagnotto?

Cagnotto swerves to avoid a pedestrian.

Deep in thought, he doesn't notice the insults flying.

He remembers lines of verse, a poem, words scrawled by an innocent soul.

What crime was he about to commit?

My God.

Cagnotto is driving erratically, true to his thoughts.

All that avant-garde and experimental theater, just to cop fame and success, so he could spend his nights with malevolent strangers?

Is this where he wants to take Bobo?

Is this what he wants to teach him?

How to become alienated and lose the innate illumination of the truth?

Cagnotto slams on the brake. A kid on a scooter points with both hands at his prick, as if to say, *Dickhead, you suck.*

And in the name of what? A concept of the theater that even he, to be honest, has yet to understand.

No.

If there is a true path here, it is that of the master who bows to the apprentice, admiring the freshness of his thinking.

Yes.

It is to Bobo's thinking that he should now attend. He will take it in hand, like a little bird, a tender young hostage to the beauty of nature. And he will nurture that *thought* so that it will bud, flower, express itself, and explode with all its delicate power.

Cagnotto wets his lips, shifting into top gear.

That's what he will do.

Back to the days of innocence.

Cagnotto will uproot the weeds of modernity that are suffocating the garden (maybe it is still thriving!) of his inspiration.

He must get back to the classics.

Yes, the classics.

No doubt about that.

Absolutely.

Metaphorically (and not just metaphorically before he had signed a contract with the region to finance his productions) the underground Cagnotto had spit, pissed, and vomited on the classics.

"Oh, how I love anew these people who are called common"— who was that quote from? Goethe? Cagnotto can't remember.

Yes, the common people.

Oh, what damage had been done to the classics by the avant-garde, the ranting when they should have been speaking to the common people. Had theater been born to address the elite?

No, never.

Shakespeare. Who did Shakespeare write for? For whores, thieves, and delinquents.

And Greek theater? The people ate peanuts watching Greek theater. Well, maybe not peanuts because peanuts hadn't been invented
yet, but they were munching on something.

Certainly, the interpretations of the classics needed to be re-
thought, brought back to the original letter and spirit. It will be
necessary to reinvent a language and gestures that are plain and
genuine, that will bring the message of the theater to ordinary folk.

He parks the BMW X5 on the sidewalk without even braking. He
waves at the bread man who's smoking a cigarette in the doorway of
the bakery.

He runs to his own building.

He rings the bell.

Then he realizes he is downstairs and grabs the keys in his
pocket with a smile on his face.

He's got to tell Bobo about his decision right away, keep him up
to date on his spiritual evolution.

Okay, he thinks in the elevator, shall I call him right away or
shall I wait fifteen minutes?

CHAPTER TEN

In Pajamas and Dressing Gown in the Sitting Room of Villa Wanda

In pajamas and dressing gown in the sitting room of Villa Wanda, Turi Pirrotta is staring curiously at a bell. For years now Pirrotta has been staring curiously at his house; since his wife Wanda learned that redecorating was an excellent way to launder money, she has done nothing but shift the furniture out from under him, switch this room with that, bang in nails, adjust walls, and hire consultants.

Here's how it works: You get hold of a bell, let's say the bell costs you five euros, you take it and you put it in a shop owned by your family under a fake name (usually under the name of the previous proprietor of the shop, who has fallen on hard times because of the protection money he had to pay you or because of the interest on the loans you advanced). You take the bell and on the bottom you put a sticker with a price on it: five hundred euros. Into the shop walks Wanda, she buys the bell, and you have just laundered four hundred ninety-five euros in one go.

And even if the tax police do come along, what can they say?

Pirrotta pictures the tax police, all serious, asking his wife, "And you say you paid five hundred euros for this bell?" You just have to look at Wanda to see she's the type who would do something as dumb-assed as that. Shit, you just have to look at the woman when she comes back from the hairdresser's.

Pirrotta raises his eyes to the heavens recalling the time his tax accountant's wife explained these financial matters to Wanda. Couldn't they just exchange gossip about their lovers like all other married women instead of busting their better halves' balls?

Where the fuck is Betty? How much fucking time does she need to get home? How long is this frigging lunch going to last?

The thought brings a happy half-smile to Pirrotta's lips. Shit, getting her married to Turrisi!

His daughter Betty not only out of his house but into Alfio Turrisi's.

Mrs. Betty Turrisi. Mother of God, how nice that sounds to Turi Pirrotta. Mrs. Betty Turrisi.

The oil business at Ispica: check!

The Mafia-war business: check!

The ball-busting-daughter-who-needs-a-husband business: check!

What more could he want from life? Only that Wanda should go to the hairdresser's a little more often.

Is Betty going to hurry up and bring him some news?

Pirrotta sighs and squirms in his chair.

The bell rings in his hand.

Pirrotta, deep in thought, jumps.

He takes that bitch of a bell and puts it down carefully between a stylized pineapple in crystal and a cigarette box in the shape of the Altar of the Nation, that mammoth monument to national unity in Rome.

The Filipina maid appears. "Mister ring?"

"Who, me? No!" Pirotta says without thinking, somewhat freaked. The maid bows and withdraws.

Pirrotta looks at the bell again.

He understands.

He picks up the bell and rings it hard.

The maid does not appear.

Pirrotta rings harder.

Still nobody.

Pirrotta takes the bell in two hands and shakes it with his whole body, as if he were strangling someone.

The maid runs in.

"Mister ring?"

"No, I was just celebrating the election of the new mayor."

The maid doesn't get it.

"Yes, I rang. Didn't you hear?"

"I hear. But I think you fooling."

Pirrotta lowers his eyes to contain the rage that is rising in him.

"Bring me a *wodka.*" (Strangely, he pronounces it as if he were a true Russian.)

"Right away, sir."

"A double, make it a double."

"Double, sir, double."

Pirrotta hears the door slam and the tick-tick-tick of Betty's heels.

He gets up, doesn't know what to do with himself, sits down, gets up; he doesn't want Betty to see that he's worried.

But hey, as if Betty hadn't already figured it out.

Pirrotta gives up and sits down carefully in the chair, his nervous hands stuck between his legs, his face hopeful.

Betty comes into the room, followed by Carmine. She stares at her father distractedly.

Her father has a dumb smile stamped on his face; shit if her mother isn't right, thinks Betty.

She tosses her bag on the sofa and just as casually throws herself down beside it.

She looks at Carmine.

Carmine raises his eyes.

Betty takes the bell.

Carmine sits down in a chair and crosses his legs.

Betty rings the bell.

Turi Pirrotta doesn't move a muscle; he watches the performance with a dumb look. Oh, how sweet it is when the children come home. He flashes a dumb half-smile at Carmine too while he's at it.

The maid comes in with the double vodka and asks, "Miss ring?"

"A cup of tea."

A cup of tea?

"What do you want?"

"Okay, I'll have a cup of tea also, darling, with a shot of brandy in it," says Carmine, dusting off the collar of his orange jacket.

"Yes, miss," says the maid, putting the double vodka down on the table in front of Pirrotta.

Pirrotta looks at the double vodka as if he has no idea what it is.

"Mama says you shouldn't drink, it aggravates your diabetes."

Oh, Mother of God, how beautiful it would be if she went to bust the balls of Turrisi every morning. Mother of God, how beautiful.

"Well, you won't tell her."

Betty smiles. "That depends."

Pirrotta gives her a look like someone who's in total agreement. "So?" he says.

"So what?" says Betty taking a cigarette from the Altar of the Nation and lighting it with a silver skyscraper.

"Your mother says you shouldn't smo—"

Betty looks up.

Pirrotta smiles. "And so? What's he like?"

"Mature," says Betty, exhaling a little cloud of smoke.

"Oh, good, good. So he's well behaved; that's interesting, no?" Pirrotta looks to Carmine for help.

Carmine's wearing an indecipherable expression.

Pirrotta hangs all his hopes on that indecipherable expression. "Okay, good. Um . . . so . . . will you be seeing each other again?"

Silence.

Carmine looks at Betty.

Betty is trying to figure out what is that thing in her hand shaped like a lit cigarette. She tosses it in an ashtray. She stretches like a cat, mewing, takes off her shoes, tucks her feet under her thighs, and says nothing.

Pirrotta looks at Carmine.

Carmine doesn't know what to say. "Uh . . . yeah, I guess so?" With a question mark.

Carmine and Pirrotta stare at Betty.

Betty is bobbing her head back and forth, trying to get the crick out of her neck.

Pirrotta and Carmine wait impatiently.

Betty interrupts the neck business. "What's to look at?"

The maid comes in with a tray.

On the tray there's no tea, only a cordless phone. "Mister Turrisi for the miss," says the maid.

Pirrotta's mouth falls open.

Carmine exhales.

"Give it to me," says Betty with a bored gesture of her hand.

The maid steps up to Betty and with a bow hands her the cordless.

Betty takes the phone slowly, removes an earring from one ear, throws it into a seashell made of porcelain, looks at her father, and says, "Hello?"

Pirrotta sits very still.

Carmine discreetly studies Betty out of the corner of his eye. He's the kind of guy who knows women well, but Betty never ceases to surprise him.

Betty picks up a glass slab with a piranha trapped inside. "No, I can't come with you to the theater."

Pirrotta, terrorized, stares at Carmine. He turns toward Betty and goes, *Yes, yes, yes,* with his head.

"No . . . no . . . no," says Betty to the cordless.

Pirrotta smooths out his pajama bottoms. Then he comes to a decision. He falls to his knees, puts his hands together in supplication, and gazes at his daughter screaming, *Yes, yes, yes,* with his head.

Betty looks at Carmine.

Carmine is embarrassed.

She looks at her father, sighs, and says, "No, tonight is out of the question. Let's talk tomorrow. And now I'm compelled to say goodbye."

Betty taps the off button and tosses the cordless on the sofa.

Pirrotta struggles to his feet, stares at the vodka, downs it in a gulp, straightens his dressing gown, and walks off without saying a word.

Compelled?

CHAPTER ELEVEN

An Immense Ham Hock Lies on Cagnotto's Plate

An immense ham hock lies on Cagnotto's plate. (Apparently his stomach is in order again.) Their two hands, joined at the table, are lit up in the flickering candlelight. Bobo has ordered a salad of fennel and arugula.

"I have nothing to give you but myself, Bobo."

Bobo withdraws his hand and scratches his neck.

"Myself. The heart of me, know what I mean?"

Bobo doesn't understand.

"Precisely!" says Cagnotto as if Bobo had replied. "I want to tell you the truth, Bobo. I don't have a penny. I was there trying to work up an idea for a new theater season and *you* came along. And I realized that I was prostituting myself."

Cagnotto smiles proudly. "I was once again prostituting myself and my art, and for what? For the hypocritical acclaim of the public whose adoration lasts only as long as the next round of applause."

"Don't talk like that."

"I will," says Cagnotto with determination, seeking Bobo's hand with his own.

"No, don't."

"Yes, I will! You made me understand. You . . . I'm, uh . . . grateful."

Bobo puts his hands in his lap.

"Don't be shy."

"No, it's just that . . ." Bobo looks around.

They're in the restaurant attached to the Stage Space, a performance complex tucked into an old brick factory that has been rehabbed thanks to European Union funds for cooperatives. Exposed volcanic stone, plain cement floors. The air-conditioning is turned down to minus zero and the room is freezing. That's why nobody goes to the restaurant attached to the Stage Space. But Cagnotto had wanted a quiet place to talk and in the summer the outdoor restaurants are wild. And they say we're in the middle of an economic crisis?

The woman manager of the Stage Space restaurant is German, the ham hocks are a German specialty, and she says that if she doesn't keep the air-conditioning up to the max her clients won't want to eat ham hocks in the summer.

"I'm going to give back to Shakespeare that which is Shakespeare's, Bobo."

"How's that?"

"You know Pasolini, De Sica, neorealism?"

Bobo is silent.

"They used street actors, like Shakespeare. Simplicity is their essence; the lack of professionalism renders the artist's message cleanly. Without actorial mediation, which is motivated, let's be frank, by the vanity of the protagonists."

"Huh?"

Cagnotto smiles, spearing his ham hock. "But Pasolini and De Sica were film artists, get it, Bobo? Films. In the movies, if a nonprofessional actor flubs his lines, gets an expression wrong, or is unable to convey an emotion, what do you do?"

Bobo doesn't know.

"Reshoot the take!" Cagnotto chews with gusto. "You follow me?"

Bobo looks at Cagnotto. He looks at his salad. He nods with his head bowed.

"But me, what do I do? I don't do *films*." Cagnotto pronounces the word *films* with a certain distaste. "So I said to myself, who are the street actors of the theater?"

Bobo looks at Cagnotto.

"Who are they?"

Bobo looks at Cagnotto as he slices off another piece of ham hock. "Don't know. Jugglers?"

"Huh?"

"Those guys on crutches?"

Cagnotto looks up, interested. Jugglers? Crutches?

"I don't know. The real tall ones."

"Ah, stilts!"

"You want to do something with stilts?"

Cagnotto smiles. "No, no, the street actors of the theater are dialect theater actors. They are the ones who can speak to the public's heart without any"—Cagnotto takes an abundant gulp of wine—"superstructure."

Bobo looks at Cagnotto.

Cagnotto nods. "Bringing Shakespearean theater back to its origins."

Cagnotto looks Bobo in the eyes. "Bringing Shakespearean theater back to its origins, just as you have restored me to mine. We must resist being determined by our respective social statuses, Bobo. What you said to me at Capomulini struck me . . . struck me deeply. You, salesclerk, and me, director: Are we going to be limited by these definitions?"

Cagnotto smiles to himself, continues. "Are we once again going to allow social position to negate our desire? Again? Then what was the use of Shakespeare? Nothing. Bobo, I'm going to stage the play in which the Bard taught us to overcome social convention, in which he showed us that the power of love cannot be thwarted by society's rules. Bobo, I'm going to do *Romeo and Juliet*. Me, Capulet, you, Montague; the theater is there to teach us. We must not fall into the trap of conformism."

Bobo looks at his salad. He shivers.

Cagnotto nods at his ham hock.

CHAPTER TWELVE

Betty Is Counting the Toes on Her Feet

Betty is counting the toes on her feet.

Carmine is certain. At first, it looked like she was merely checking the condition of her toenail polish. But instead, Betty (Carmine is sure of it) is actually counting the toes on her feet. She's keeping count with her index finger, her face absorbed in her task.

Betty sometimes goes off in her own world like this, doing apparently strange things. Carmine knows that in moments like this Betty is planning something. Getting deeply involved in apparently innocuous activities is her way of camouflaging herself.

The bright pink polish the same color as her dress.

"You want to talk?"

"Four, five, si . . . about what?"

Carmine sighs.

Betty shrugs her shoulders. She rests her chin on her knuckles and gazes into the void with excessive interest.

"Sweetheart, look, you don't have to explain to me, but give me at least a clue. That's all I need, just enough to satisfy my curiosity. What are you planning to do?"

"You're curious?"

Carmine reflects. "Yes."

"That'll teach you not to help me when I need you."

"I must have been distracted."

"You weren't one little tiny dick distracted."

Carmine gets up. He checks his fly. "Okay, so, see you later."

Betty stares at him.

Carmine smiles. "Don't get them in trouble."

"Who?"

"See you later." Carmine struts out, both injured party and victorious.

Betty watches him, making a *so what?* face. "Asshole. What the fuck does he know? Faggot."

She checks, stretching her neck, that Carmine has really gone, then gets up on tiptoes to see that nobody else is around.

Back on the sofa, she takes the cordless and stares at it dumbly.

"Oh, yes," she says. She grabs her bag, takes out a slip of paper, and punches in a number.

"Alf . . . Mister Turrisi, no . . . ah . . . listen, you must forgive me for bothering you, yes, yes"—Betty makes a face, rolling her eyes as if to say, *Shit, what a jerk this Turrisi*—"the fact is"—Betty turns conspiratorial—"no, no, you mustn't call me at home, no, of course I don't mind, but my father, um, I beg you, don't even call me on the cell phone, my father checks the incoming calls and what if I forget to delete them? I beg you, please don't get me in trouble, no, no texting either. Oh, God, I've got to get off now. I'll call you back."

Betty hangs up. She tosses the cordless to the other end of the sofa and sits back down.

Wanda makes her imperial entrance into the sitting room, followed by her assistant, who is weighed down with packages. She drops, exhausted, into a chair, takes off her shoes, massages her feet and her swollen ankles, flashes a smile at her daughter, glances with distaste at her assistant, and tells her, "Fine, we're finished for the day, give the stuff to the maid." She waits until the young woman is gone, then gets up and hurries over to her daughter's side, hugs her happily, cheek to cheek, sits back down, smiles, and says, "Tell me. Everything."

"You want me to get married?" says Betty, getting right to the point.

Wanda makes a serious face, tips her head to one side, pouts her lips so as to hollow out her well-upholstered cheeks, gazes at Betty very seriously, and nods firmly.

Betty raises her right arm, puts it over her head and down, grabs her left jaw with her right hand, and tries to wiggle the crick out of her neck. She repeats the operation with her left arm and her right jaw. The damn crick just won't go away.

Wanda watches this operation with interest. "Aren't you a little young for neck problems?"

Betty throws her head back, points the fingers of both hands under her chin, and pushes. No luck, the crick won't budge. She loses interest in these operations and turns to look her mother in the eyes.

Wanda smiles. She begins to explain. "Your father, as you know, is a dickhead. And this Turrisi is another dickhead." Wanda thinks. "Actually, I think Turrisi is more of a dickhead than your father. That Baronessa Faillaci, baroness my ass, was gobbling him up at that lunch at Palazzo Biscari. He's got real estate in London, he's got a collection of English cars, he's grabbing all the land in the province of Siracusa where they say there's oil, but above all, they say, he has intellectual pretensions. And take my word for it, Betty, there's no dickhead more dickhead than one who has intellectual pretensions."

Wanda looks at Betty. Betty doesn't look convinced. "And I'll bet he's a pansy too," she adds.

Betty looks at Wanda.

Wanda sighs. She makes a *no* with her head. "Betty, don't make the same mistake your mother made. *My* mother said to me, 'Riddu the Cement-Mixer has a hard-on all the time.' I didn't want to listen to her, back in the days when he used to come and pick me up in the Mercedes. 'If he has a hard-on, I'll make it disappear,' I said. And my mother, who was smart, your grandmother, know what she told me?"

Betty goes *no* with her head.

"She said, 'You think that'll be easy?' How right she was, your grandmother. You ought to get married to someone like this Turrisi. Don't make my mistake and marry someone who likes to . . ." Wanda stops, not wishing to sound vulgar, and raises her right hand with a closed fist to make a *fuck* gesture.

Betty is staring at her elbow.

Wanda looks at Betty. "Betty?" she asks.

"Yes."

"How come you aren't saying anything?"

"Me?"

Wanda rests her elbow on the arm of the chair and begins to massage her brow, looking worried.

CHAPTER THIRTEEN

Have You Ever Been in Sicily when the Hot Wind of Love Blows over the Land?

Have you ever been in Sicily when the hot wind of love blows over the land? Cagnotto walks happily along Via Etnea, this morning like every morning an explosion of almond and lemon granita, smells of *pasta reale* melting in the heat and cannoli just out of the oven, whiffs of vanilla and almond from all sides mingling with the unmistakable smell of moisturizer and carotene (which deepens your tan.)

Cagnotto is drunk with happiness even though he can't go to the beach. He can't go because now he has a proposal and if he gets to work right away he can have his new production on the stage by September.

He's got an appointment with Falsaperla, the culture commissioner for the province. The culture commissioner for the province of Catania deals with distribution. While the culture commissioner for the city of Catania takes care of culture in Catania, and the culture commissioners for towns in the province of Catania take care of culture in their hometowns, the culture commissioner for the province distributes. The culture commissioner for the province is very pleased with his duties: He sends an artist to Pedara and he sends an intellectual to Trecastagni. He keeps track of political favors and tries to accommodate everyone as best he can. He has an important job: by oiling the wheels of culture on the slopes of Mt. Etna, he keeps the machine purring.

"We'd rather you continue with experimental theater," the commissioner is telling him as he flips through some papers: Cagnotto's CV and his new proposal.

Cagnotto's benevolent smile hardens on his face. He tilts his head to one side. He doesn't know what to say.

The commissioner burrows in the piles on his desk to find the remote control for the air conditioner. He picks it up and fiddles with it, pointing it upward toward the machine.

Cagnotto looks upward.

"You know what I mean, no?" says the commissioner, shaking the remote.

"Um . . ."

The commissioner makes a *no* with his head, it's not clear whether to the remote or to Cagnotto.

The commissioner is wearing a summer jacket in a check pattern, a shirt of red stripes, and a multicolored regimental tie.

Cagnotto is hypnotized by all the colors.

He's also strangely fascinated by the extremely long hairs that sprout from the commissioner's ears.

"You know, the dialect theater companies won't like it, they're in trouble—"

"But—"

"Listen, Cagnotto!" snorts the commissioner tossing the remote on the desk, "what's all this about dialect theater?" The commissioner grabs the phone and punches a button. "You made your name in avant-garde theater, read this, it's your CV. And let me say, you wouldn't have a CV like this if *we* hadn't helped out." The commissioner slams down the phone. He gets up. He looks at Cagnotto and walks resolutely toward the door. Cagnotto notices that the commissioner's sleeves reach down almost to his fingernails. The commissioner opens the door wide. "Gnazia-a-a, how does this fucking air conditioner work?"

With the door wide open a gust of air comes in and lifts Cagnotto's CV off the table, sending it sailing past his nose.

Cagnotto follows with his eyes.

Gnazia comes in sighing.

"Why didn't you answer the intercom?" the commissioner asks her.

"Huh? I was on the phone."

"And what were you doing on the phone?"

Gnazia stares at the commissioner with contempt.

The commissioner is silent.

Cagnotto decides there must be something going on between Gnazia and the commissioner. Only a guy who's *involved* could be so silent.

"So what's wrong now?"

"That thing"—the commissioner indicates the air conditioner—"doesn't work."

"What do you mean, it doesn't work?" Gnazia strides to the commissioner's desk, takes the remote in hand, stares at it, looks up at the air conditioner, looks at the window, sees the drapes that are swirling around, and throws Cagnotto an investigatory look as if to say, *Did you open the windows?*

Gnazia tugs at her skirt, walks firmly toward the windows, and closes them, being sure to make a lot of noise. "The air conditioner works fine but the windows have to be kept closed or the heat comes in from outside."

"And who opened the windows?" the commissioner says.

Gnazia eyes the commissioner with loathing and goes out without saying another word.

The commissioner heads over to the windows and makes sure they are shut tight. He has to think of everything around here!

He goes back to his desk.

Cagnotto still has the courteous smile glued on his face.

The commissioner gazes at Cagnotto with a *who the fuck is this? who let him in here?* look. "So where were we? Okay. So what's this about dialect theater? You need to keep doing that stuff, the avant-garde, and that other stuff, experimental theater, otherwise they'll say the government isn't responsive to young people."

The commissioner nods to himself with conviction. Everyone knows that young people matter. "And anyway, I'd have a revolt on my hands from the dialect theaters all over the province. It's not like you can just get up in the morning and bang! improvise dialect theater."

The commissioner waves his hand as if to say, *Are you going nuts here?*

"But, Commissioner, it's not my idea to have them perform in dialect, the proposal explains that we need dialect actors because they are the 'street actors' of theater. You know, Pasolini, De Sica, neo-realism, well, they all used str—"

"I get it, Cagnotto, I get it," says the commissioner, interrupting him. "Are you cooling off now?"

Cagnotto doesn't understand.

The commissioner nods toward the air conditioner with his chin.

Cagnotto still doesn't get it, and so the commissioner points toward the air conditioner once again, jerking his jaw up twice in rapid succession.

"Ah . . . yes, I see, yes, it's working."

The commissioner is all smiles. He turns his attention back to Cagnotto's business. He looks around on his desk but can't find the CV. Aiming a suspicious stare at Cagnotto with one eye, he grabs a random sheet of paper and shoves it in front of his nose, pretending it is Cagnotto's CV.

"Just between us, Cagnotto, we're cutting back funds for dialect theater because the future of the slopes of Etna lies in food festivals. Don't you read the papers, Cagnotto? Forget neorealism. You come in here and pitch me neorealism. You think that's how a guy becomes commissioner for culture?" The commissioner tosses Cagnotto's fake CV on the desk and snaps his fingers. Then he joins his two hands together in his lap and looks serious.

"The future of the slopes of Etna is called oenogastronomy."

"Of Etna?"

"Cagnotto. I'm amazed. You didn't know that the future of culture is going to be in local color? Bronte pistachios, Militello sausage, *fritto misto* from Iacicastello? Take my word for it, money for dialect theater is going to be scarce. So do what you're good at, that stuff, the avant-garde."

Cagnotto shifts in his chair. He tugs at the hem of his jacket, which has gotten stuck under his rear end. "Commissioner, look, this proposal of mine *is* avant-garde, I'm interested in the realism of the street, the unadorned realism of the str—"

"Hey, I'm sorry, Cagnotto, but here I see the words *dialect actors*," says the commissioner, picking up a random page.

Cagnotto stares at the pages of his proposal and his CV, lying on the floor.

"I say to you Cagnotto: avant-garde. We must be *experimental*. This is Sicily. We have to show those cocksuckers up north what we're capable of."

Cagnotto is about to say something.

The commissioner stands and sticks out his hand. "Fine, Cagnotto. I've given you my advice. Now you write me a proposal with that stuff of yours, the weird stuff, and then . . . let me think"—the commissioner thinks—"in a few months, when the winter season is on, come back and we'll see what we can do. Happy?"

CHAPTER FOURTEEN

A Patron, a Piazza, an Amphitheater

"A patron, a piazza, an amphitheater." Seated in the bar of the Yacht Club, Commissioner Paino is trying to explain to the Contessa what Cagnotto so desperately needs.

Paino hunkers down into the jacket of his blue linen suit worn over a white polo shirt, glancing around with a conspiratorial air.

The members of the Yacht Club are playing cards. Because you need a boat to be a member of the Yacht Club, everybody has one, although no one has ever seen any of them on the water. Most likely the boats are employed in betting, they probably use them like chips. The Contessa, for example, to join the Yacht Club, had bought a motorized rubber speedboat and baptized it *DBMB* for *Divine Bianca Maria Beatrice*, one of the Bourbons who had been queen of something, although many suspected the initials stood for Don't Bust My Balls.

Cagnotto had called the Contessa asking to see her because he wanted to ask a favor, and when you're asked a favor, says the Contessa, it's a good idea to get a second opinion, because the one who's asking you the favor isn't likely to tell you the truth. So she's asking Paino.

"Falsaperla closed the door in his face," says Paino. "Cagnotto wants to do something in dialect, Shakespeare or De Sica, I couldn't understand which, you know how Falsaperla is when he explains things. Falsaperla has sent out a memo in which he invites all commissioners to stick to tradition, to stay away from events that involve 'contamination,' and to promote the local color of the region."

"Falsaperla talks like that?" The Contessa is in pale blue linen complete with hat.

"No, he's got a press office. They write the memos for him."

The Contessa makes the usual vague face she always puts on when somebody tells her about the workings of the democratic system. Once upon a time there was a king and everything was simple. Even if he was a cretin, there was only one of him and it was easier to manage.

"To tell the truth, I don't understand the memo myself. So I called the culture commissioner for Pedara to ask what the hell Falsaperla meant by 'contamination.' I was worried that if I wanted to do the Slopes of Etna Wine Festival I would have to include in the application to the department yet another application for a quality control certificate from the food and wine inspectors, and I thought Falsaperla was losing his mind and as far as I'm concerned, as you know, I wouldn't mind if Falsaperla lost his mind, so I keep an eye on him and his memos. The commissioner for Pedara told me that Falsaperla is still lucid, although I'm not sure how long the light of reason will last because he's getting it on with Gnazia, and Gnazia is an expert at driving men crazy, you know who I mean, Gnazia?"

The Contessa nods, looking the other way. As if she couldn't care less about such matters.

"The commissioner for Pedara told me that 'contamination' referred to Cagnotto. Cagnotto wants to break into the dialect business, that is to say he's looking for culture funds, and as punishment, he's not getting any work anywhere this summer."

"So he doesn't have any money for his show? And he wants money from me?"

Paino smiles. "At this point all he needs is a piazza. A sponsor. Otherwise he can't put on his performance, even if he coughs up the money himself."

"And why's that?"

"What do you mean, why? Where's he going to put on a show, in summertime? He can only do it in a piazza. And who owns the piazza? Me, I mean we, the commissioners."

The Contessa puts on an *I love this!* face. "And so, in the summertime, it's up to you commissioners to decide which performances are put on?"

Paino nods contentedly.

"I see."

"Then if he wants to do the financial side, that's his business, but he's got to take care of the box office, the royalties, and all the rest. It's up to him. I just put the amphitheater at his disposal."

"And you've got an amphitheater at San Giovanni la Punta?" The Contessa, who in her youth had buzzed around in her Spider looking at archaeological remains (or so she said), had never heard of an amphitheater at San Giovanni la Punta.

"You didn't know that?"

"Listen, I'll do you this favor, though in my opinion Falsaperla is already crazy. I'd say he's positively dangerous. Are you sure you want to make an enemy of him?"

Paino flashes a sardonic smile. "Who? Falsaperla?"

CHAPTER FIFTEEN

Rosalba Quattrocchi's
Salumeria Is Unctuous

Rosalba Quattrocchi's *salumeria* is unctuous. All *salumerie* are unctuous, and Sicilian *salumerie*, in the summer months, are especially unctuous. But Rosalba Quattrocchi's *salumeria* beats them all. The fat is not due merely to the hams and cheeses, the mackerel fillets in oil and the wheels of Gruyère perched on little marble columns. The unctuousness of the Quattrocchi *salumeria* is a swish of status, an oozing exhibit of opulence.

Jano Caporeale and Cosimo Cosentino enter the *salumeria*, looking around a little bit bewildered. The Quattrocchi establishment makes them slightly nervous, especially since Caporeale had once refused the advances of "Signorina" Quattrocchi, fatally forgetting that the "young" lady let them both buy on credit.

"Shit," Cosentino had confided to Caporeale, "I can't bring myself to call her *Signorina*, have you looked at her?"

"But you've been calling her Rosalba for years and you even use the *tu*."

"Exactly, that's what I'm getting at, I'd prefer to address her as *Lei*."

"Well, look who's here. Our great actors on the dark way!" says Quattrocchi, who has seen them come in and gotten a little bit confused between Dante and his *dark wood* and the Great White Way.

Signorina Quattrocchi is sitting behind the counter reading a gossip magazine, turning the pages, and licking her index finger with great pomp and circumstance.

Caporeale tugs at his jacket in a most dignified way, looks at Cosentino, nods, and says, "Watch it, because you're speaking with two Shakespearean actors."

Quattrocchi, not taking her eye off the magazine, twists her mouth up in a little smirk of sarcastic admiration. "In other words, you've come to settle your account?" she says, squinting an eye at something, a photo or a caption.

Caporeale tries to get Cosentino's eye.

Cosentino is staring at a basket of salami.

"Given that I appreciate the fact you didn't call me at home to remind me, I'm here to say that the dark way is with us no more. We got a call from Cagnotto, who wants us for his new piece."

"Who?"

"Cagnotto. The theater director, experimental theater. Don't you read the papers?" Caporeale looks to Cosentino for approval. Cosentino is turning over a tin of tripe with great curiosity.

Quattrocchi, by way of reply, lifts the magazine so they can see.

Caporeale frowns with contempt. "Cagnotto is a director who's famous all over Italy. If he keeps it up you'll be coming to see us downtown at the City Theater."

Another smirk of sarcastic admiration. "I've got a season ticket at the City, including a seat for the opening night. And if they put *you* on down there, I'm canceling. And just for your information, I didn't call you at home because I knew that sooner or later you'd be stopping in here."

"Shit, and I'm telling you that I'm doing Shakespeare with Cagnotto."

"Yeah, and what does that mean? That you'll pay your bill?"

Caporeale is silent.

Quattrocchi smiles. "Okay, you can stuff your sandwich with the script. Any more cultural discourses to deliver, you and your *cumpare*?"

Caporeale and Cosentino are plowing down Via Ventimiglia with their heads bowed. They're in the upper Civita quarter, between the Archi della Marina and Corso Sicilia. The whole block, not long ago, was the domain of prostitutes. The people of Catania like to say with pride that theirs is the only Italian city to have a red-light district. But then, right on Corso Sicilia a couple of years back, they had held the World Conference on the Exploitation of Women. The mayor really had to scramble to get everything cleaned up. Now the only professionals here are the transvestites, who because they own the apartments can't be sent away. Poor things. They had put in a lifetime of hard labor, managed to save up and buy their apartments, either directly or as fronts for unnamed others, they had rented the apartments to Afro-Sicilians, the black hookers had displaced the white hookers, then the mayor had cleaned up the block under threat of force majeure (and luckily he had an excuse, otherwise who knows what would have happened), and the transvestites had had to get back into their fishnet stockings and earn a living. It wasn't a very pretty picture. Transvestites grow old too.

The vacant apartments are used by the Afro-Sicilians as warehouses for their high-tech trade. They're there at the street corners and zebra crossings, in their running suits and their sunglasses, controlling the territory. Who knows why these Afro-Sicilians like controlling the territory so much? They're so intent on controlling that they even give the evil eye to Caporeale and Cosentino. Along the sidewalk, half-wrecked automobiles are parked, blankets thrown over the seats, with plasma-screen TVs and home entertainment units inside. Down at the end of Via Ventimiglia you can catch a glimpse of the sea.

"But are you sure?" Caporeale begins. "I mean, we know Cagnotto, could this just be more of his bullshit?"

Cosentino is lost in thought. "Huh?"

"The money. Are we sure he has the money? I already told those guys in the bar we're doing Shakespeare. And if we don't?"

"No, no, Cagnotto is in tight with the commissioners," says Cosentino, still a bit dreamy. "I had a word with Pippo Rattalina the *capocomico*, the boss of the dialect stage."

"Nice *guy*, he's forgotten all about us old veterans."

"Hey, we're not *that* old."

"So why don't we get any work anymore?"

"What do we care about dialect theater? All they need is four punks and two cockteases, the ones who know the right people, and they can put on a show in the piazza. He says we shouldn't work with Cagnotto."

"And what the fuck difference does it make to Rattalina? And why the fuck did you call him?"

"I didn't call him. I ran into him at the bar and I wanted to make him jealous."

"Make who jealous, Rattalina?"

Cosentino nods.

Caporeale makes a *fuck, what an idiot you are* face. "And what did he say to you?"

"He said there are already too many impresarios around and that Cagnotto's going to get into trouble."

Caporeale makes a face like, *That was something that had occurred to me too.*

"But I reassured him. I told him we were not going to be doing dialect theater. I told him we were doing something from Shakespeare."

"So you started out trying to make him jealous and you ended up trying to reassure him?"

Cosentino makes a face that suggests he hadn't looked at things in that light. "I also told him we weren't going to be performing in a piazza, we were going to be performing in a loft."

"Where are we going to be performing?"

"In a loft. Everyone knows that Cagnotto works in lofts."

"Not in the summer, because you fry."

Cosentino hadn't thought of that.

"And so?"

"And so what?"

"What did Rattalina say?"

Cosentino stares at Caporeale, then averts his eyes.

Caporeale grabs him by the arm and makes him stop walking. "What did he say?"

Cosentino makes a face like, *Do I really have to tell you?*

Yep, you really have to tell me, and fast.

"He said, 'It's up to you.' "

"What did he say?"

"It's . . . up . . . to . . . you."

Caporeale thrusts his hands into his hair. "So that means we'll never work for Rattalina again. Shit, let's hope that Cagnotto really has the money. Fuck, I even told my sister I was going to do Shakespeare. And already she's on my case that at my age I should settle down and get married."

"At sixty?"

"My sister, when she has something on the brain—"

"So why don't you marry Quattrocchi?"

"You're the one she likes, not me."

"Who, me? No, sir. You saw how sour she was. The one she's in love with is you. Nothing so furious as a woman scorned."

"Who, Quattrocchi?" says Caporeale, stunned.

Cosentino nods. "You look at her from the outside and you see Quattrocchi. But never forget, inside Quattrocchi, even if you can't see it, is a woman."

CHAPTER SIXTEEN

Contessa Salieri Likes It When They Kill People

Contessa Salieri likes it when they kill people. She said so to Dr. Cosenza, her psychoanalyst. She told him she particularly likes it when they kill people she knows. She specified that she was telling him this not because she felt guilty about it, but because she knew you were supposed to tell your psychoanalyst everything.

Dr. Cosenza told this to his colleague Dr. Farina, and Dr. Farina said that probably Contessa Salieri had repressed something, like that she had done something nasty in the past and now she likes it when there's evil in the world because it makes her feel better about herself, and he advised Dr. Cosenza to continue with the analysis until what she had repressed came out.

Dr. Farina, wanting to show off, told all this to his mistress Baronessa Ferla, and Baronessa Ferla told Farina that the only thing Contessa Salieri had repressed was the memory of the male organ, which she hadn't laid eyes on since the days of the national referendum to abolish the monarchy.

She also told him that the Contessa was constantly spreading bullshit because she didn't have anything else going on in her life, she was bored out of her mind, and she had decided to go to a psychoanalyst because she had read in *Vanity Fair* that wrinkles could be psychosomatic, and since there was no longer anything to stretch with all the face-lifts she'd had, otherwise she'd rip, she had decided to go to Dr. Cosenza.

She had gone to Cosenza and not to Farina because she knew that Farina was going to bed with Baronessa Ferla and she didn't want her business to be known all over town. Baronessa Ferla tumbled out of bed thinking that in any case she now knew all about the Contessa's business.

Cagnotto knows nothing about any of this, and has asked to see the Contessa to obtain a *raccomandazione*, to get her to put in a good word. Cagnotto feels rotten.

He has made a promise to the actors that the play will go on. And if you make a promise to actors, and maybe they decline another job, and then you don't go ahead with the play, you can forget about those actors.

He had made a promise to Caporeale and Cosentino, those assholes, and they had gone and had a fight with Rattalina.

But above all, he had made a promise to Lambertini! Who, with all her connections to the commissioners, if you made her a promise and then the show didn't go on, you could consider yourself a dead man.

There's something perverse about events sponsored by the departments of culture. To present your proposal you need to have your proposal in hand. But how can you have the proposal if you don't already have the funds? To put together a theater company you need funds, but to get funds you need the company. This is how things work in Sicily, in any case, and Cagnotto is beginning to feel faint.

Before talking to the Contessa, Cagnotto had tried asking Lambertini, with a distracted air, "But, um, among the important people you know, what do you think, might there be someone, obviously taking into account other obligations, someone who might want to buy my . . . our Shakespeare?"

And Lambertini had replied, "Are you trying to tell me you don't have the sponsor or the money and that the play isn't going to happen?"

That's how Lambertini is, she prefers to keep her connections to herself and save them for her recitals.

Lambertini's "recitals" are select pieces in which she presents herself onstage with the player of a musical instrument (usually a piano or a cello), and as the notes begin to swell, she plucks out her hair like chicken feathers, rips her clothes, yells out voices in her head, slaps herself all over until she drops to the floor, kicks her feet, whacks the stage, gives a couple of head-butts to the musical instrument, and, depending on the piece she's performing, either swoons, dies, or kills herself. This description comes courtesy of Caporeale.

According to Caporeale the version she does best is the one in which she kills herself. And in fact, every time he sees one of Lambertini's recitals in which at the end the actress swoons or dies a natural death, without fail Caporeale will comment, "But how come she didn't kill herself?"

Without the backing of Falsaperla, Cagnotto would not only fail to get a piazza, he wouldn't even have a dark corner in which to mount his Shakespeare. You had to have a permit, you had to have traffic cops to direct traffic, you had to have crowd control.

Why couldn't he have come up with the usual experimental bullshit that they always gave him the funding for?

His only hope is the Contessa.

When the Contessa gives her backing to something, there is always a little article about it in the paper. And a little article in the paper is something a commissioner would do anything to obtain. Even making an enemy of Falsaperla, if necessary.

Of course, it is usually a little article in the society pages, not on the theater pages, but what does a reader of *La Voce della Sicilia* care if an article is in Society or in Theater? The Contessa is his only chance to persuade a commissioner to give him a piazza, a street, a dark corner.

Before getting out of the car, Cagnotto looks at himself in the mirror. The self-tanning lotion he has smeared on his face has fortunately given him a nice orange tennis-court color. He steps out and promptly loses himself among the pathways of the Contessa's garden.

Waiting for Cagnotto, the Contessa and the Baronessa, sitting at the white wrought-iron table at the side of the pool, hurl at each other, from behind sunglasses speckled with rhinestones, glances of mutual loathing. The Contessa has put on a straw hat big enough to be a sombrero and a giant pin to close the décolleté of her bathing suit. The Baronessa knows the Contessa is wearing that hat because otherwise her makeup would melt under the sun, and the pin is there to cover up the wrinkles in her cleavage.

The Baronessa is wearing a scarf on her head and huge sunglasses. The Contessa knows that the scarf is there to conceal the fact that the Baronessa didn't make it to the hairdresser, and the big sunglasses are necessary because at poolside, with the sun in her face, you can see the flesh-colored makeup covering the black rings under her eyes.

Cagnotto, finally back on the right path, sees them sitting there all tarted up like that and feels freaked.

The Contessa alone already scares him, and in the company of the Baronessa, sitting by the pool in the sun, she's a walking horror. He has come to plead for a *raccomandazione*, he has to humiliate himself, prostrate himself at the (disgusting) feet of these two who know nothing of Art and who in an hour's time will be telling everyone in town how he's fallen. Forced to plead for a *raccomandazione* after a lifetime of successes.

"Contessa! Baronessa! What a pleasure to see you both." Cagnotto manages an acrobatic bow to kiss their hands and narrowly misses falling into the pool. He looks around and sees there's no chair.

The old witch did that on purpose, Cagnotto feels certain. Cagnotto is there to beg a *raccomandazione* and of course the Contessa couldn't pass up the fun of seeing him casting around for a chair. Cagnotto is also sure the Contessa had the table put right up by the edge of the pool on purpose.

"Sit down, Cagnotto. Always so elegant."

Cagnotto grabs a chaise longue and drags it toward the table. He sits down carefully and feels the button on his jacket about to explode. He unbuttons it, then feels the buttons on his shirt exploding. This operation complete, Cagnotto looks at the Contessa and the Baronessa and doesn't know what to say. "Gorgeous place," he says. The Contessa's pool, lemon-shaped (so she says; the Baronessa calls it "mussel-shaped"), is protected from the view of her neighbors (her cousins) by a row of olive trees.

The Contessa nods and takes a sip of her almond milk.

"Would you like something to drink?"

"Oh, yes, thanks, almond milk?" says Cagnotto, adding a question mark because it sounds more chic.

"Certainly!" the Contessa practically shrieks with joy, but doesn't call the maid or anyone. "You said on the phone that you had a problem."

"I admire you so much. I've seen all your plays. Tell me, what are you working on now?" The Baronessa had bided her time so she could interrupt the Contessa's remarks in midstream. Otherwise, where was the fun in it?

Cagnotto doesn't know which of the questions to answer. So he says, "No, yes," then collects his thoughts and replies to both at once. "I want to do an experimental version of Shakespeare, and that's the problem. There was a misunderstanding with the culture commissioner for the province. He got the idea I want to do dialect theater."

"And you don't want to?"

Cagnotto smiles, shaking his head *no*. "No, no. I just want to use dialect actors, but there won't be any dialect on the stage. Dialect actors are the *street actors* of the theater. Like Pasolini, De Sica, neorealism . . ."

"Did you hear that? The commissioner for the province didn't get it," says the Baronessa to the Contessa.

Cagnotto sees his mistake. "No!" he shouts. Then, smiling affectionately, almost tenderly, he goes on, "The commissioner was magnificent. I see his point. He has to consider what all the theater companies in the province want. No! He did everything he could, really."

"Ah, I see," says the Baronessa.

"Dear Falsaperla. He needs to find a proper tailor, however," says the Contessa, speaking from the high vantage of being a countess with respect to the Baronessa.

Holy Mother of God, how Cagnotto would love to dish a little dirt about Commissioner Falsaperla, his air conditioner, his probable thing with Gnazia (which his intuition had picked up on and which no one else in town yet knew about). Hey, the Contessa herself had given the green light. But the Baronessa seems to him a little bit unreliable, and anyway it's always better not to gossip about a commissioner in the presence of a baroness.

Cagnotto stares at the olive trees, pretending not to have heard. Why, oh, why hadn't the Baronessa just stayed home?

"But I've already spoken to Paino! He's delighted to host your play at San Giovanni la Punta!" says the Contessa happily.

The Baronessa is annoyed. Why isn't the Contessa joining forces with her against Cagnotto? "Wonderful! Paino is doing wonderful things at San Giovanni la Punta!"

The Contessa and Cagnotto give the Baronessa a *there you go again with your bullshit* look.

"But . . . how did he know?" says Cagnotto, ruffled, to the Contessa.

"These things are known," says the Baronessa with a laugh, with reference to Cagnotto's problems.

"Paino learned that the commissioner for the province wanted to recommend your new production to the commissioner for Pedara. But he's been following your work for some time. He absolutely must have you put on the show at San Giovanni la Punta. In the amphitheater."

Amphitheater? Pedara? San Giovanni la Punta? He had gone there to ask if she was willing to be a "godmother" to Shakespeare and she had already gotten him a political patron. He is bowled over. This Contessa is a real lady! Maybe, given her age, she is a little vague, like she forgets to put out chairs for her guests, but that's normal, these *nobili*, the real ones, are not used to thinking about the practical details. That's what servants are for. This is what the real aristocracy is about. Not like the Baronessa, new aristocracy, ruder than the bourgeoisie. Another school altogether, the Contessa. Certainly they didn't make countesses much older than this!

"Obviously, Paino too has a problem, Cagnotto. The money has dried up," adds the Contessa.

"Hey. No problem. At all!" exclaims Cagnotto, getting up happily.

"No, wait, Cagnotto, wouldn't you like to have a swim?"

Cagnotto exchanges a look of gratitude and complicity with the Contessa.

"Rehearsals, Contessa, rehearsals!" Cagnotto bends to kiss her hand, and then in a burst of affection tries to grab her and kiss her on the cheeks, despite the sombrero.

He bids a chilly farewell to the Baronessa and goes off deep in thought, teetering dangerously on the edge of the pool.

"Now, where did you get that? Did you also hear the rumor that he's crossed swords not only with Falsaperla but also with Rattalina?"

The Contessa takes a sip of almond milk. "Crossed swords? No, no. Arturo begged me to put in a good word with Cagnotto. He really wants to host his play at San Giovanni la Punta." The Contessa puts the glass down carefully on the table. "Luckily I'm old now and such things don't interest me anymore. Otherwise I'd be concerned that Arturo is going over to the other side. Which reminds me, yesterday I spoke with Dr. Farina's wife. She told me he no longer has, how can I say, the *enthusiasm* he once had."

"I'd better go," says the Baronessa.

All alone, the Contessa telephones Paino. "Arturo. It's done. You have a free show by Cagnotto. No, I have no idea. What the hell do you think I care about where he gets the money?"

CHAPTER SEVENTEEN

Paino Phones
Falsaperla

Paino phones Falsaperla. "I'm going to host Cagnotto's show here at San Giovanni la Punta . . . No . . . no, I don't know where he's getting the money. No, not from me. Are you crazy? It's a free performance, what do you want me to do? Tell me about it, tell me about it. They were going to grab the show for Pedara. Yes, yes, I know. Your guidelines, your memo."

Falsaperla yells into the phone, "Now everybody's going to want to know why, if there was a free show by Cagnotto available, I gave it to you."

"And what are we supposed to do? Not let him work because he's not asking for a penny?"

"Exactly. Otherwise how's he going to know who to be grateful to?"

"He'll be grateful to me because you didn't even offer him a piazza."

"You'll pay for this, I swear I'll make you pay for this."

Gnazia appears at the door. "Could you stop yelling, because I'm on the phone too? Thanks."

Paino has slammed down the receiver.

Paino is calling *La Voce della Sicilia*.

"This is Commissioner Paino of San Giovanni la Punta. You remember me? That time we did the finals of Queen for a Night, no, what was it called, that beauty contest we did here in the amphitheater. Certainly we're doing it again this year! It's called Miss Local Color and obviously we would be honored to have you as the president of the jury for the finals. No, no, don't mention it. Listen, I wanted to give you a tip. You know Cagnotto? The avant-garde director? We're going to do his upcoming play here in San Giovanni la Punta. The Contessa Salieri will be present too. The nobility, the slopes of Etna, you could do something like 'Shakespeare, the aristocracy, and a weekend in San Giovanni la Punta,' what do you think?"

Falsaperla too calls *La Voce della Sicilia*, only Falsaperla has the advertising budget of the province in hand and he speaks directly to the managing editor. "It's Falsaperla. Cagnotto's new performance does *not* have the sponsorship of the province. He's doing it at San Giovanni la Punta, paid for by God knows who and I don't want to know, and therefore, on our side, there's no advertising coverage."

Falsaperla grabs the remote and ups the ventilation on the air conditioner.

"Yes, we'll be doing food festivals in the coastal towns. Uh-huh, I think we'll advertise them. Yes, yes, the future of the slopes of Etna is definitely in local color. Food and wine, that's right. Which brings me to something I wanted to say: I'm going to call the ad department because I think maybe it would be nice to have an insert, say eight pages, how many editorial pages could you give me? By the way, did

I say that Cagnotto's new show doesn't have the sponsorship of the province?"

Falsaperla tries to get his feet up on the desk. "That's very good of you. No, no, sure, I've read the proposal. What Cagnotto presented was a real mess. It lacks *structure*. Structure. He's good, of course, but there's no structure. Otherwise, I would have sponsored him. I don't understand how Paino could have . . . sure, they're young and they want to be noticed, I know . . . I know . . . I know."

Falsaperla gets his feet up on the desk. "I know."

He takes the remote of the air conditioner in hand. "I know."

At that very instant Cagnotto is looking for a parking place on Corso Sicilia. He doesn't have a clue how you go about getting a mortgage on an apartment. He just hopes it won't take too long. In front of him looms a giant concrete building, his bank.

CHAPTER EIGHTEEN

Ridi, Pagliaccio . . .

Ridi, Pagliaccio . . .

Seated in a leather chair in the calm of his wood-paneled study, Mister Turrisi takes refuge in opera.

The week has passed much like the equatorial climate that for some time has possessed Sicily, due to chlorofluorocarbon emissions that, according to some, are provoking the alternating blistering heat and violent downpours that make the fruits of the earth grow fat and sensual.

Similarly, Turrisi's mood has swung from melancholy to wild ecstasy, such as he experienced as an adolescent, buffeted by hormones, in solitary afternoon pleasures, when, having stolen a motorbike and found a secret hiding place in a courtyard baked by the sun, he was unable to determine if the emotion he felt was erotic pleasure (an ineffable mystery whose existence he'd learned of thanks to the explicit stories he'd heard from older companions) or merely the result of a digestive process which had reached its natural climax.

She calls, she calls, she says she'll call, but she doesn't call.

What the fuck was going on? He had written a letter to Milord and Milady, permission had been granted, the lunch had been a great success, and then came the mysterious call. He was certain, however, that Betty had feelings for him, and that made it possible to endure the distance between them while he waited to learn why.

Fuck if it made it possible; however, Turrisi knew that Englishmen behaved this way, they were calm and collected.

Devoting himself to Literature and the Fine Arts was the ideal way to prepare himself for their next encounter. Betty belongs to the younger generation, she hadn't grown up, as he had, in a time when art didn't fill your stomach, and even though the supermarkets had been full of food, the hunger in Sicily had been, how did you say? Ah, yes, atavistic. No, Betty's generation is completely different, they all go to university, they read the newspaper, they *know*. To tell the truth, his father and Betty's father would be the same age today, if his father hadn't . . . Turrisi squelches the thought of his father. Already he's listening to opera, all he needs now is to start thinking about his father and begin to weep right there in front of Lino.

Lino too is young, and *knows*.

. . . e ognun applaudirà!
Tramuta in lazzi lo spasmo e il pianto;
in una smorfia il singhiozzo e 'l dolor . . .
Ridi, Pagliaccio, sul tuo amore infranto . . .

. . . and all will applaud!
Make mock of pain and tears;
And grin with sighs and woe . . .
Laugh, Clown, for your broken heart . . .

The recording is from the famous production with Maria Callas (soprano) in the role of Nedda, Giuseppe Di Stefano (tenor) as Canio,

Tito Gobbi (baritone) as Tonio, and Rolando Panerai (baritone) playing Silvio.

Turrisi nods as he follows the libretto and the music, seated on
the edge of his chair, his hands clasped at his chest, his legs crossed
at the ankles, his eyelids heavy. Turrisi, deep in his heart where it is
difficult to dissemble, above all to himself, thinks that Ruggero Leoncavallo's *Pagliacci* is just a story about Nedda, an actress and a slut,
who has married a miserable two-timed comedian, Canio, so she can
use him. Nedda won't go to bed with Tonio (a hard-up case who tries
it on because he knows she's a slut) because he's an intellectual but
a little bit of an asshole, while at the same time she wants to go to
bed with Silvio, the peasant, who's totally dumb but has a nice body
because he works in the fields.

However, Turrisi is convinced that there must be something more
to the story, I mean, how could a guy become an opera composer just
by telling the story of a common slut?

However, opera is full of sluts. That's the impression he has
gained since he began to learn about this new art form. He knows
that this impression is due to the fact that he grew up with a mother
who was obsessed with postwar hardship, who was always saying,
"It's macaroni that'll fill your stomach." But now Turrisi can't wait to
connect to the new generation. And so he has hired a consigliere,
Lino Marchica, a *deep* young man with a university education, who's
instructing him in opera. Turrisi is not ashamed of his own ignorance.
After all, his ignorance has not prevented him from owning a bank in
London. But he knows it's right to get advice from those who know
better.

Studying opera. There couldn't be a better way to spend his time
in order to impress Betty Pirrotta, who, Turrisi is certain, is fed up
with living at home with that arriviste father of hers who drove a
cement-mixer in his youth, and with Milady, who had gone to work at
a glove factory, when nobody, not even in Sicily, had bought a glove
in years.

He and Lino had studied the *Cavalleria rusticana*, *La Bohème*, and now they are studying *Pagliacci*. Lino had explained to him that you said it like that, *Pagliacci*, without the article. Turrisi takes the stereo remote that's sitting between his legs and lowers the volume. It's the signal that he wants an explanation.

Lino, who looks like he's about twenty, rimless glasses, a mass of dark curls, a narrow tie with a white, short-sleeved shirt, sits in front of him on a sofa covered with books. He looks at Turrisi and scratches his head. Pietro had found him Lino. It was amazing how many people Pietro had gotten to know selling sandwiches at Pietroburger.

Turrisi nods, he's ready to listen.

"*Pagliacci* deepens opera's *verismo* tradition, which begins to focus more attention on the conditions of Southern Italy," Lino begins.

"Right!" says Turrisi, giving the armchair a whack.

He looks at Lino, decides his reaction was a little over the top, flashes a polite smile, and says, "Right!" but this time with his voice lowered and with a little punch of his right fist onto his left palm. Yes, that's better.

"It was staged in 1892 at the Teatro dal Verme in Milan, with Arturo Toscanini conducting. Other works of the period that belong to the same school of *verismo*, inspired by Giovanni Verga, include *Mala Pasqua!* by Stanislao Gastaldon, an opera that follows the same plot as *Cavalleria rusticana* but which had little success."

"The same as Mascagni's?"

Lino nods.

"Poor bugger. With that name. Go on, go on."

"*Mala vita* by Umberto Giordano . . ."

"Shit, *Mala Pasqua*, *Mala vita*, sounds like *crime* opera." He sniggers.

Lino's expression doesn't change.

Turrisi stops laughing. He coughs. "No, no, you're right," he says.

"*Vendetta sarda, un mafioso . . .*"

Turrisi's about to say something.

Lino interrupts him. "Never mind."

Turrisi nods.

"*Pagliacci* was inspired by a true story, which Leoncavallo probably heard from his father, a Calabrian magistrate."

"Magistrate?"

"Magistrate," says Lino, looking bored.

"Calabrian?"

Lino nods *yes* again.

Turrisi makes a disgusted face.

"It seems to refer to a crime that took place at Montalto Uffugo."

"What a dumb name. Go on, please."

"A company of jugglers and acrobats had come to town and a servant of the Leoncavallo family, a man named Gaetano, began to pursue one of the actresses. Her jealous husband slit both their throats on the night of Ferragosto."

"Impossible!" Turrisi gives an *impossible!* shake of his head.

"Impossible?"

"You think Leoncavallo would write an *opera* about an actress getting it on with a servant?"

Lino makes a funny face. He thinks. "But—"

"Never mind, go on, go on . . . with a name like *Gaetano*!" Turrisi flashes a superior smile.

"The poetics of *Pagliacci* are spelled out in the prologue, in the voice of Tonio . . ."

Turrisi drops his eyelids to half mast again. "Tonio," he says, nodding. "Now, there's a name that belongs in an opera, not like Gaetano."

Lino picks up a book. He flips through it looking for the right page.

"Here it is:"

Io sono il Prologo
poiché in scena ancor
le antiche maschere mette l'autore,
in parte ei vuol riprendere
le vecchie usanze, e a voi
di nuovo inviami.
Ma non per dirvi come pria:
Le lacrime che noi versiam son false!
Degli spasimi e de' nostri martir
non allarmatevi! No! No!

I am the Prologue
since on the stage today
the author uses ancient masks,
partly to revive
the old customs, and to
send me to you anew.
But not to say as once was done:
The tears we shed are false!
Of the pain and of our martyrdom
have no fear! No! No!

Lino looks at Turrisi.

"No! No!" says Turrisi, alarmed. "For God's sake."

Lino looks at his shoe. "The author's intentions could not be more different from what we see in, for example, Shakespeare's *Tempest*, when Prospero lays down his mantle, saying . . ." Lino looks for the book:

Lie there, my art. Wipe thou thine eyes; have comfort.
The direful spectacle of the wreck, which touch'd
The very virtue of compassion in thee,
I have with such provision in mine art

So safely ordered that there is no soul—
No, not so much perdition as an hair
Betid to any creature in the vessel
Which thou heard'st cry, which thou saw'st sink.

Turrisi's mouth falls open. "But wait, we haven't studied *The Tempest* yet."

"Yes, we did. We studied all the works of Shakespeare."

"Sure, we did Shakespeare, but we didn't do *The Tempest*."

"Um . . ."

Turrisi looks at the young man, then looks at his watch. "Okay, I've got another appointment now."

Lino shrugs. He picks up his books while Turrisi says, "Excellent, very good. Nice, *Pagliacci*."

Turrisi gets up from his chair in excellent spirits, singing, *Ree-dee Pagliac-cio*, under his breath. From time to time Lino has this habit of playing literary critic and starts laying on such quantities of bullshit that Turrisi can't take it. The idea here is to get the bare bones, they can do criticism another day.

Lino goes out with his books under his arm.

Turrisi slams the door behind him, hurries over to the stereo, fiddles with the knobs, and sits down in his armchair. Forget about literary criticism, he knows better. Opera should be memorized. He once met a guy in Catania who knew every opera in existence by heart, and the guy sat there for hours in Cosimo's bar listening to romantic arias about ill-fated lovers. Ill-fated lovers are very popular with young people.

Forget about literary criticism.

Turrisi closes his eyes and, following the melody with his mouth pursed up in a heart shape, purrs:

Stridano lassù, liberamente
lasciati a vol, a vol come frecce, gli augel . . .

Crying on high, flying
free, flying like arrows, the birds . . .

Turrisi's face clouds for a moment.

Betty hasn't called.

Art is the ideal cure for a heart sick with love, no doubt about it. But how perfect it would be to be able to resolve matters of the heart the same way you resolved business matters.

A little bomb, a nice explosion, and you never had to worry about it again.

He softens once more.

Lasciateli vagar per l'atmosfera
questi assetati di azzurro e di splendor
seguono anch 'essi un sogno una chimera
e vanno, e vanno, fra le nubi d'or.

Let them roam the air
hungry for blue skies and for splendor
they too chase a dream, a chimera
diving, diving, among the golden clouds.

Curtain.

ACT TWO

Celebrity
as Will
and Idea

CHAPTER ONE

Why, Then Is My Pump Well-flower'd

"Why, then is my pump well-flower'd."

In the Civita quarter of Catania, a debate is under way about this line of Shakespearean verse and how to interpret it.

Everyone has something to say about it.

Melo, nephew of the proprietress of Zia Tana's *pasticceria* in Piazza San Placido, has something to say about it, he has an architectonic interpretation.

The Zia Tana *pasticceria* stands in Piazza San Placido right in front of the "doors of shame," the doors to the house of the pornodialect poet Micio Tempio, whose caryatids holding up the balcony (one male in the center and a female on either side), constructed according to the express design of the poet, are masturbating disrespectfully over the heads of the pedestrians.

"He's touching his prick and so you can touch yours too," says Melo every time Caporeale stops to eat a *cassatella* and relax from the rigors of rehearsals.

'Nzino, proprietor of the seltzer kiosk under the Archi della Marina, has something to say about it. He's totally against it because he cares about hygiene and he can't stand those guys who scratch their crotches ostentatiously and then come over, drink a seltzer with salt and lemon, and people see them, and the glass always seems dirty even if he disinfects it with lemon.

Ketty (short for Concetta) has something to say about it. She's Saro's daughter, runs the tourist shop selling postcards and puppets under Porta Uzeda, and is acquainted with the critical dispute because Rosa, wife of the auto-body mechanic Paolo, told her about it. Ketty, getting a touch overheated, tells Caporeale that Leonardo DiCaprio, in *Romeo + Juliet*, grabs his prick and so therefore he not only *should*, he *must*, grab his too.

Zu Mimmo has something to say about it. Since he sold the emporium he owned up above, on Via Pacini (where they've now opened a megacosmetics store), he's loaded with cash and spends his time hanging around and shooting the shit, and he says no, he never saw Peppino DiCapri touch his prick, just imagine if while he was singing *Champagne, per brindare a un incontro*, he had gotten up from the piano, grabbed his crotch, and given a big tug, as if he were a thing, a rock star or a whatyamacallit, an Ip-Op singer.

This matter of grabbing his prick, the more Caporeale wants to keep it silent, the more everyone is talking about it.

For the rehearsals, Cagnotto has rented the old Matador Theater, a little space where amateur companies used to perform, until they decided it was better to accept money from the government rather than try to rely on ticket sales, and where only the front three rows, in Formica-covered plywood, are still in place, because the rest were torn up by the proprietor, who wanted to use the place as a warehouse for his men's/ladies' underwear shop.

It's suffocatingly hot among the boxes of thongs, but then it's not like they could rehearse out-of-doors, and there's not even a crappy air-conditioning system at the Matador, so the actors frequently escape in order to walk around outside, among the rogue parking lot attendants, the people in bathing suits waiting for the bus at Piazza Alcalà that will take them to the beach, the tourists wearing Birkenstocks, and the students who stay in Catania with the excuse that they have to study for their exams because they don't want to return to their hometowns and go insane.

And in this oversized brothel of traffic and sandals, street salesmen and fishmongers, *limoncello* and churches, and above all of people who never mind their own business, Caporeale refuses to touch his prick while delivering the line "Why, then is my pump well-flower'd."

Cagnotto had appeared two days before, deeply tanned because he had spent a week at Sharm el-Sheikh with his boyfriend, with this thing that in order to respect the Bard's spirit, his ardent passion for double entendres, his humble extraction, and also the . . . what was it that he had said? . . . the heterogeneous composition of the audience, the line "Why, then is my pump well-flower'd" should become, in his deliberately provocative translation (Sharm el-Sheikh, said Caporeale, had fried Cagnotto's synapses): "My prick is getting as hard as the point of my shoe."

And that wasn't all.

He also wanted Caporeale, who *also* had to wear a pair of tights that even Nureyev would have been embarrassed to be seen in, to grab his prick ostentatiously, while looking at the audience. Fifty respected years on the stage, sixty on his birth certificate, and he had to grab his prick in front of the whole city.

"And maybe you could emphasize the gesture by letting your

legs go weak," said Cagnotto, pushing his pink eyeglasses up on his nose.

Caporeale froze when he heard that comment.

He kept his head bent over the script.

Already there was this line that he had to say that was in itself, well . . . All that was missing was to have to let his legs go weak. Right, *weak*.

That asshole Cosentino had started to titter silently (Cagnotto might not notice but Caporeale, who had known him for a lifetime, certainly did), and that slut Lambertini had nodded, looking professional (hey, for a slut like her what difference did it make, a touch of the prick here, a touch of the prick there), and then that homo Cagnotto had added, "Got it?"

Caporeale had slowly lifted his head, had looked first at Cagnotto, then at Cosentino, and then at Lambertini, and had pronounced the words slowly so his views would be clear. "Not even if you each give me a blow job one by one." (Pause.) "And now that I think of it, not even if you give me a blow job all together."

Then he walked off indignantly and bitching to himself while Cagnotto tossed the script up in the air, yelling at him to get fucked and screaming, "Ingrate!" after him.

After this came two days of *get-fucked*, insults, spite, quarrels (and many chuckles from Cosentino, who of course didn't have to touch *his* prick at all).

Besides Rosalba Quattrocchi (I mean, with this business of having to touch his prick, every time he had to pass her shop he went all the way around the station so as not to be seen), Caporeale had told just about everyone that he was acting in a Shakespeare play. And already he couldn't count the number of times he'd been ridiculed, and the jokes on the telephone, when you come home tired after a rehearsal, sit down to relax and watch the TV news, and the phone rings and some asshole says, "Caporeale, pay attention to those rehearsals, you know on opening night you could grab for it and miss?"

And Caporeale had replied, "Well, then, we'll call your sister, who in living memory has never missed once."

CHAPTER TWO

It's the Story of an Actress Who's Married and Who's Being Courted by Tonio

"It's the story of an actress who's married and who's being courted by Tonio, an actor in her company, not her husband, but she doesn't yield to his courtship," Mister Turrisi is telling Betty, who's looking *avid* for culture.

Luckily the beach at San Giovanni li Cuti is crowded with gay beefcake, so at least Carmine has something to look at and be entertained by. Otherwise he'd have to go and bash his head against those rocks, see those rocks? Having to listen to Turrisi tell Betty about *Pagliacci* without the article.

She's hanging on every word that escapes his lips, that little mustache.

Turrisi is dressed up like Lawrence of Arabia, with a white linen shirt, white linen trousers, and a pair of loafers in leather so fine they look like condoms. Carmine is acquainted with them, the black condoms that taste of licorice. Who isn't? They sell them in the machine at Pegaso, the gay discoteque on the beach, where in summer a bunch of boys crowd around the pool and in winter a bunch of boys gather in a circus tent. Thank heavens there's no shortage of gay guys in Catania, thinks Carmine, letting his mind wander.

Carmine's nerves are shot.

Betty had told him she had a date for lunch with Turrisi at San Giovanni li Cuti.

So Carmine had asked her once again what she had in mind.

"Mind?" Betty had said, making an *I don't understand* face.

At the beach at San Giovanni li Cuti you don't tan much because the sand is volcanic, i.e., black, and it sucks up all the sun. At the beach at San Giovanni li Cuti the black sand isn't the only thing that sucks.

Do forgive Carmine's lewd thoughts, but when Betty acts like this it drives him nuts.

So he's concentrating on a guy, waxed all over, who arrived on a bike, no shirt, bandanna, glistening with self-tanning lotion, all oil and Vaseline, so that you can't figure out how the bike didn't shoot out from under his butt while he was parking. (And let me see that beautiful butt!)

The guy is wearing a super-tight bathing suit so you can see he's not well hung: this is the latest fashion among gays in Catania, to promote competition with gay tourism in the Far East. Because everyone knows that Sicilian males are super-hetero, they *love* women and like to show off incontrovertible proof of their virility, so when you're looking for a gay guy you have to travel all the way to the Far East because those big pricks are scary.

However, little pricks can also be found in Catania, there's no need to travel all those miles.

Betty is smitten with the idea of the faithful wife.

She too, who knows why, is dressed up à la Lawrence of Arabia.

White linen shirt and pants, a hairstyle parted on the side and drawn back so she looks like a little gay guy herself.

Turrisi, when he saw her, practically keeled over with love.

Because, in Carmine's opinion, Turrisi is a little bit gay himself. But because he wants to play the Sicilian male he has to approach queerdom very cautiously, little by little. And at this moment Betty is the archetype of a gay guy with a prick so small it doesn't exist at all.

How does she do it? How does she *know*? She's like a slut version of *Victor/Victoria*.

"So she whips Tonio in the face and goes off to watch the birds."
Whips? In the face?

Oh! Che volo d'augelli
e quante strida!
Che chiedon? Dove van? Chissà!

Oh! What a flight of birds
and what cries!
What do they want? Where do they go? Who knows!

says Turrisi, signaling to the waiter.

Carmine agrees about the flight of birds. He's wearing a blue silk damask suit and is dissolving in the heat. He's less in agreement with Betty, who sighs, her eyes turned heavenward, "Where do they go? Who knows!"

Betty not only knows perfectly well where the birds are going, she knows how to blow them out of the sky with a shotgun, bam bam.

"But then Silvio the peasant arrives."

"Ah, Silvio," says Betty, sighing again.

Turrisi smiles.

The guy with the bandanna is greeting other gym-toned males in a masculine way. They grab each others' veiny forearms lasciviously.

Non abusar di me
del mio febbrile amor!
Non mi tentar! Non mi tentar!
Pietà di me! Non mi tentar, non mi tentar!
Non mi tentar!

Don't take advantage of me
of my fevered love!
Don't tempt me! Don't tempt me!
Have pity on me! Don't tempt me, don't tempt me!
Don't tempt me!

Shit, she says it five times, five. In case that cretin Silvio doesn't
get it.

To which Betty replies, "Hey, look, your outfit is just like mine."

Carmine twitches.

"What?" says Turrisi.

"Nothing, I was thinking."

She was thinking.

She was thinking?

And what was she thinking about?

Carmine shifts on his seat. He waits a moment.

The waiter arrives, black hair combed back, white jacket too short, arms too long, hands too big, ears that stick out. Every time Carmine comes to San Giovanni li Cuti all the hair he no longer has (electrolysis) stands up.

Turrisi is hypnotized by Betty.

Who is looking at her hands folded in her lap. Head down.

Carmine says to the waiter, "An almond *semifreddo*?"

The waiter smiles.

"With chocolate on top."

"Melted?" says the waiter.

Carmine rests an elbow on the table. Are they trying to make an ass of him? Then he snaps back. "And you two?"

Between Betty and Turrisi the thrill of love is palpable, it's humming on their epidermises.

And they wonder why you turn out gay?

"What?" asks Turrisi. "Yes, for me too."

Betty, rather than order anything, smiles.

"Three," says Carmine. Then he turns toward the beach without so much as a glance at the waiter because he knows this will drive him crazy.

Turrisi glances around with a conspiratorial look. "Bathing suit?"

Betty smiles again, her head bent. "My father . . ." she says.

Carmine is paying attention now.

"My father . . . wouldn't like it."

Turrisi gives the table a whack.

Everybody turns to look.

This time Turrisi has his head bent.

He's patting his napkin.

Her father wouldn't like it? We'll see . . .

CHAPTER THREE

Pump Means Shoe

"Pump means *shoe*. Decorated in a floral pattern. It means *shoe*: pricks have nothing the fuck to do with it. I asked my niece, who knows how to use Intranet," says Caporeale.

A table has been set on the stage. The scripts are lit by little table lamps that Cagnotto bought from some North Africans on the sidewalk. The setup is quite professional, and despite the heat Cagnotto's happy.

He's told Bobo that there have been disagreements about how to interpret one of the lines. He told him that all of Shakespeare's poetics could be found in that single line. Things between him and Bobo have improved immeasurably since they went to Sharm el-Sheikh. Cagnotto had taken a mortgage on his apartment and now that he had cash in his pockets again, decided to permit himself and his new love a week of interpersonal reflection in Africa. Bobo had been very concerned about Cagnotto's health. But now he could see he was in good form and was much relieved. At Sharm, all the shades of uncertainty had vanished from his face and the week had been a source of infinite inspiration. Not just the mise-en-scène, the idea of using dialect actors as the street actors of theater, De Sica, Pasolini, neorealism, the recovery of Shakespeare's authentic spirit going back to the origins of his signs and signifiers . . .

"You mean Internet," Cosentino corrects Caporeale.

"Whatever the fuck you say," says Caporeale. He's had his arms crossed for two days, signifying his dissent.

"No, no," says Cagnotto, "the interpretation isn't so simple."

Lambertini is following the discussion with great interest. Her eyelids lowered behind intellectual glasses, her lips hanging open to reveal extremely white teeth. ("It's like when she's not screwing, they're switched off," says Caporeale.)

"We must not forget," adds Cagnotto, "that the double entendre plays, in Shakespeare's language, a leading role with respect to the broader use of poetic devices ranging from metaphor to allegory, to the active linguistic deconstruction that manifests itself in the energy released by—"

"Go fuck yourself," says Caporeale. Without metaphor or allegory.

Caporeale joins the tip of the index finger on his right hand to that of his thumb and draws a vertical line in the air. "Go fuck yourself. It's that simple."

Cagnotto makes a peculiar move with his head, like he's been Tarantinoed, and also with his hands, as if he's playing tambourines. Then he suddenly puts his fists on the table, stares at Caporeale, nods, and says, "So it's that simple? Well, here's what I have to say to you. I say to you that the meaning of 'Why, then is my pump well-flower'd' has to be sought, etymologically, in the following question: the *pump*, what does it stand for?"

Cagnotto turns to Lambertini as if for enlightenment.

"Um . . . oh, no, wait, don't look at *me*," says Lambertini.

Cosentino and Caporeale lock gazes. *Oh, no? And if not you, who?*

Caporeale turns away; he's offended, indignant, and doesn't want anyone to see he's about to burst out laughing.

"The confirmation comes with the line pronounced by Mercutio a moment later," insists Cagnotto. " 'Sure wit! Follow me this jest now till thou hast worn out thy pump, that, when the single sole of it is worn, the jest may remain, after the wearing, solely singular,' where, as you can see, the word play involves *jest*, which means gesture as well as joke or pun, and *sole*, which refers to a shoe but also means alone, and in fact Romeo replies, 'Oh single-soled jest, solely singular for the singleness!' in which the sole is no longer of the shoe, but is, and this is the point, a pedestrian pun, in the sense that the pun stands on its own two feet, it works theatrically, only so far as it is pedestrian, down to earth, anchored, shall we say, to the popular language of . . ."

Caporeale drops the corners of his mouth and rolls his head from side to side as if to say, *How much bullshit can he produce in one go, Cagnotto?*

". . . and so the sole of the shoe, understood as a humble play on words, restores to the word *pump* all its demotic meaning of *prick*." Cagnotto takes off the pink glasses and looks around expectantly.

Cosentino looks at Cagnotto, then at Caporeale, then he looks at Lambertini.

Lambertini, all practical, looks at her watch and in the most casual way possible says, "I mean, what the fuck are we supposed to do with this prick?"

CHAPTER FOUR

Paino and Falsaperla Are at Each Other's Throats

Paino and Falsaperla are at each other's throats because of Cagnotto's production. And needless to say, Contessa Salieri is fanning the flames with a fancy poolside dinner that everyone will be talking about for a week because everyone in Catania knows that Paino would like to screw over Falsaperla and become culture commissioner for the province.

The Contessa, when she explains worldly and political matters, is always a little vague and you can never tell if she's being serious or has gone senile.

The Contessa says that commissioner for culture is a very sought-after job because you have only a tiny budget and do not commission public works and so it's very unlikely that anybody will go and kill you.

Everyone who wants to get into politics in Sicily but doesn't have real guts ends up being commissioner for culture. And of course you get to meet a lot of people, go to a lot of parties, decide who becomes an actor and who doesn't, who becomes a playwright and who doesn't.

Commissioner for culture, the Contessa further maintains, is a very important job because you don't have to confront, how do they say, market forces, because the market destroys culture, people don't understand, they're stupid and watch television, and so they don't go to the market to purchase culture, which is *tough going*, and that's why we have a commissioner for culture, so that even if nobody wants culture, he goes and gives it to them anyway.

Since Falsaperla has the backing of his party, will get elected in any case, and doesn't need anyone to mount an election campaign for him, the Contessa has decided to support Paino, so that at least he has to feel grateful to her. Otherwise what's the point of mounting a campaign?

When she thinks about what's going to happen tonight the Contessa is as close as she can get to remembering what an orgasm is like. Along with Paino, obviously, she has invited Falsaperla. And Falsaperla, the last thing he's going to do is say no to a society event at which Paino will be present.

The Contessa has also let the wives know that if they wish they can have a midnight dip in the pool. (On the invitation she has written "moon-bath" to let them know to bring their bathing suits.)

She's had her hairdresser come to the house because she wants to personally supervise the pool buffet, which is supposed to be abundant. If a politician dies in the pool because he has a *congestione*—if too much blood goes to his stomach because he ate too much, and he passes out and drowns—the value of your property goes up. You can never figure out when the Contessa is fooling around and when she's being serious.

"What did the yoga instructor say?" she yells out to someone while the hairdresser fiddles with her hair.

. . .

The Contessa had them put candles along the path that leads through the garden. Every ten yards she's also stationed a waiter dressed in a white jacket who's standing very still. The waiters are in a good mood because they know that there are many gay politicians, whose acquaintance they hope to make. The gay politicians, by way of thanks, will get you a job with the city. Anyway, that's what they say, and the Contessa neither confirms nor denies, she merely says, "Until you blow him or he blows you, there's no way you can be sure." Some people think the Contessa is completely out of her mind. Others think she is merely being a countess and is therefore sane.

The Contessa says that once upon a time things were done the same way, but instead of the gayish male waiters they had slutty girl waitresses. But that's gone out because today gay guys are in.

The Contessa wants to be clear about this because, who knows, they might label her politically incorrect. When it comes to whores, male and female, there's no shortage in Catania, thank heaven.

The men arrive at the party with their wives on their arms. Not that the wives like being on the arms of their husbands, but the path that leads to the pool is a dirt path, and so in order not to take a dust bath they have to glom on to their husbands' arms. The husbands, who knows why, are usually shorter than their wives, probably because of the heels, and so the ladies try to glom on, lose their grip, and trip all the same. The wives lose their cool in a low voice because otherwise it's not chic. Usually, the blame goes to the husband, not to the heels.

The Contessa says that the guests, before they arrive at the party, must be tested: first you make it hard for them to find a place to park, then you make them walk down a dark path lit by candles with the gay waiters, and finally, when they arrive, you treat them badly and don't acknowledge their presence. The Contessa says the point of this is to get the husbands and the wives to quarrel, so that they won't say a word to each other all evening, but will talk to other people out of spite, and then you have a good party.

The Contessa, when she says these things, looks very serious. You want to tell her to stop fooling around, but then you get to the party and there are husbands and wives who are practically tearing each others' ears off in front of everyone, and you realize that the Contessa, silly as she sounds, is not entirely dim.

Commissioner Falsaperla comes in all sweaty.

He's wearing a three-button jacket, all three buttons buttoned, and on his arm is his wife. Commissioner Falsaperla is trying desperately to quarrel with his wife because the Contessa has also invited Gnazia to the party, and Gnazia, when she sees him come in with his wife, gets into a vindictive thing where she starts to play the slut with everyone if you don't keep an eye on her.

Falsaperla's wife knows all this perfectly well and so she doesn't get annoyed when her husband doesn't find a parking place, doesn't get cross when she sprains her ankle on the path, and doesn't get angry now when her husband says to her, "Let go of my arm, I'm hot. Is this shirt you bought me polyester? How many times do I have to tell you not to buy me polyester because it gives me an allergy? Fuck, I'm burning up. And let go of my arm."

Falsaperla's wife, who married him for just this reason, is damned if she's going to detach herself from the arm that belongs, yes, to her husband, but also, let us not forget, to the culture commissioner for the province of Catania. It's all very well about Gnazia, who lets him blow off steam in the office sometimes so that when he comes home he doesn't bust her balls, but a party is a party and Gnazia can go drown herself in the pool if it means so much to her.

The Contessa, who up to now has not acknowledged anyone, as soon as she sees Signora Falsaperla glued onto her husband's arm, unsheathes (that's the correct term for it: *unsheathes*) her smile (lips that draw back like a glove, lines at the corner of her mouth like rubber bands ready to spring), approaches the couple, and says, without preamble, "Signora! What a pleasure! You *will* let your husband spend a little time with us too, won't you?"

But if the Contessa is a bitch and likes to stir things up, Signora Falsaperla is no slouch. And so she replies, "Oh, but I see so little of him that tonight I don't intend to let him out of my sight!"

Commissioner Falsaperla, sweatier than ever, aims an interrogatory glance at his wife. Then he casts around the room looking for Gnazia. Mother of God, what a miniskirt she's got on. A fog descends on Commissioner Falsaperla: the nervous sweat is pearling on his glasses. He takes them off and tries to wipe them on his jacket sleeve, which has plenty of excess fabric.

"Are you looking for Paino?" says the Contessa. "He's here! You know the party's in his honor, don't you?" she adds happily.

Signora Falsaperla turns a gaze of contempt on her husband. Paino? Is there anybody who doesn't know that Paino is trying to destroy Falsaperla?

"Arturo-o-o-o," trills the Contessa.

Turi Pirrotta has the most beatific dick-face on the planet tonight, because the Contessa has invited both his daughter Betty and Alfio Turrisi and he can't wait to exchange a few pleasantries with his future son-in-law.

Holy Mary, how sweet it is! He's sucking on a skewer of pineapple and strawberries and his wife, Wanda (who was busting his balls all afternoon, telling him to hurry up and get ready or they'd be late), as soon as they got to the party had put on a big face, made it clear she wanted him to bugger off, and left him alone by the buffet table. Damn, he is enjoying himself. The reflection of the moon sparkling in the pool, the piped-in music from the fifties.

The commissioner for public works for Siracusa walks by, not even bothering to look at him. Pirrotta nevertheless aims a smiling bow in his direction: just wait until his daughter marries Turrisi, and then the commissioner for public works for Siracusa can get stuffed where he should be stuffed. Pirrotta's giving the skewer a noisy workover with his tongue, otherwise, where's the beauty in it?

Tino Cagnotto is struck dumb with amazement and excitement. He had come in with Bobo and there were all these waiters along the path giving him languid glances, so that Bobo had turned to stone on his arm from jealousy. Mother of God, how Cagnotto loves it when Bobo gets jealous.

The waiters know that they have to aim the languid glances at the older one in the suit, not at the younger one with the flashy shirt open to his navel.

And now here's Paino, who has grabbed his arm and is taking him around introducing him left and right. Cagnotto hears the Contessa shouting, "Arturo-o-o-o," and feels Paino grip his arm and steer him toward the call of the Contessa. Cagnotto sends a look of love at Bobo. Bobo stares back with a look that says, *Go ahead. I'll wait for you here in my heart's solitude, I'll let the others have some of you but only tonight and only because it matters to you.*

Standing next to the Contessa is Falsaperla.

Paino holds on to Cagnotto's arm as if he were made of gold.

"Falsaperla!" exclaims Paino. "Look who's here, Cagnotto!"

Cagnotto sees that Falsaperla is even more sweaty than he is. His wife's got him in a hammerlock on her arm, poor bugger.

He's not going to pass up such an occasion, is he? Never! So Cagnotto says, "Commissioner, my friend, you know what? With Paino, I managed to resolve that whole business."

Falsaperla looks at his wife fearfully.

"With Paino?" says his wife.

Commissioner Falsaperla doesn't know what to say.

Signora Falsaperla says to Cagnotto, "I'm a great admirer of your work. What's this you've resolved with Paino?"

"My new play, *signora*. With your husband, unfortunately, there were some problems."

Signora Falsaperla looks at Cagnotto. Then she looks at Paino and then at her husband. She looks at her husband as if he were scum.

The Contessa is beaming.

Mister Turrisi has come with Pietro of Pietroburger. He had told him not to dress up like Elvis because this was going to be an elegant evening. "Exactly!" said Pietro, to make it clear that Elvis attire *was* elegant.

Turrisi had gotten him a double-breasted suit, he'd sent down to Via Etnea for it. Pietro had put on the suit, but with a white Elvis turtleneck and a pair of Ray-Bans.

Turrisi thinks the result is pretty good.

Carmine is weaving down the path.

Betty, in her red and gold damask minidress, takes a step and twists her ankle. She takes another and falls. It's amazing how this complete inability to walk is considered sexy, but then, men are like that, they're total morons.

Right now, however, Carmine is not focusing on the mysterious harmony of Betty's gait. He's focused on the shit that Betty is plotting. She's there hissing incomprehensible stuff into his ear.

Betty looks at the candles along the path.

Okay, it's great to have a gay guy for a friend, they even say so on the sitcoms, but the sitcoms don't show you what happens when the gay guy starts busting your balls. In the sitcoms the gay guy appears only when you need him, offers girl advice, makes you gay stuff like complicated drinks and soufflés; he doesn't come to your house and bust your balls.

"Hey, Carmine, if you've got a case of pussy-hysteria without having a pussy and you don't know what to do about it, there's no way I can help you."

Carmine stands immobile.

Nailed to the path.

He looks at Betty's ass, which continues to twitch back and forth between tripping and twisting.

A waiter, frozen in place, is looking at him with a smile.

Carmine flashes him a look that says, *Listen, don't go playing queer on me now that I've got a serious problem on my hands.*

Betty, nervous and annoyed that she's been brought to a party of old people, joins her father to establish that she's here, but as if to say with all her bored being, *Yes, I'm here, but only because you made me.*

She settles herself with her hands joined in front of her stomach, agitating her handbag, her legs twined together, and her hip cocked to one side.

Turi Pirrotta looks at her with love.

Crazy, he thinks, once upon a time a babe that stood around like that, they would have sent her to the insane asylum. Now they all come crawling, all nuts with their tongues hanging out, crazy how times change. Shit, those fruit skewers are tasty, where am I going to get myself another one?

The culture commissioner for Montelusa is saying to Lambertini, "You have no idea what a mess you've gotten yourself into."

The culture commissioner for Montelusa is scary to look at, he's a kind of Mercedes on two feet.

Lambertini smiles serenely.

The culture commissioner for Montelusa looks at his glass, his mouth opens in a smile as if the top's coming off the Mercedes, and he walks off without saying a word.

The culture commissioners for Avola, Noto, Pachino, and Marzamemi, respectively, hurry over to Lambertini.

Good God, how Lambertini loves it when the commissioners compete for her!

Caporeale and Cosentino are unrecognizable.

They're both wearing blue suits. The only difference is that Caporeale has on a blue shirt while Cosentino has on a white one. Both shirts are well unbuttoned, showing off chains with crucifixes, baptism, first communion, and confirmation medals, and other trinkets nestling among the white chest hairs. Their entire savings have been invested in these suits, but it's not like you get an invitation from the Contessa every day. The Contessa had said she would be honored to have as her guests two pillars of the Catania theater. Nobody had ever called Caporeale and Cosentino *pillars* before.

"Hey, let's go and grab a drink and sip it on the edge of the pool," says Cosentino to Caporeale.

Shakespeare, thinks Caporeale, is destroying Cosentino's brain stem. And he doesn't even have the responsibility of playing Romeo. He only has to play Mercutio, and above all, he doesn't . . . Caporeale raises his eyes to the heavens. Hey, better not to think about it.

Cosentino has all the effervescence of the sidekick, while Caporeale has that momentous responsibility that weighs on his shoulders as he works himself into the character.

"Grab that drink."

Cosentino walks up to the table where the *aperitivi* have been poured and gazes happily at the glasses. Meticulously, he selects two, gives one to Caporeale, and moves to the side of the pool.

Caporeale stares at him with an expression that says, *Wow, how dumb.*

Cosentino, having taken his place at poolside, begins to rotate the glass, making an elegant motion with his wrist.

Caporeale joins him and watches the glass rotate.

Signorina Quattrocchi, who has plastered rhinestones all over herself like caciocavallo cheese sprinkled on tripe, comes over on Gnazia's arm.

Caporeale sees her and looks at Cosentino in terror.

Cosentino stops rotating his drink.

Quattrocchi and Gnazia are standing in front of them. "Show me what you do when you grab yourself," says Quattrocchi to Caporeale.

Pirrotta stops licking the fruit skewer halfway down. Oh, shit, Turrisi is here. How come he's brought Pietro? He was worried they'd try to blow him away in the Contessa's villa? Where the fuck is Wanda, who knows how to handle these public relations things? Pirrotta, seized with panic, turns toward Betty.

The way Betty looks, you'd think the Contessa's garden was made of quicksand. She has her big toes crammed together, her legs in an X, her shoulders hunched, her head cocked to one side, a big face. She looks like she's deflating and needs a little pumping up.

Turrisi appears in front of him.

Pirrotta gives him a social smile. He doesn't know what to say. He looks at Betty.

Betty's staring at the pool.

Pirrotta turns back to Turrisi.

Turrisi, all serious, says, "Good evening."

Pirrotta gives him a real smile. "My friend!" he says, then stops, not knowing how to continue.

Where the fuck is Wanda?

"Good evening," says Betty in a feeble voice.

Pirrotta, all smiles, begins, "So you . . ."

And stops there.

Because Turrisi has turned on his heels and gone.

Pietro's still standing there. Motionless. Looking at him.

In Pietro's Ray-Bans you can see Pirrotta, puffed up in the reflection of the lens, turn toward Betty with a questioning look.

Then Pietro too turns on his heels and is gone.

Signora Musumeci's already got her bathing suit on.

She wants to be the first to jump in the pool so that everyone will ask her whether the water's cold. She's wearing a blue suit with a kind of scarf braided into the front that becomes a sash at the level of the navel and winds around behind where it joins up with the tails of the flower blossoming on her shoulders, whose petals fall like a pleated cape over her back.

Signora Musumeci, her bosom thrust out and wobbling on her expensive sandals, passes in front of Carmine.

Carmine raises a hand to his chest, looking around for Betty.

If I don't have a heart attack tonight, I never will.

Oh, Lord, Betty looks like St. Rita or St. Genevieve or St. Somebody on her way to martyrdom. She's there by the buffet table with an expression on her face like she's just been unjustly crucified. There's her father who's trying to ask her something.

She's, like, destroyed.

Carmine walks over, pretending enthusiasm.

The Contessa has used citronella candles and the smell makes him want to throw up.

Turi Pirrotta is saying something to his daughter: "What the fuck is going on? What the fuck happened?"

He sees Carmine.

"Carmine, what the fuck is going on?"

Turrisi, there in the heart of the Catania aristocracy, gazes with the eyes of a man denied justice at the pain-seared orbs of his forbidden love.

He exchanges a glance of complicity with Pietro.

Pietro can't exchange glances because he's wearing Ray·Bans, but you can see that at the very least he's stung by the same thirst for justice as Turrisi.

"Turrisi. Is it true that you can run into Hugh Grant in Notting Hill?"

Pietro smiles, who knows why.

"Huh?" says Betty, coming to. She straightens her legs and uncocks her hip.

Pirrotta looks at her, then at Carmine.

Carmine is an ode to joy. "Signor Pirrotta, did you get a look at that pool? What *atmosphere.*"

"Carmine, give me a break. What's happening with Turrisi? Didn't you go to lunch at San Giovanni li Cuti?"

Carmine nods, looking at Betty.

Betty has a wounded look.

"He came here, then he went there," says Pirrotta, scandalized, to Carmine.

Carmine nods as if to follow with interest Pirrotta's reasoning. "He came here, then he went there," he says.

Right, says Pirrotta with his face.

Carmine, not knowing what to do, stares at Betty.

Betty, in a trembly voice, says, "Maybe . . . he's shy," and bites her lip, which is also trembling.

. . .

"Do you know Cagnotto?"

Paino is euphoric. He wants to introduce Cagnotto to Turrisi, the emerging Catania entrepreneur who seems to own a couple of theaters in London.

"I haven't had the pleasure yet."

Cagnotto is about to piss, he's so excited.

"Signor Turrisi, obviously we're expecting you at San Giovanni la Punta for the opening of *Romeo and Juliet*. That is what you're calling it, no, Cagnotto?"

Cagnotto looks uncertain, though smiling broadly. "Hmm, yes. That's the working title. You know, Shakespeare."

"Romeo and Juliet?" asks Turrisi, curious.

Cagnotto nods, gratified. "Let's say it's a new interpretation in the light of neorealism."

"Betty, sorry, they tell me you have to move your car." Carmine drags Betty away, leaving Turi Pirrotta standing there still trying to figure out what the fuck *shy* means.

He feels someone touch his arm.

Snapping around, he finds Commissioner Falsaperla.

Falsaperla had been elected by *him*. Or so he seems to remember. It isn't like he can keep track of all those politicians he has helped to get elected. And what was Falsaperla? Oh, yes, commissioner for culture. Pirrotta wondered why the party had to bust his balls to get him to help elect a guy who was going to become commissioner for culture. Why the fuck should Pirrotta give a fuck about culture?

"Yes?"

"Pardon me, have you got a moment?"

Are we insane here? Once upon a time commissioners for the

budget, for planning, for housing, or for health came to see him, and now here comes a commissioner for culture and he touches him on the *arm*.

Pirrotta glares at him. "What's up?"

"Paino is dangerous."

"Who?"

"Paino."

"And who the fuck is that?"

Falsaperla points with his chin at Paino.

Paino is laughing cheerfully with Turrisi.

Pirrotta's wearing the face of a pit bull.

He writes me the *pizzino*, the message, he busts my balls at home, I let him go out with Betty, he doesn't say a word to me, and instead he is yukking it up with Paino?

Falsaperla nods. "You know who Cagnotto is?"

"Who?"

"If you have a moment I'll explain."

Pirrotta looks once again at Turrisi.

Then he turns abruptly toward Falsaperla and says, "Okay, explain."

"Betty, what are you up to? Betty, Betty, Bettee-ee-ee!"

Betty smiles. She has this thing, that when other people get neurotic, she's happy. And the more she's happy, the more the others get neurotic.

Meanwhile, the ladies are all undressed, or so it seems to Carmine, they're hobbling, waddling, and lurching toward the water in an explosion of sequins and straps, pink roses and stalks of wheat, cameos, tiaras, and rhinestones, one-pieces and bikinis, push-ups, C-cups and D-cups.

Maybe it's the light of the candles that flicker and enhance, maybe it's the citronella that's poisoning him, but to Carmine it looks like a zombie movie.

Wanda is doing yoga.

The Contessa has set up a yoga corner for those who want to do transcendental meditation by the light of the moon. The yoga instructor is pressing on Wanda's abdomen, trying to explain to her how to get in touch with her vital center. Wanda's got a very deep expression on her face.

CHAPTER FIVE

The Next Day Turi Pirrotta Is Knotting His Necktie with Care

The next day Turi Pirrotta is knotting his necktie with care.

He's wearing the darkest one he has.

He combs his hair back carefully, buttons his double-breasted jacket, checks his cuff links, and sprays cologne abundantly around his head.

When he's all suited up like this he looks exactly like Ernest Borgnine.

He even has the gap between his incisors, and he had his dentures made so you couldn't tell they were dentures.

He walks downstairs purposefully.

His wife is lying on the sofa with a slice of eggplant draped over her brow.

Wanda opens one eye.

She sees her husband.

She picks up the slice of eggplant carefully, puts it on a tray with

various other vegetables, rises calmly, sits up, and says to her husband, "Don't do anything stupid."

Pirrotta nods.

He lifts his trousers to preserve the impeccable crease and sits
down in an armchair.

"I'm going to destroy him."

Wanda doesn't know what to say. She had been so nice and relaxed at the Contessa's party. "You can't expect him to ask Betty's
hand in marriage already, they've only seen each other twice."

Pirrotta nods as if he found what Wanda was saying rather con-
vincing. "I'm going to destroy him."

"I told you not to do anything stupid. Be patient and let me take
care of this, it's a woman's thing."

"No, sir, this is a man's thing. My daughter went out with that
guy twice"—Pirrotta shows Wanda the number two with his index
and middle finger—"and in a public place. I'm not going to put up
with disrespect like that, not to my daughter."

"Shit, Turi, before Turrisi came along do you know what kind of
a line there was?" stretching out her arm in a gesture that might
mean *get stuffed* or it might mean *a line from here to Acireale.*

Pirrotta nods again firmly, he's completely in agreement with
what his wife is saying. "Right, but it's not like the others came to the
house or sent me a *pizzino* of good intentions."

Wanda lifts her eyebrows and turns her head to one side as if to
say, *This too is true.*

"And not to mention the fact that Betty, poor baby, went out with
that shithead to please us."

This too is true.

"Yesterday she was there, with that tragic look on her face . . .
no, don't let me get started!" Pirrotta gives the arm of the chair a
smack. "And that dickhead was playing the cocktease with the
baronesses, with the countesses, with the commissioners, and even
with the faggot director. Why the fuck write me the *pizzino* if when

you get to the Contessa's house you don't even deign to *look* at my daughter? He did it on purpose. He did it on purpose to show disrespect in front of the whole fucking city."

"Nothing at all?"

"Nothing. I told you, Wanda, don't get me agitated, because I'm already stressed. He came, he said, 'Good evening,' and he went. Pietro was there, he looked at me, and then he walked off too."

"And what did he say to Betty?"

"He didn't say a fucking thing, nothing, it was as if the poor baby didn't exist."

"And what did Betty say?" Wanda's trying to keep him talking because sometimes when he talks Pirrotta calms down.

"Don't make me think about it, or I can't be responsible for my actions. You know what she said? She said that maybe he was *shy*. Shy, right! You should have seen how he was whoring around with the countesses and the baronesses and with Paino."

"Well, maybe he's shy with Betty because he loves her."

"Right, my ass. There was Betty, poor baby, who was just about to cry in front of me. Carmine had to drag her off with the excuse she had parked the car badly."

"But doesn't Betty have a driver?"

Pirrotta flashes a sardonic smile and the wounded-victorious look of a man who's thinking, *Yeah, that's what I'm telling you.* He starts yelling again. "She doesn't know, poor baby, that men are scumbags and pieces of shit."

"Turi, take it easy, because you're getting me worried."

"The one who should be worried here is neither you nor me. I'll tell you who should be scared shitless. I'm going to talk to Falsaperla and then we'll see."

"Falsaperla? What's Falsaperla got to do with it?"

Pirrotta jumps up.

Wanda looks at her vegetables.

CHAPTER SIX

Apart from Caporeale, Everyone's Tired and Happy This Morning

Apart from Caporeale, everyone's tired and happy this morning. You think Cagnotto was going to give them a day off rehearsals and pass up the chance to review the party? They all look pallid under their tans from sleeplessness, but happy.

The happier they are, the more Caporeale feels pissed off. Today, even though he's got his arms prominently crossed to show he's indignant and offended, nobody seems to notice. Theater people are real scumbags, give them a taste of success and they behave like bastards.

Cagnotto and Cosentino look like they've been sharing a bed for a lifetime, they're so affectionate with each other. And then there's Lambertini, radiant and *mussed*, as only a great blabbermouth knows how to be radiant and mussed.

Caporeale gives them a dirty look.

No one notices.

Caporeale can't stop thinking about his meeting by the poolside with Rattalina.

That bastard Cosentino had left him alone and gone off with Gnazia, a woman whom everyone in Civita had known for a lifetime (need I say more?) and who, since she had gotten that job at the province, had become intolerable. First she got a new wardrobe, or so they said in the neighborhood, politely, because who knows, one day you might need a favor from the province. To Caporeale it seemed that Gnazia was wearing the same clothes as always. Just that before they used to say that Gnazia dressed like a slut, and now she wore designer. Anyway, Gnazia had taken Cosentino by the arm (Holy Mary, what a minidress Gnazia had on!) and then all three, Gnazia, Quattrocchi, and Cosentino, had gone off without asking him along. Some friend.

And that was when Rattalina appeared.

Caporeale was uneasy in Rattalina's presence on account of that meeting Cosentino had told him about. *It's up to you*, Rattalina had told Cosentino, making it clear that Rattalina was finished with the two of them, and who knew what else. Who knew what else? Rattalina had control of the dialect theater halfway across Sicily, he plagiarized musicals, he plagiarized dramas, he even plagiarized TV shows, and sometimes, to raise the tone of his company, he got a singer from the Sanremo Song Festival, one of the losing ones, to come down to Sicily. Rattalina was a Neapolitan. He had started out as a surveyor at the land office, and Caporeale is always a little nervous about people who come from nowhere and make a career. It's not like this is America, where they have the *Merican dream*.

And then Rattalina gives Caporeale the creeps because he has a Neapolitan accent. But not a high-class Neapolitan accent, no, he has a Neapolitan-Brazilian accent. Caporeale calls it that because once he had been in a comedy where there was a Neapolitan faggot transvestite who wanted to speak Brazilian because that's how they talked in the *work environment.*

Even if Rattalina, so he says, has all his clothes made by a Neapolitan tailor and, say his colleagues, tries to make it with all his actresses, he still has the accent of a Neapolitan Brazilian faggot transvestite.

Whatever.

Rattalina had even made a rapid bow in his direction and Caporeale couldn't figure out whether he was making fun of him or not.

But meanwhile Rattalina was looking ever so serious and intellectual.

"Good evening, Caporeale."

Caporeale stared at him. "Good evening, *Dottore.*"

"Look, I wanted to compliment you on the party."

Caporeale looked around. It wasn't his party, was it?

"Everyone here is talking about your performance . . ."

Caporeale half nodded and then looked the other way as if to say, *And you think that's my fault?*

"No, no, Caporeale, we all know that fellow, um, Cagnotto, is a, as you say, a fine director . . ."

Caporeale, his head pointed away, studied Rattalina with one eye.

Rattalina was nodding firmly as he spoke. He seemed to believe in it.

"However, Caporeale, I too am interested in the theater, the real thing . . . certainly it's not like in the summer they can sell out all the spaces doing Brecht, otherwise the audience will head off to the beach, they're on vacation, after all . . . But I too am a man of culture."

A humble Rattalina Caporeale had not only never seen before, he'd never even heard mention of. But knowing how these things worked, seeing as how he'd never been to a party at the Contessa's before, for all he knew the Contessa could be a Mafia boss and Rattalina was trying to warn him. What the fuck did Caporeale know about high society and stuff like that?

Rattalina looked left and right with a conspiratorial air, and then took his arm and in a low voice asked, "But, um . . . this thing that you . . . you go . . . you thing . . . I mean, you touch yourself down there?"

Caporeale snapped his chin up as if he were looking skyward to see whether some bird was doing its business on his head. "We're discussing it. It's a question of point of view. Classical theater versus modern theater."

Rattalina drew back as if he were astonished by the cultural level of these remarks (or like somebody who's getting ready to spit in your face). But then he moved forward again, very cordial, he could have been talking to a university professor, and asked, "No, please, you must explain: how, what, and why?" Rattalina nodded very rapidly, inviting Caporeale to elaborate on the matter.

Caporeale looked around.

All the actors, pretending to be somewhere else, were watching, all curious to know what Rattalina and Caporeale were being so chummy about.

"There's Mercutio in the part of Cosentino," Caporeale said, putting his hands in his pockets and confusing Cosentino playing Mercutio with Mercutio playing Cosentino. But then you try being on Rattalina's arm.

Rattalina nodded.

"Mercutio complains to Romeo that the night before, he had disappeared."

Rattalina nodded twice.

"And Romeo apologizes, saying that *his business was great.*"

Rattalina shifted slightly and peered into Caporeale's face. "And that's when you touch it?"

Caporeale looked down at Rattalina. He looked down at him because Rattalina's head only came up to his shoulder.

"No, actually—"

Rattalina, drawing close once again, said, "Oh, right, it seemed . . . no, no, not at all . . . it seemed strange to me, such a *heavy*, um, thing." Rattalina made that gesture with his head again, inviting him to continue.

This time Caporeale moved his head back a little.

So what was up, was Rattalina trying to make a fool of him?

Only, Rattalina's face was all interested and deferential.

"And then Romeo and Mercutio talk about courtesy, about *bowing in the hams*, about a curtsy . . ."

"Ah, yes, sure. Cagnotto does these things so well."

"What?"

"No, I mean *these* things, the Shakespeare thing." Rattalina made a revolving gesture with his hand, inviting him to continue. He was much too interested and didn't want to get lost in the details.

Caporeale pulled his head back again. He couldn't pull more than his head back because Rattalina remained glued to his arm.

"Romeo says that Mercutio is very good at *bowing*."

"Bowing?"

"Yes, bowing," said Caporeale with a serious face.

"Oh, I see, so tell me, does Cosentino make this bow?"

"This I have no idea yet. We're still doing the sit-down read-through."

"Sit-down?"

"We sit down and read."

"Sure, sure, and then what?"

"And then Romeo tells him that he's good at bowing and Mercutio replies that he's the very *pink* of courtesy."

Rattalina jumped back.

He looked at Caporeale.

He put his hands on his prick.

He grabbed it.

He started to wag it back and forth like a madman. "And you do . . . this shit . . . this shit?"

Then all of a sudden he dusted off his hands, leaned toward Caporeale, and hissed in his ear, "Got any idea, Caporeale, what I'm going to say to you when you and your dear *cumpare* come back to me looking for work?"

And then he was off as quickly as he had appeared.

The way it looked to Caporeale, Rattalina seemed to waddle ever so slightly and the back of his neck was all burned by the sun and a tiny bit sweaty.

Caporeale hears applause.

"So, can we begin the rehearsal again?" Cagnotto is saying. "Come on, no resting on our laurels! Caporeale, what's up? Lost in thought? I hope that yesterday's success made you realize that this production is going to be an *event*. We're not just performing Shakespeare, we're contributing a little piece to the history of theater. Caporeale, I trust we've banished your doubts about my direction?"

Caporeale makes a rotary gesture of his hand as if to say, *Hey, totally banished.*

Cagnotto puts on his pink glasses and picks up the script. "Okay, let's begin. Here we are: Romeo apologizes for having disappeared the night before. 'Pardon, good Mercutio, my business was great and in such a case as mine a man may strain courtesy.' "

Cagnotto smiles and raises his eyes to the heavens, relishing the poet's verses.

"And Mercutio replies: 'That's as much as to say, such a case as yours constrains a man to bow in the hams.' "

Cagnotto shuts his eyes in delight. "And Romeo: 'Meaning, to curtsy.' "

Cagnotto thinks. He turns to Caporeale. "Okay, now here you,

Caporeale, could make a nice bow. You know, with a polite swish of your hand."

"I have to bow?" says Caporeale, stunned.

Cagnotto nods, immersing himself once again in the play. "Mercutio replies: 'Thou hast most kindly hit it.' "

Cagnotto jerks his head around like when you come out of the shower and shake to dry off your hair; Shakespeare's words are running through him like shivers of pleasure. "And Romeo: 'A most courteous exposition.' "

Cagnotto smiles and turns to Caporeale. "Here, Caporeale, you need to make another bow with, you know, your kidneys tucked in a little." Cagnotto puts a hand on his back and arches it.

"What am I supposed to do?"

Cagnotto, still seated, puts a hand on his back, bows, and then arches. "Like that."

Caporeale crosses his arms again.

Cagnotto nods distractedly, continuing to read. "And Mercutio exclaims: 'Nay, I am the very pink of courtesy.' "

Cagnotto nods. "Here you, Cosentino, should raise your clenched fist, with your fist clenched like a real man!"

Cosentino raises his clenched fist like a real man, puffing himself up and making what's left of his biceps vibrate.

"Perfect, Cosentino. Perfect."

Cosentino makes a face at Caporeale as if to say, *Hey, take that!*

"And Romeo again: 'Pink for flower.' " Right, that's perfect, and now you, Caporeale, should close your fist too, that's right, and then open it gently, in a, you know, feminine way."

"In a feminine way," says Caporeale, leaving out the question mark.

"Like *this*." Cagnotto tightens his fist and then opens it, sinuously, like an orchid flowering in the soft dawn of spring.

Caporeale, his arms still crossed, looks at Cagnotto's hand.

Cagnotto says, "And you, Mercutio, reply, 'Right,' and you, Caporeale . . ."

Cagnotto looks at Caporeale.

Caporeale is making strange movements. He has spread his arms as if he wanted to do calisthenics or was stretching, then he wiggles the fingers of both hands, raises his arms, lowers them, grabs his crotch, and yells, "You mean this great, big, hotheaded, crazy dick!"

Cagnotto snaps his head up. "Perfect, Caporeale, that's perfect!"

Cosentino is very annoyed.

And so is Caporeale, who was referring to the orchid.

CHAPTER SEVEN

God, What a Jerk You Are

"God, what a jerk you are."

"Huh?"

Commissioner Falsaperla's rear end is just visible under his desk.

"What are you doing under there?"

Commissioner Falsaperla, in reverse, comes out of his desk with the remote of the air conditioner in his mouth. "Ightfeght . . ."

Gnazia puts her hands on her hips. She waits for the commissioner to stand.

Falsaperla rises laboriously. He dusts off his hands. He takes the remote out of his mouth and says, "It fell."

Gnazia looks at him.

"The remote," says Falsaperla, as if to excuse himself.

"That remote is messing up your mind."

Falsaperla shrugs his shoulders. What the hell does Gnazia know about the letters and the forms and the requisitions you need to file before they give you an air conditioner? She plays the lady, she receives the proposals, and sends them on to me. She thinks that because I'm the commissioner I have a magic wand?

"Why the fuck did you have it in your mouth?"

Falsaperla, moving back behind his desk, makes a pushing movement with his hands. "Otherwise how was I going to push myself?"

"To push yourself?"

Commissioner Falsaperla sits down. He puts the remote in the remote holder (he had brought it from home, it's a dish with a blue ribbon attached to it, given out at the baptism of his neighbor's son, little Vincenzino) and crosses his hands on the desk.

He looks at Gnazia.

Gnazia really enjoys a good quarrel.

Okay.

She has to make him pay because at the Contessa's party the commissioner spent the whole evening with his wife on his arm.

"To push myself, yes, Gnazia, to push myself." The commissioner begins to gesticulate like a mental patient, Gnazia has been tormenting him all morning. "I was under the desk, I picked up the remote, but I cannot, Gnazia, walk backward on my knees without using my hands. Because if I don't lean on my hands, I have to push the baricenter back so as not to end up with my face on the floor, but I can't go back because I'm under the desk and if I raise my rear end"—Falsaperla imitates a bear getting up on its hind legs—"I butt my head."

Falsaperla calms down and crosses his hands again. "Is that enough of an explanation for you or do you want me to go into the details?"

Gnazia looks at him with sarcasm and contempt, reproach and repugnance. She says, "Pirrotta's out there, do I tell him to wait because you're having problems with the remo—"

Falsaperla slams his hands on the desk and jumps up. "Fuck,

what a bitch you are." He runs to the door. "Dottor Pirrotta!" he screams. "Please! Come in! Please! Holy Mary, what a surprise! Come in!"

Pirrotta makes his entrance into the commissioner's office.

Gnazia looks at both of them with open disgust and walks out, slamming the door.

The commissioner is smiling even more brightly.

Pirrotta looks around.

"But what an honor! Coming here to see me in the office! And I thought you were joking. You, coming here to see me. But what an honor. What an honor! What can I offer you, what can I get you? Would you like a coffee? Shall we call down to the bar? Please, do sit down, you'll have to excuse my humble office but this is what the government provides." Then he remembers that he was elected thanks to Pirrotta's vote-buying. "Not that I'm complaining, oh, no! I have everything I need here, a desk, a TV, a computer, there's the air cond—"

"Nothing for me," says Pirrotta, sitting down.

Falsaperla races around behind his desk and takes his place. He joins his hands together and smiles at Pirrotta.

Pirrotta looks at him impatiently. "To get right to the point, Commissioner . . ."

"Yes!" says the commissioner. He says no more.

"You told me you had some ideas."

"Oh, yes, yes, sure, certainly." Falsaperla stares at the remote, then turns his gaze away so as not to lose his concentration, picks up a pen holder, moves it, picks it up again, and moves it back where it was. "So . . ."

Pirrotta waits.

"Okay, this is what I've understood. There's Paino, who wants to screw us."

"He wants to screw us?"

"Yes, that is, us, our wing of the party."

"Uh-huh," says Pirrotta, who still doesn't understand why the party wants him to produce votes for a culture commissioner who counts for nothing.

"And behind Paino, as I'm sure you know, is Turrisi."

"No, that I didn't know."

Falsaperla nods gravely. "It's a conspiracy. A conspiracy."

Hey. It seems to Pirrotta that this Falsaperla is behaving like a moron today. A conspiracy? Of what? Turrisi has copped all the petrochemical rights from Ispica to Ragusa, and why should he give a shit about Paino, another culture commissioner, and not even for Catania, or for the province, no, for San Giovanni la Punta, which is famous because they have a movie theater that shows films on Sunday morning, period?

It starts like that, slowly, slowly, bit by bit, filtering in.

Pirrotta is beginning to understand why they made Falsaperla culture commissioner. Probably they had started out to give him Health, then they realized he was a jerk and gave him Culture. "Okay, but how do I come in?"

Falsaperla smiles as if to say, *Gotcha!* He picks up the phone, dials a number. "Hello?"

Falsaperla gives Pirrotta a conspiratorial look.

"Yes, yes, it's me. I'm here with Dottor Turi Pirrotta." Falsaperla laughs. He covers the receiver with his hand and says, "They send their greetings," then, in a whisper, "from *La Voce della Sicilia*."

Pirrotta makes a face like, *And why the fuck am I supposed to care?*

Falsaperla flashes back a look that says, *Don't worry, don't worry, I'll take care of this, relax.*

Pirrotta sits back with an expression like, *You do whatever you want.*

"Do I know Cagnotto's production?"

Falsaperla nods violently in Pirrotta's direction, *Yes, yes, I know it.*

Pirrotta glances back with a look that says, *What's this all about?*

"Yes, yes . . . I know Paino behaved badly . . . yes, I know . . . I know . . . I know . . ."

Falsaperla makes a face that says, *The usual throat-clearing.*

Pirrotta sees the remote in the remote dish. He reaches out his hand.

Falsaperla grabs his hand.

Pirrotta looks at Falsaperla.

Falsaperla, leaning forward over the desk, the phone still on his ear, his hand on the remote, smiles, going, *No, not that, that's not important.* He leans back. "Right, I know what I told you . . . I know . . . I know . . . listen a minute."

Falsaperla nods vigorously, *There we go, now they're listening, the throat-clearing is finished.* "I want the evening to be a success . . . yes, that's right . . . yes, I know what I told you . . . I know . . . I know . . . but now you do what I'm saying . . . sure . . . sure . . . my responsibility . . . sure . . . I said yes . . . yes . . . eight pages for the food festivals . . . I said yes . . . but listen now about Cagnotto . . . it must be a success . . . a big success. That's it, then. 'Bye."

Falsaperla hangs up contented, puts his fingertips together, and smiles at Pirrotta. "Get it?"

Pirrotta shifts forward until he's sitting on the edge of his chair and rests his forearm on the desk. "Get what?"

"It's going to be a big success. If *La Voce della Sicilia* says so, we can believe it."

"And what does that mean?"

"It means there will be a big crowd. Reporters, photographers, and VIPs. Some things"—Falsaperla makes a fast movement with the right corner of his mouth, *smack!* like a wink without the excessive intimacy of a wink—"the more people the better, no?"

Pirrotta looks at Falsaperla and sits back in his chair. "Certainly, it's a play, so the more people the better," he says, trying to figure out where Falsaperla is going with this reasoning.

"What did I say?" says Falsaperla, laughing.

Pirrotta makes a hard-to-decipher gesture with his head.

Falsaperla continues. "Turrisi will be there, Paino will be there, Cagnotto will be there. Let's hope nothing goes wrong . . . know what I mean?"

Another hard-to-decipher gesture from Pirrotta.

Falsaperla laughs again.

"No, no," says Pirrotta, "let's certainly hope nothing goes wrong. With all those *people!*"

Falsaperla tilts his head to one side and raises his eyebrows as if to say, *Am I or am I not a genius?* "Things in a public place, as you know, there have to be people. If there's nobody, then nobody will go around talking about it, and the thing doesn't have any meaning."

"Sure, otherwise what meaning does it have?"

"That's what I say," says Falsaperla.

When he gets back home Wanda asks, "Well? How did the meeting with Falsaperla go?"

"If the guy's a jerk it's not my fault. Is there any almond milk in this fucking house?"

CHAPTER EIGHT

Cagnotto Is Having His Toenails Trimmed by Bobo

Cagnotto is having his toenails trimmed by Bobo. He's stretched out on the zebra-striped sofa with an ice bag on his head. "I can't bear Caporeale anymore. That ingrate! Oh, God, my head, what time is it?"

Bobo puts down the nail file. "Three-thirty. Polish?"

Cagnotto leaps up. "Are you crazy? It's late! How do I look?"

Bobo, seated on the ottoman, looks up at him with admiration. "You look gorgeous."

Cagnotto's wearing a black silk dressing gown lined with red over red silk pajamas.

Around his neck is a pink feather boa.

Cagnotto smiles. "I'd better take this thing off or they'll think I'm gay." He takes it off and hides it under one of the sofa cushions.

"Idiot," says Bobo, smiling.

Cagnotto touches Bobo's nose with the tip of his index finger, then pulls back quickly. *"Hunk."*

This morning they had called from *La Voce della Sicilia* asking if they could send a reporter for an interview about his new play. Cagnotto had gotten the call on his cell phone while they were at the Matador. If only they were giving him fewer problems, the actors, he would have invited the reporter to come directly to the rehearsal. He would have had her talk to Caporeale, to Cosentino, to Lambertini. But they were still thinking out the interpretation and Cagnotto was afraid the actors would say something dumb. And so he had said into the phone, "At home?" as if on the other end of the line they were asking to come to his house. "Fine, then, if that's what you want, at my house." Cagnotto had repocketed the phone, spreading his arms as if to say, *They insisted on coming to my house.*

The doorbell rings.

Cagnotto throws himself on the sofa.

Bobo gathers up the pedicure equipment into a towel and runs to hide it away, yelling, "Get the door!"

An aging retainer wearing white livery crosses the sitting room. He walks kicking his legs forward as if he can't take another minute in this house full of crazies.

"Yes?"

The old guy pushes the buzzer and then opens the apartment door to wait for the elevator.

Bobo comes running back in shouting, "Get the door!"

The old guy's look is impenetrable.

Bobo, very nervous, asks, "Did you open?"

The old guy, in front of the elevator, nods slowly, twice.

"Baby!" Bobo runs over to Cagnotto.

Cagnotto is imitating Paolina Bonaparte as sculpted by Canova in the style and posture of Venus.

"What are you doing?"

"Huh?" says Cagnotto with a start.

"What's this *look*?"

Cagnotto doesn't understand. He checks to see that the dressing gown and pajamas are in place.

"Sit up!" Bobo orders.

Cagnotto stares at him.

"Sit up!"

Cagnotto sits up.

"Cross your legs."

Cagnotto crosses them. He puts his hands together on one knee. He looks up.

Bobo runs to a table, grabs a book, runs back, and slaps it into Cagnotto's hand.

Cagnotto nods, takes the book, and begins to read with his elbow on his knee. Then he makes a funny face, looks at the cover, *Madame Bovary*, a look of horror crosses his face, but once again he fakes an interest and begins to read.

Bobo races to the other end of the sitting room, where there's the "musician" setting with the piano. He leans on the piano.

He hears the door of the elevator open.

He hears the reporter say "Good afternoon," to the old guy.

Bobo springs.

He manages to meet the reporter just as she's stepping into the apartment, but on the run, as if he were just passing through by chance. "Oh, good afternoon."

"I'm the report—"

"Yes, I know, I know. Follow me. You'll pardon me then, I'll be off."

The reporter follows him, looking around.

Bobo sends Cagnotto a look of anguish.

The reporter is a cross between a harpy and a wife, you can see that she's just been to the hairdresser because she had an appointment with a director, and you can see that the hairdresser was pitiful. The typical mix of envy and resentment. She walks like a drunk on her high-heeled wedge sandals. Bobo can hear her rolling across the floor behind him. Her sweat stinks of nervousness and rancor. Bobo wishes Cagnotto would lift his head from that book so he could warn him with his eyes.

Cagnotto continues to read with great interest.

"The reporter is here . . ."

Cagnotto is deep into the book.

Bobo is standing in front of him.

Cagnotto lifts his eyes distractedly.

He sees Bobo's face.

He opens his eyes wide.

Bobo sends him a forced smile.

Cagnotto remembers to smile.

Bobo steps back. "The reporter . . ."

Cagnotto looks at the reporter.

Cagnotto looks at Bobo.

He thinks he's going to pass out.

The journalist holds out her hand.

Cagnotto stares at the hand as if it were a piece of decaying sushi. He says, "Please sit down," pointing to a chair on the other side of the room.

The reporter says thanks and runs her hand through her hair, filling the room with the smell of crappy hair spray. She sits down on the sofa right next to Cagnotto.

The old guy appears. "Would you like something to drink?"

"A coffee," says the reporter, wiggling a behind as big as Piazza Europa and settling into the sofa as if she intended to sit there for the rest of her life.

CHAPTER NINE

Betty Is Stretched Out on the Sofa on Her Stomach

Betty is stretched out on the sofa on her stomach, her hand limp on the carpet. "Carmine, will you calm down?"

Carmine is pacing nervously around the living room. He jumps into an armchair and perches on the edge. "Okay, shit, just tell me what are you up to, why are you up to it, and what made you do it?"

"Lay off."

"No, I won't lay off because there has to be a reason, people don't do things without a reason. So what's your reason?"

The hand comes to slowly, it rests on the carpet and pushes down weakly. Betty sits up, moving like a tree sloth. Now her two little hands lie limp on the sofa cushions, palms facing up.

Betty gazes with interest at the arrangement of objects on the table. She looks thoughtful. Laboriously, she leans toward the table, moves a bust of Socrates made of quartz to the right and a Big Ben made of colored glass to the left.

She falls back on the sofa, lifts her legs, one by one, and places her two little feet in the space she has cleared.

She looks at Carmine, exhausted. "Carmine, it's not so complicated."

Carmine is still looking at the bust of Socrates.

"What am I supposed to do? It's not like Turrisi totally turns me off. And what's more, if they want me to, I can even marry him, but, like, when I'm old and decrepit, like, I don't know, thirty. You have to be crazy if you think that I want to get married at my age, like the little girls down in San Cristoforo."

"And you can't find a way to make this clear to Turrisi, who doesn't get it?"

"Carmine, you're a gay guy, you don't know about *guys*. You know about gay guys but that's different."

Carmine looks annoyed, as if he's about to go down with a hysteric fit.

Betty, calm, puts the brake on. "If I let Turrisi know I don't go for him he'll never stop insisting. He'll think I'm doing it because I'm a female, and because I'm a female, that I don't understand."

"And actually you do understand?"

Betty looks down at Carmine from an immense, galactic distance. "My father and Turrisi both want me to get married. They've been enemies all their lives. And now that they've discovered that there's oil in Ispica, well, guess."

"Oil?"

Betty nods. "Luckily there's oil. Because in this business neither Turrisi nor my father can afford to do something stupid. They're picking up the land at auction." Betty smiles. "Public auction, get it?"

"Auctions?"

Betty nods with an expression that says, *Auctions, can you believe it?*

"Auctions, what's so strange about that? That's how you buy things when there are several people who want to buy them."

The immense, galactic distance increases by light-years. "Carmine, let me tell you. You really don't understand fuck-all."

Carmine, puzzled, tries to think about this business of auctions.

Betty sighs, rolls her head back, and looks at the ceiling.

Turi Pirrotta comes into the living room and finds his daughter sprawled on the sofa with Carmine on the edge of a chair, looking at her with a puzzled face.

"Aha!" says Pirrotta. "We've now got to the point where my daughter has to be *consoled*."

Carmine snaps around to look at Pirrotta, not knowing what to say.

Betty slowly turns her head the other way and rests her cheek on the back of the sofa.

Pirrotta stares at Betty, the way it looks to him his daughter has turned her head to one side so as not to let her father see she's crying.

Pirrotta looks at Carmine scandalized. "We'll see if I let this continue. We'll see!"

Pirrotta goes out yelling nasally, "Wanda! Where the fuck are you, Wanda?"

Carmine is silent.

Betty, who is trying to work the crick out of her neck, says in a low voice, "There's fuck-all he can do about it."

CHAPTER TEN

Shit, Listen to This

"Shit, listen to this."

The reporter had begun with an architectonic description of Cagnotto's apartment, a house "designed to be inhabited by the intellect" where "minimalism has been abandoned in favor of ethnic color . . ."

"Are you listening Bobo?"

After this came an overview of his work.

"Get it, Bobo? They're doing an overview of my work."

An overview that used words like *contamination, avant-garde,* and *experimentation, an artist who wouldn't be out of place in New York.*

"I certainly wouldn't be out of place."

And then it continued with the interview itself, in which Cagnotto's words were faithfully reproduced.

"Good work! Now, this is journalism. Not like those guys that put stuff you don't want in your mouth. Bobo, has anybody ever put stuff you don't want in your mouth?"

Cagnotto had spoken of "theatrical neorealism, capable of bringing the Italian cultural Renaissance to international prominence. Pasolini, De Sica, Pirandello! Romeo is played by a sixty-year-old actor to suggest, in stage terms, the eternal adolescence of the *idea*."

(Caporeale had called up, furious. "I'm fifty-nine years old and if you keep this up you can get Lambertini to grab *her* prick. Why didn't anyone interview the actors?"

"You're sixty-four."

"Fuck if I am."

"No, I mean, like Pascoli, theatrical fiction is the genuine reality that can draw the young into the world of culture.")

The article went on to say that "Shakespeare's relevance must be credited not to Shakespeare but to those directors who know how to reinterpret his work."

"Shit, did I really say that? Let's hope the English don't hear about it. But okay, if the reporter thought it was true, and wrote it in the paper, it must be true. Right, Bobo?"

Paino had called to congratulate himself for the article. He was proud of the way they had played up the event. He had been the one who got in touch with the paper. Cagnotto had said to Bobo, "The credit is all mine, what does Commissioner Paino have to do with it?" And in fact Commissioner Paino had nothing at all to do with it, the credit belonged to Commissioner Falsaperla and his phone call.

Paino had suggested he give a dinner. Commissioners like dinners, especially when they're given by other people. "We've got to cultivate the terrain," he said. Create interest. The article was a starting point. They had to move fast. He was wasting his words because Cagnotto, the idea of giving a dinner, he had already had all by himself, you think he wasn't going to give a dinner on the day there was a front-page article about his Shakespeare?

The Contessa had called to congratulate *herself* for the article. The credit was due to her *raccomandazione*. She had also asked if she could invite some of her friends. Cagnotto replied that it would be an honor for him.

In the "Victorian" sitting area, Cagnotto dictates, "So write this, Bobo: 'Rotten Apples.' And tell it to the shop down below where they make those candied apples. Next comes 'Human Kindness Ravioli with Pork Sauce.'"

"Human kindness?"

Cagnotto nods. "Human kindness as in 'the milk of human kindness,' *Macbeth*. We can't do veal intestines because they give the calves powdered milk now and they don't taste of anything, so that if we want human kindness we will have to eat ricotta ravioli with pork sauce. Oh, and then we'll have a cheese course and we'll call it . . . um . . . Mad Cow Lady Macbeth, and on the menu we'll write, 'Come to my woman's breasts.'" Cagnotto makes like he's offering a woman's breasts. "Oh, and the menu should be printed, like, on parchment and rolled up with a red ribbon and sealing wax stamped WS. What else? Oh, yes, obviously, Merchant of Venice Ham, sliced thick, and a sparkling wine, I don't know, a Lambrusco or a Sangiovese, nice and fizzy, and on the menu we'll write, 'Toby Belch, from *Twelfth Night*.' What else? Oh, yes, our heroine. See that table there?"

Bobo looks at the table.

"Okay, that one I want served with Marzipan Juliet and on the menu write, 'Good thou, save me a piece of marchpane,' and tough shit for anybody who doesn't understand the reference. Tell Prestipino that I want the marzipan in the shape of poison vials."

CHAPTER ELEVEN

Bruno Pirronello, Photographer of *La Voce della Sicilia*

Bruno Pirronello, photographer of *La Voce della Sicilia*, is bent over his camera bag fiddling with his lenses.

All around him Casa Cagnotto is bustling with preparations for the party.

Sitting in silence in the back seat of the Mercedes, Turi Pirrotta looks a lot like Riddu the Cement-Mixer tonight. Even Wanda, who never has anything to say to him except that he should go screw himself, is impressed. He looks younger.

The driver too is particularly silent.

Wanda is gnawing at her lip because she doesn't understand what's going on, and when Wanda doesn't understand, her nerves flare up. She wants to have everything under control. But tonight she's not going to risk overplaying the wife, because she remembers, with rage and with affection, with hatred and with love, with relief and with nostalgia, the days in which, if she said something wrong, Riddu would give her a slap that . . . Wanda doesn't like to confess even to herself the unthinkable thought.

Maybe her daughter Betty also needs a man who would give her a slap. Okay, times have changed, but when you got a nice slap out of nowhere that set your whole face on fire, you did feel like a wife. That is, of course, if you had married for love. And Wanda had married Riddu the Cement-Mixer for love. She used to watch him from the balcony on Via Vittorio Emanuele when he drove by in the cement-mixer and blasted that crazy horn he had picked up in Germany. Tadadadadadada, the theme song of *The Godfather*. Wanda felt her insides churn around like a cement-mixer.

But then time had moved on and Riddu turned into Turi, the cement-mixer turned into a Mercedes, the apartment turned into a villa, and Wanda's hair rollers turned into a beauty salon. Not that Wanda is complaining, God forbid, but sometimes, when there's a full moon in springtime and a warm breeze that brings you the scent of fried eggplant, Wanda thinks that she wouldn't mind going back to Via Vittorio Emanuele to hear the sound of the cement-mixer as it butted aside the garbage bin to park, and Riddu stumbling in, half soused, demanding that she do her sacred duty as a wife. He had those pitch-black curls that Wanda stroked all over while he told her, "Now we'll see if you calm down, you little slut, you slut . . ."

The orange lights illuminating the marvels of the Sicilian Baroque shine off Turi's mute face.

"Turi?"

"*Chi bboi?*"

Mother of God, when he started talking real dialect!

"What's wrong?"

Turi looked at her and his left eyebrow rose right up onto his forehead. Damn! Wanda was tempted to tell the driver, "Stop the car, stop, we're getting out here and going to get the cement-mixer. I said stop!"

Casa Cagnotto is all tarted up for a Shakespeare party that all of Catania will soon be talking about. Cagnotto is wearing his super-tight black jeans, a large white shirt, Hamlet-style, and on top, a skin-tight damask vest, Juliet-style. ("Looks like a bodice, no?") All in all, he resembles a flute player in a Sicilian folk dance company. He looks at himself in the mirror and feels quite elated.

He turns to Bobo and pats his cheek. "Bassanio, then do but say to me what I should do that in your knowledge may by me be done, and I am prest unto it."

"Huh?" says Bobo, looking uneasily at the lace on his shirt and the floppy suede boots.

"The Merchant of Venice."

Bobo's face is puzzled.

"You don't know how much a reason you are, Bobo, for the occasion that tonight we've set about to stage. If Art is Art, as Art is, then artists are the slaves of beauty."

"Shakespeare?"

Cagnotto goes *no* with his head. "No, just Cagnotto in love." He raises his arm, hides his face in the crook of his elbow, and walks away from the mirror.

Bobo gives his own reflection another look.

Mister Turrisi's Aston Martin arrives with tires squealing at the roundabout, the high-pitched sound wafting all the way down a deserted Corso Italia.

It happens all the time, Turrisi's tires always squeal when he gets to the roundabout because his Aston Martin has the steering wheel on the right and he's unable to stick to the curves, never mind a roundabout.

That's why Pietro, even if his hair is plastered against the window by the centripetal force of Turrisi's driving, looks relatively relaxed.

Relaxed, however, is not what Turrisi is, he's holding on tight to the steering wheel to keep from ending up in Pietro's arms.

Pietro realizes that something is wrong only when Turrisi parks the car; he doesn't brake and sidle up slowly to the sidewalk, as he usually does to avoid scratching the rims of the wheels. He parks at high speed, coming to rest with one tire on the sidewalk.

Turrisi gets out of the car like a demon and slams the door like this was an old Fiat 127.

Pietro gets out, looking at Turrisi curiously.

Turrisi's hair is a mess, the long part that covers the top all stiff with Brylcreem has flopped over and fallen down on one side like a cocker spaniel's ear (thanks to the roundabout).

Pietro wants to say something but Turrisi, who now seems calmer, adjusts his double-breasted pin-striped jacket and with a wave of his arm, puts the hair back in place.

"Mister Turrisi," says Pietro, walking around the car, "pardon me if I take the liberty of saying so, but you need to calm down."

"I'm extremely calm."

"Just give me the signal, Mister Turrisi, just give me the signal, and Pirrotta, you can consider him disposed of. Rest assured, I've already given it a thought."

"You haven't given it one fuck of a thought," says Turrisi, walking toward the door.

"No?" says Pietro, who has joined him at the door and is studying the names on the bell.

Turrisi fluffs up the carnation in his buttonhole, stretches his neck because the collar of his shirt is a tiny bit tight, and says,

"It's not like I can blow away my father-in-law! Ring, lean on it!"

"Okay, but we don't have to go around putting up posters. Who would know who did it? Where do I ring?"

"Cagnotto," says Turrisi, who's still trying to stretch out his neck imprisoned in the collar of a shirt with fine red stripes.

Pietro squints to try to read the names. He gives up, turns to Turrisi, and says, "I can't see either."

"No, I would never do something like that to Betty. And that's not even the point. Move."

Pietro moves. Turrisi gets close to the intercom.

"So what is the point?"

"There it is, Cagnotto." Turrisi rings the bell. "It's . . . um . . . I have some affairs in Ispica and so that business will have to wait."

"Who is it?"

Turrisi steps back and signals to Pietro to announce their arrival.

Pietro puts his mouth up to the intercom. "Mister Turrisi."

The door opens.

In the elevator Pietro says to Turrisi, "With all due respect, sir, what the fuck does Ispica have to do with it?"

Turrisi looks at Pietro with one eye, then looks back at himself in the mirror. He sighs, adjusting the loose knot of his tie. "Pietro, Pietro, everyone knows I'm sitting on the countryside from Ispica to Ragusa, and everyone knows that Pirrotta would like to get his hands on that land too. If Pirrotta disappears, who do you think they're going to come after?"

"Oh, I see, so now that Pirrotta's interested in the Ispica countryside, we have to accept that he can't disappear?" Pietro is indignant.

"No, he can't disappear. I've told you this twelve thousand times, we cannot fuck around here. Otherwise they'll send in the tanks again."

Pietro bursts out laughing, thinking of the time Italy sent the army to Catania to fight the Mafia. There were tanks and soldiers on street corners behind bulletproof glass shields, and there were kids on motorbikes who, to fool around, were throwing firecrackers at them.

"Anyway I'll think of something," says Turrisi, smiling to himself.

The elevator stops at Cagnotto's floor.

The door opens.

"Mister Turrisi!" exclaims Cagnotto, dressed up as . . . dressed up as the driver of a Sicilian painted cart?

Pirronello's flash goes off: *Mister Turrisi in front of the elevator door, Cagnotto smiling and approaching for a cheek-to-cheek at the center of the frame, behind them a guy with a late-model Elvis forelock and teardrop Ray·Bans shoves a hand in front of the camera.*

Pirrotta's driver slows to a halt in double file in front of Cagnotto's building. He gets out of the car buttoning his jacket, opens the door for Turi Pirrotta first and then goes around to open for Wanda.

Turi Pirrotta looks disgustedly at Turrisi's Aston Martin listing off the sidewalk.

Wanda stares at him, worried.

In the elevator, Pirrotta rests one hand on the wall, his head down.

"Turi, you've had something on your mind since this morning."

Pirrotta lifts his eyes. "It's for me to know, what's on my mind."

Wanda bites her lip and tries to pat his head.

Pirrotta jumps back. "Are you nuts?"

Wanda retracts her hand nervously.

"Don't touch me or you'll get burned," yells Pirrotta.

The elevator arrives at Cagnotto's floor.

Pirrotta leaps out.

Wanda yells after him, "Don't do anything stu—"

Pirronello's flash goes off: *Turi Pirrotta coming out of the elevator like a demon, his hands messing with his hair. Behind him his wife, Wanda, her face contracted in a worried frown, tries to contain him.*

Falsaperla has told his wife he has a political meeting to discuss Paino, who wants his job, Cagnotto, who's in cahoots, and Pirrotta, who might be able to intervene. "Oh, Lord, my nerves!"

"And is Gnazia going to be there?" his wife had asked him.

"Who? Have you got anything for a headache? Mother of God, what a headache. It must be the stress."

This Cagnotto is turning out to be a genuine ball-buster. He even had the nerve to call him in the office to invite him to his Shakespeare dinner.

It was like he was doing it on purpose, twisting the knife in the wound.

Fuck, these faggots could be vindictive!

And then, a true Machiavelli, he had invited Gnazia, taking advantage of the fact that she answered the office phone. "Commissioner," that big old faggot Cagnotto had said, "I'm holding a Shakespeare dinner. Tonight! You'll come, no? I've also invited Gnazia! So nice, Gnazia! What a splendid person. Lord, what a nice person!"

Gnazia, nice? A piece maybe, but not *nice*.

Tonight she hasn't said a word to him, to the commissioner, who is feeling a bit of a fish out of water. All by himself, he circles the marzipan table watching Gnazia, who won't even concede him a glance.

What a bitch! Gnazia wants all of Catania to see me chasing her from party to party. Hey, I'm the commissioner, you're the secretary. You're the one who's supposed to hover over me, bringing me an *aperitivo*.

Fat chance!

She's there gabbing away with her distinguished friend the *salumiera* Quattrocchi.

Falsaperla runs his finger along the edge of the table.

"Commissioner!"

Falsaperla raises his eyes and sees a flowing blond mane tossed by the pounding wind of a desert sunset. "Signora Lambertini!"

Lambertini joins her hands under her chin, a mortified expression on her face. "You see what I'm reduced to, Commissioner, working with Paino at San Giovanni la Punta?"

Falsaperla takes a rapid glance at Gnazia, who's already on alert, turns around and takes Lambertini by the arm. (There, you talk to Quattrocchi!)

Lambertini slams into Falsaperla with her cleavage at nose level.

Gnazia lifts her chin slightly, to make it clear she hasn't noticed anything.

"Tonight I want you to stop busting my balls and enjoy yourself. There will be lots of gay guys like you." Betty is looking at herself in a tiny mirror.

Carmine stares at her with disdain. "And what are these clothes you're wearing?"

Betty doesn't reply.

"You want to drive him crazy, that guy?"

"What guy?"

"What do you mean, what? Turrisi."

"Oh, him."

"Shit, look how many people," says Cosentino, elbowing Caporeale.

"Let's hope they get here fast, because I already have an appetite."

The elevator is unloading barons, baronesses, baby baronesses, countesses, baby countesses, *cavalieri, commendatori,* Knights of Malta, white mantle and black, Red Cross officers, Rotary, Rotaract and Lions Club officials, volunteer society members, priests, military officers, and other professionals.

"Shit, look at all those people." Cosentino is excited.

Caporeale adjusts his blue jacket with a quick movement of his shoulders. "Word got out that I am going to touch my prick onstage and people have come to see this great wonder of nature."

Cagnotto, gnawing on his thumb, is looking around for the Contessa. He sees her: she's at the center of a huddle of lady aristocrats who are hanging on her every word. You can tell they're aristocrats because they would like to dress like tarts but they haven't succeeded. Too many midiskirts, too many little blouses, too many pleats.

Cagnotto breaks in. "Contessa!"

The Contessa stares at him, annoyed at the interruption. Never interrupt a countess in mid-discourse.

"Some Human Kindness?" says Cagnotto pointing at the buffet where they are already serving the ricotta ravioli with pork sauce.

The Contessa and the other aristocrats stare at him weakly.

"Fine, maybe later."

"You should have come to see me sooner, *signora,*" Falsaperla is telling Lambertini in a low voice as he leads her toward an empty corner of the room. (Take that, Gnazia!)

"But I imagined that you were terribly busy," Lambertini replies, leaning over a bit more in case he hasn't had a good look at her tits.

Falsaperla is hypnotized. "But for you, my office is our office."

Falsaperla's head is spinning. Lambertini's perfume, it's coming right out of there, where her tits in a push-up bra make a giant crevice.

A waiter offers a tray with flutes of champagne to Gnazia and Quattrocchi.

Gnazia smiles, takes a flute, her little finger extended, and continuing to smile says to Quattrocchi very clearly so that everyone can hear, "Okay, I'm going over there and setting fire to those tits. You wanna make a bet?"

Pirronello's flash goes off: *Betty Pirrotta in a black silk minidress that runs from her nipples down to her hips, an S of rhinestones over her stomach, strides out of the elevator, her panther gait emphasized by boots that run halfway up her thighs. Behind her Carmine cranes his neck, curious.*

Turrisi, in a foul temper, looks at Cagnotto.

Paino is saying to him, "Mister Turrisi, this show has to go to London, to London!" Then he turns to Cagnotto. "You know, Cagnotto, that Mister Turrisi has theatrical interests in London."

Cagnotto can't understand why Turrisi is giving him such an ugly look.

"Sure," says Turrisi, "in London!" It sounds like a threat.

Cagnotto looks at Paino, makes a *huh?* expression with his face.

Paino is enthusiastic.

Turrisi catches sight of Betty. He doesn't know who to be pissed at, so he's pissed at Cagnotto. And because he doesn't know what to say, because Cagnotto, poor bugger, hasn't done anything, he merely gives him a dirty look.

"Where the fuck has he gone to make out?" Gnazia asks Signorina Quattrocchi.

"Huh?" Quattrocchi, in a dress with a flower pattern in paillettes, is looking at Caporeale. "Gnazia, look at him, it's true I can't stand him but isn't he handsome?"

Caporeale looks around, jiggling something metallic in his pocket. Beside him Cosentino is trying to act indifferent.

Gnazia tugs at her leopard-print miniskirt, unbuttons a button on her blouse. "Tell Caporeale that if he marries you, I'll get him a job at the province, we'll get him a pension, and then we'll make him *capocomico.*"

Quattrocchi smooths her dress down over her sides. "*Capocomico?* Can I tell him?"

"Tell him. I'm going to look for the commissioner and when I find him I'm going to make sure he ends up like that." Gnazia points to the leopard skin stretched out on the floor.

Betty has scoped out the party in a blink of her eyelashes, has calculated the geometry of the sitting room with respect to the position of the guests. Since she doesn't intend to stay long at this fucking party, because afterward she intends to hurl herself into Catania nightlife, she needs to move fast, and well.

She decides to stand and admire an abstract painting hung in a strategic position. She lowers a delicate veil of sadness over her suntanned cheeks. Oh, Lord, how hard it is to appreciate the joys of art when the torments of love plague your heart!

Betty's gaze manages to harpoon that of Turrisi.

On her face, the expression of a wife visiting her husband in prison. Separated by destiny, by institutions, by watchful society.

"Pardon me," says Turrisi abruptly to Paino and Cagnotto, striding firmly over to Betty.

Betty's eyes widen in terror.

Turrisi looks determined. This situation, somehow or other, must be resolved.

Betty's eyes reflect even more terror.

"Signorina, please, I'd like—"

"Oh, God, my father!" yells Betty in a loud voice.

Turrisi whips around.

There's no one there.

He turns again to face Betty.

But Betty has disappeared.

"No, but I, I wouldn't, ah, dream, because, ah, of coming. I mean, to your office," Lambertini, her eyes cast down, is stammering.

Falsaperla looks up from her cleavage for a moment, to catch the expression on her face.

Lambertini, out of the corner of her eye, sees Falsaperla's questioning look.

Lambertini nods, as if Falsaperla has understood.

Falsaperla hasn't understood.

"I don't understand."

Lambertini nods furiously, she knows that Falsaperla has understood, and then some.

No. Falsaperla hasn't understood.

"You," says Lambertini, enunciating the words, "are a married"—pause—"man."

Falsaperla, it's like he's gotten a slap in the face.

"Me?"

Lambertini nods vigorously while she searches for something in her bag. "You!" says Lambertini, a tormented heart.

Falsaperla gazes once more at her cleavage and begins to sweat.

"So you're also a connoisseur of art? Mister Turrisi, what are you doing here all alone?"

Turrisi turns around to find the Contessa.

Half a second ago he was talking to Betty and now here he is talking to the Contessa.

The Contessa is important, she's an aristocrat, and for the English, aristocrats *matter*. It matters to him too, the aristocracy. He simply can't wait to invite a couple of truckloads of aristocrats to London to show that he too has highly placed friends. This doesn't make it any better that half a second ago he was talking to Betty and now he's talking to the Contessa.

Turrisi looks at the Contessa with the eyes of a man who's losing his grip. Then he jumps to attention, fumbles out a "Pardon me," and disappears.

The Contessa looks at the painting. In her opinion it's a piece of shit.

"But you're perspiring," says Lambertini as she continues to rummage around in her bag.

"Me? Married?" Falsaperla is trying to understand what he has already understood perfectly well but which he feels he has not understood sufficiently yet.

"May I?" murmurs Lambertini.

"Huh?" Falsaperla raises his eyes.

Lambertini, ready with a Kleenex, pats his upper lip.

Falsaperla, taken by surprise, stretches forward to assist in the operation.

Gnazia screams.

Falsaperla turns toward Gnazia.

Gnazia, perturbed, spins around on her heels and says something like, "Lipstick!"

Falsaperla looks at Lambertini and says, "I'll be right back."

Pirronello's flash goes off: *Gnazia running somewhere, you can see that she's running because her fists are clenched and her arms are well clear of her sides, behind her a purple-faced Falsaperla stretches out an arm to stop her. Farther back is Lambertini, who's carefully putting a Kleenex back in her bag.*

"Commissioner!" Pirrotta grabs Falsaperla's arm on the wing.

"Signor Pirrotta!" exclaims Falsaperla, glancing around for Gnazia. Shit, don't let me think about what damage Gnazia could do if I don't hurry up and explain that there was no lipstick and that Lambertini was only wiping the sweat off my lip. Shit, don't let me think about what damage she could do if I don't even try to explain it to her.

"I came especially to see you!" Pirrotta announces.

Falsaperla, in a state of panic, smiles.

Pirrotta pulls his head back a little. "Are you in a hurry? Changed your *mind?*"

"Changed my mind?"

Pirrotta brings his head closer, winks, and says in a low voice, "Changed your mind about that idea of yours? Come, come with me." Pirrotta drags him over to a more crowded corner of the party.

"I was about to tell him, that thing about the *capocomico*," says Quattrocchi to Gnazia.

"*Capocomico?*" says Caporeale.

Quattrocchi hasn't yet told him this thing about the *capocomico*.

Gnazia looks at both of them as if she's never seen them before.

"Problems?" Gnazia asks him.

Quattrocchi smiles, she looks around.

Caporeale looks at Quattrocchi.

Quattrocchi doesn't understand.

If Quattrocchi, who is Gnazia's friend, doesn't understand, how is Caporeale supposed to get it?

Caporeale turns toward Cosentino.

Cosentino is staring into space.

"You were saying?" says Quattrocchi, her head tilted slightly to one side, her gaze frantic, a wide, tight smile.

"Come on, come on, Commissioner! How about a nice photo?" Pirrotta is dragging Falsaperla around the party. (Where the fuck has Gnazia gone?)

"You, take our picture."

Pirronello's flash goes off: *Pirrotta, straight-backed, cheerful, and contented, has Falsaperla tightly by the arm. A purple-faced Falsaperla looks the other way, terrorized.*

"Again, another one!"

Pirronello's flash goes off: *Pirrotta, straight-backed, cheerful, and contented, has Falsaperla tightly by the arm. A purple-faced Falsaperla still looks terrorized but this time stares at the camera with the expression of someone who's forgotten to smile. Next to them, at the edge of the photo, there's Turrisi in half profile.*

Pirrotta sees Turrisi and, in reaction, squeezes Falsaperla's arm even more tightly.

Turrisi doesn't know what to say, he'd like to say something that would convey, at the same time, discord, loathing, offense, regret, contempt, arrogance, dignity, superiority (but not too much, you need a touch of obsequiousness in case Pirrotta decides to feel guilty one of these days), and then injured love, desire for revenge, disenchantment, the last flicker of sentiment in a soul ravaged by cynicism, and what else? Oh, yes, indifference. Turrisi concentrates all his energy on honing his tone of voice and says to Pirrotta, "Good evening."

Pirrotta pauses a moment. Then he also says, "Good evening."

"Good evening," says Falsaperla, who hasn't understood fuck-all.

Turrisi says again, "Good evening," turns on his heels, and is gone.

Pirronello's flash goes off: *A purple-faced Falsaperla finally grins as he stares at the camera but this time Pirrotta isn't smiling. He's looking with loathing at the back of Turrisi's neck, which is disappearing.*

Pirronello's flash goes off again, just to be sure: *Same scene as before except that this time, where Turrisi's neck had been, is the profile of a guy with a forelock and a pair of teardrop Ray-Bans.*

Cagnotto's on his knees.

He's fooling with the CDs. There's a hint of nervousness in the air and he wants to put on some music.

Who the hell is always messing up his CDs?

Cagnotto's expression softens from annoyance to tolerance, he's just remembered that it is he himself who is always messing up his CDs. Bobo is extremely methodical about these things. He needs to remember to attach a sticker, something written; these burned CDs all look the same. He picks one, makes a *who knows?* face, and puts it on the CD player.

The *Ride of the Valkyries* comes on.

Everyone turns to look at Cagnotto.

What the fuck, the *Ride of the Valkyries*. The CDs fall from Cagnotto's hands. The *Ride of the Valkyries* is his music for intimate occasions. It's like someone has just discovered his collection of porno DVDs.

Betty, sitting alone on a sofa, begins to tap her foot to the music. She's staring, with great interest, at a candied apple.

Carmine comes in, all out of breath. He sits down, looks at her.

Betty hands him the apple as if she wanted him to taste it.

Carmine looks at the apple, looks at Betty, looks at Pirronello.

Pirronello's flash goes off: *Carmine stares at the camera fearfully. Next to him is a bright red apple.*

It's a shame that in a photo you can't hear music, thinks Pirronello.

The Summer Sunset Sends Torrid Waves over the Amphitheater of San Giovanni la Punta

The summer sunset sends torrid waves over the amphitheater of San Giovanni la Punta. People are taking their places, lingering to chat.

The chief press officer of San Giovanni la Punta is in heaven. Two days ago he hadn't been anything like chief press officer. But Paino had wanted to do things right, yes, he had, so he had scrounged up some kind of contract, he had hired Tafuri, who covered the San Giovanni la Punta soccer matches for *La Voce della Sicilia*, three euros per article, and he had offered him the job of chief press officer for the city. He even told him he would get him benefits. Tafuri hasn't understood what kind of a contract it is, contracts with the public administration are complicated, but hey, shit, this is a government job! His grandmother is elated; his wife has gone to the manicurist to get her toenails painted. Paino had even made sure there was a little box of business cards in his office: *Fabio Tafuri, Chief Press Officer for the City of San Giovanni la Punta.* For the time being, Paino had said, he would have to make do with the telephone number of the receptionist, but he was going to get his own internal line. Tafuri looks around even though there's no one else in the room, apart from a lectern they've moved from some middle school classroom to serve as a desk, pulls an envelope out of his pocket, and for the first time in his life snorts cocaine. White powder on the lectern like the white powder on the desk of a PR ace in Los Angeles. Warm air scented with jasmine wafts through the window.

Cagnotto, surrounded by agitated types all wanting to ask him something, is looking at a tubular metal construction about ten feet high, positioned in the center of a gravel-covered open space, the stage, in the middle of the amphitheater.

Paino comes up smiling. "Have you seen how many people there are? They don't get crowds like this at Monte Carlo." Paino thinks, Monte Carlo! He must tell Tafuri.

"By the way," says Paino, "the chief press officer of the city is ready to talk to you whenever."

"What's that?"

"What?"

"That."

"That?"

Cagnotto nods.

"Romeo and Juliet's balcony, and below it, Friar Lawrence's cell."

"No, it looks like the thing they put up when they restore a building, but there's no building behind it."

Paino looks at the tubular scaffolding and nods. "As I said. An allegory, in short."

"A what?"

"Allegory," says Paino smiling.

"Of what?"

"Oh, well, that I couldn't tell you. I'm the culture commissioner, you're the director. Aren't you the one who did the sketch?"

"I, the director, say take it down immediately. I didn't think you were going to make it out of metal pipe."

Paino goes *no* with his head. "Impossible, we paid for it and now we have to use it. We can't fool around like that with public money."

The man from the bar down in the piazza comes up, a white cap on his head. "Excuse me."

Paino and Cagnotto look at him.

"In the toilet down at the bar. Something's going on. Could you come quickly please, all my clients are leaving and the owner's going to take it out on me."

In the bar there are customers with little pastries and big pastries, with ice-cream cones and ice-cream cakes, with granitas and brioches, all of them anxious about and interested in the shrieks and sounds coming from the toilet.

Paino and Cagnotto look back and forth at each other. Paino shoots off in the direction of the toilet, very nervous. Cagnotto shoots off with greater equanimity. Lambertini's scenes before opening night are famous. Lambertini, the scene she makes before opening night above all in a new venue where she's never acted before, she does it for several reasons. To prepare the audience, to attract attention, to provide journalists with an anecdote so that the next day, writing up the story, they will steal space from the other actors and give it to her. She does it because it's fun, and finally, she does it because, before opening night, Lambertini is hysterical for real.

Lambertini has a chair and is bashing the machine you use to dry your hands, shouting, "I am Lambertini-i-i-i!"

The amphitheater, pride of San Giovanni la Punta. Built ten years ago of concrete and gravel. Come to rest in the public gardens like the mother ship of ET. Designed by Surveyor Intelisano, brother of Chartered Accountant Intelisano, who's responsible for the Baroque accounts of the city of Noto. Twenty rows of seats in reinforced concrete that soar over a gravel-covered open space where beauty pageants have been held, Martoglio has been performed, and the most famous DJs of Radio Etna International have appeared. "The amphitheater of San Giovanni la Punta: the missing link between ancient Greek theater and rogue construction in reinforced concrete," says the Contessa.

Paino is very proud of this definition. Reinforced concrete is the very essence of Sicily's terrific economic success.

Sooner or later they'll appreciate it; sooner or later, the amphitheater of San Giovanni la Punta, tourists will be coming to see it.

Times change, maintains Paino. Even the Baroque, when they first built it, scandalized people, he says.

Seeing Paino and Cagnotto come running, Lambertini finally calms down. She surveys them with contempt, puts the beat-up chair back in front of the washbasin, sits down, and says, "Obviously, I'm not going up there."

"Where?" says Cagnotto, all understanding.

"There, on that thing."

Paino says, "Where? On the balcony?"

Lambertini nods *yes* decisively, crossing her legs and getting ready to sit there for a month until the matter is resolved.

Paino nods, he's in complete agreement with Lambertini.

Cagnotto begins to shake his hands and his head as if he's trying to calm down from a hysteric fit that's overtaking him. He looks at

Paino with disdain and says calmly, "Elizabethan theater was like that, Rosanna."

"Oh, yes? There were *tubes*?"

Cagnotto goes *no* with his head. "No, there were no structures made of scaffolding. But there were . . ."

Paino nods.

Will you stop nodding when you have no idea what I'm talking about?

Paino nods as if to say, *Sure, I'll stop nodding but I agree.*

"There was *abstraction*," says Cagnotto, finding the right word.

"That's right!" says Paino.

Cagnotto sends him a dirty look.

"Abstraction, allegory," says Paino.

If you shut up I'll take care of this, says Cagnotto's expression.

Yes, yes, sure, I'm listening.

"Know how they changed scenes in the Elizabethan theater, Rosanna?"

"Of course, they used posters."

Cagnotto is annoyed.

He had been sure that this business about the posters was going to convince her. On the Elizabethan stage they changed scenes using posters, on which they wrote "woods" and the stage became a forest, they didn't need to use a single tree. If in Elizabethan theater all you needed were posters, just think what a splash you could make in Elizabethan theater using scaffolding. But instead the scaffolding, it seemed, continued to bother Lambertini. "That's right," says Cagnotto, trying to buy some time.

"And so, that thing they built out there in the amphitheater, you call that a poster?"

"We can put one up," says Paino.

Cagnotto and Lambertini glare at him.

"A poster, I mean. On scaffolding, posters are fine, they often put them up, like, to say 'don't walk under' or 'falling objects.' "

"Right, and then maybe you'll get them to make me a paper hat, know what I mean? Like a boat, made out of newspaper," says Lambertini, miming a hat shaped like a boat made out of newspaper perched on her head.

"A hat?" Paino doesn't understand.

"Commissioner, allow me," says Cagnotto.

"Go ahead, go ahead."

"Rosanna, listen," Cagnotto resumes, "neither is Caporeale the right age for Romeo."

Lambertini screws up her face and squeezes her eyelids as if to say to Cagnotto, *Okay, you make even a hint of a suggestion, I mean a hint, that I'm not the right age for Juliet and I'll show you what a hysteric fit is.*

"Let's put it this way: the only real element in the Shakespearean mise-en-scène, that is the Shakespearean mise-en-scène that I have in mind, is you."

Lambertini relaxes her eyelids but not the rest of her face.

"Let's say you're the only character on the stage who is anchored to tradition, otherwise, you know, and I'm being serious here, that I wouldn't have chosen you, if I chose you it's because you have a good classical foundation, like in the ancient Greek theater of Siracusa."

Lambertini lifts her head slightly as if to say, *Go on.*

"Caporeale, Cosentino, the stylized balcony, they represent the artistic pact we make between representation and audience," Cagnotto goes on, "that magical theatrical folly in which everything is something other than itself."

"Precisely," says Lambertini, who doesn't understand fuck-all but likes it when they say *difficult* things, especially when they say difficult things talking about her.

"You represent the line of continuity between Shakespeare and our time."

"So if I go up on the scaffolding, I'm the only normal one?"

"Exactly!" says Cagnotto.

Lambertini, it seems that this thing that she's the only normal one, she likes.

She gets up, smooths down her skirt. "Fine, I'm going to put on my costume, but I want wisteria."

"Wisteria?" asks Paino.

"Yes, Commissioner"—Cagnotto steps in—"some wisteria. Can't you get some wisteria as"—Cagnotto thinks of a term that will speak to a commissioner—"as a *floral ornament* for the scaffolding?"

"Ornament? No problem. We'll get it right away with Interflora."

Lambertini comes out of the toilet smiling, on Cagnotto's arm.

Cagnotto too is smiling broadly.

Paino streaks out of the bar, announcing to his fellow citizens, "Sorry about the delay but we have to wait for the ornament."

His fellow citizens nod seriously, *Of course, if the ornament's not here, the show can't go on.*

Lambertini apologizes to the customers in the bar. "Pardon me, pardon me, it was my voice and body exercises, the Swarovski method of releasing tension."

"Holy Mary, she's got a method like the crystal swans," says a very elegant lady at the bar, although her ice-cream cone is dripping on the taffetta rose that decorates her enormous bosom.

Caporeale, in his own small way, is freaking out inside the tent pitched next to the amphitheater to serve as a dressing room. "I'm not going out."

Cosentino is in his stage costume, all ready to go on. He's wearing bloused trousers in red and blue stripes that close at the knee. A vest with wide shoulders from which emerge the orange sleeves of a shirt that's also bloused. "But they're great, these costumes!"

"Yours is!"

"No, no, mine is great, but so is yours."

Caporeale comes out of the tent, also wearing a shirt with bloused sleeves. He's holding a jacket on a hanger in front of him to cover his lower half.

"Stop that!"

Caporeale removes the jacket and says to Cosentino, "And what's this for, to emphasize my great punch line?"

Caporeale's wearing the white tights of a nurse or a bride, and at crotch level, a codpiece that greatly enhances his private parts.

"Shit! For sure, Quattrocchi's going to want to marry you now!"

Caporeale turns on the point of his dainty floral-patterned shoes and marches back into the tent.

"Just kid-ding!"

Tafuri doesn't notice he's sweating. The piazza of San Giovanni la Punta "thronged" with people, the amphitheater with its "ornament." Tafuri's taking notes in a notebook in preparation for the press release that will mark the emergence of San Giovanni la Punta as . . . what was that city the commissioner had mentioned? . . . ah, yes, Monte Carlo.

Tafuri sees Cagnotto and Lambertini crossing the piazza. His fellow citizens are looking at them with awe. This morning there had been a page in *La Voce della Sicilia*, a full page of photos of the Catania social world at Cagnotto's house. There were *nobili*, there was the upper crust, there were actors, it was enough to make you gaga.

Tafuri, "informal" in gray flannel trousers and a blue blazer with gold buttons, a notebook in hand, a camera around his neck, races toward the director and the actress.

"Excuse me, excuse me, Commissioner Paino tells me you want to make a statement about"—Tafuri looks at his notebook—"allegory."

Cagnotto's about to open his mouth.

Lambertini sends him a frosty look.

"No, I think any statements on that must come from Signora Lambertini."

"Rosanna," specifies Lambertini.

"Okay," says Tafuri, "so do you mind if I ask you a couple of questions, Rosanna?"

Lambertini looks at Cagnotto. "And who told this guy he could address me as *tu*?"

"But you yourself said . . . you said 'Rosanna,' " stammers a mortified Tafuri.

Lambertini smiles. "I said Rosanna because they often write Rossana or even Rosa Anna or Rossella, and you need to write Rosanna, all one word and with one *s*. Got it?"

Tafuri nods and takes notes.

"Fine, and then write that I am the only normal one and everyone else is insane."

Tafuri looks at Lambertini, then at Cagnotto.

"Pardon me, I'll leave you folks to it," says Cagnotto, walking away.

"Can you see her? Huh?" Turrisi, seated very uncomfortably on the amphitheater's concrete risers, is looking around trying to catch sight of Betty.

Pietro signals *no* with his Ray·Bans.

Turrisi sets his jaw and pounds his knee.

"Take it easy, Mister Turrisi, take it easy."

The Contessa sits tall in the second tier of seats, the first tier having been reserved for the *notabili* of San Giovanni la Punta. There are cards with the names of the commissioners, the professors, the *dottori*, the *avvocati*, the *cavalieri*.

The musicians are tuning their instruments.

To the right and the left of the Contessa, a huddle of minor aristocrats is patiently awaiting the start of the show, fanning themselves with colorful fans.

The Contessa looks at the diamond she wears on her index finger, bends over, and takes a fan out of her handbag too.

She pauses for effect, looking around.

Then she shows off her prize like a peacock's tail: a fan that's twenty inches long, in bone and seventeenth century lace, the real thing because the lace is a tiny bit yellow, the way precious old things turn yellow.

The fans near the Contessa stop fanning, like they're shy and ashamed of themselves compared with this majestic piece of history.

The Contessa leans over toward Baronessa Ferla on her right and murmurs, "When it comes to fans they can kiss my ass."

Cagnotto feels something damp and pleasant stamped on his cheek. It's a smell he recognizes. Bobo, wearing a white suit and pointed black patent leather shoes, has kissed his cheek in public, even though half of Catania is here in San Giovanni la Punta tonight.

Cagnotto turns with his eyes shining. "That's the first time you've kissed me in public."

Bobo looks down. "You deserve it."

Faced with such a romantic gesture, Cagnotto doesn't know what to say. He had kissed him on the cheek in front of . . . Cagnotto looks around. The crowd is thronging in from the piazza to occupy the steps of the amphitheater, they only have to wait until the sun goes down and the lights can be turned on.

And there, in front of everyone, Bobo had gone and done this, rendering their relationship practically public. Cagnotto is touched and astonished. He hadn't expected it. He really doesn't know what to say: a kiss in public, among gays, is a really old-fashioned gesture.

Turi Pirrotta is like a man on Valium.

His wife Wanda is watching him, puzzled. Pirrotta seems to be serenity itself. He is able to sit there all relaxed on those reinforced concrete risers as if they were velvet theater seats. He's fooling around happily with his cell phone. Wanda, perched on the sharp edge of reinforced concrete, doesn't know what to think. It's not easy for a wife not to have one fuck of an idea what's going through her husband's mind. For sure he's not sending text messages to his mistress Rosina, because when he's sending text messages to Rosina, Turi is all preoccupied not to let Wanda know, as if in this day and age a wife doesn't know when her husband has a mistress. So when your husband has that whole conspiratorial look like he's sending text messages to his mistress you don't worry about it, particularly if you know that dickhead of your husband, it would never even cross his mind to give up the ease of family life and set up house with his mistress. But instead, if you can't figure out what the fuck is going through your husband's mind, if one minute he looks like he wants to start a bloodbath, and the next minute he looks cool, then he turns twitchy again, and then relaxes, you worry, because it means there is something that has touched his soul, and not just his prick.

The only thing that keeps Wanda from really worrying is that Turi, if he's acting like this, it must be because he's thinking about something to do with his daughter Betty. Yes, that's an encouraging thought. Still, there's this thing that bothers you, that you've been married for a lifetime and you don't understand fuck-all what's going on in Turi's head at this moment.

There's this thing that bothers you, and let's be honest, this curiosity, because you didn't think he was capable of it, Turi (who's turning into the spit and image of Ernest Borgnine). You didn't think that he could put things in question and surround them with a, how did they say in the movies? . . . ah yes, *an aura of mystery.*

Wanda has not yet figured out whether she likes all this or whether it's a sovereign ball-buster.

Turi Pirrotta looks at his wife Wanda and smiles.

Wanda turns toward the tubular scaffolding and, without letting Turi see, bites her lip.

What the fuck is going on?

"Ridi, ridi—"

"Huh?" Pietro turns toward Turrisi, who's been talking to himself for half an hour.

"I said, *Ridi, ridi.*"

"But I'm not laughing, Mister Turrisi."

"And what do you have to do with it?"

"Huh?"

"Ree-dee . . . Pagliac-cio," Turrisi begins to sing in a low voice with the look of a madman on his face.

"Mister Turrisi, in my opinion you're too involved."

"E ognun . . . applau . . . dirà!" Turrisi goes on singing, staring at Pirrotta.

"My respects, Contessa!" Falsaperla bows as he prepares to sit down in front of the Contessa. "Have you met my wife?"

"Good evening," says the Contessa, continuing to whip her fan back and forth undaunted, without bothering too much about Falsaperla's wife.

Falsaperla's wife, who on social occasions likes to play the wife, as do most wives present tonight at San Giovanni la Punta, says to the Contessa, "Pleased to meet you, Contessa! I read so much about you in the paper. Warm tonight, isn't it?"

The Contessa replies with her fan, which stops for an instant, very tense and still, and then starts up again, whipping back and forth at a speed that's just a tiny bit faster than before. Translation from fan language: *Oh, how about this one, certainly it's hot, otherwise why am I fanning, so you're Falsaperla's wife, if you really want to have a conversation come up with something better or otherwise just sit next to your commissioner husband, play the commissioner's wife, and don't bust my balls.*

The lady aristocrats sitting next to the Contessa don't fail to appreciate the exquisite finesse of that reply delivered with just a tiny hesitation of the fan.

The fans of the lady aristocrats applaud the performance with a little flurry of activity themselves, as if to say, *Whoa, did you see what the Contessa's fan said to Falsaperla's wife?*

We certainly did!

Gnazia . . . is . . . practically . . . naked.

Not that she isn't wearing clothes, no, it actually looks like she took a lot of trouble. She's wearing a little blouse like the lady aristocrats wear, but apparently she spent the whole afternoon forgetting to put on a bra, so that every which way you look her tits are visible, tits that "in Civita, not to boast, but the dressmakers used to call me in to do the bustier fittings."

Oh, and where is the skirt? That's a skirt? More like a belt, that is.

He'd better sit down and shut up and not wag his tail, thinks Falsaperla, because when Gnazia gets like that, she's capable of going and telling his wife that he's going to bed with Lambertini.

Because, say what you will, anything the fuck you like, but Falsaperla has got an equilibrium at home like you could only dream of, with his wife who doesn't bust Gnazia's balls and Gnazia who doesn't bust his wife's.

It's true, both of them bust Falsaperla's balls, but between them, the cohabitation, all things considered, is pacific.

All he needs is for Lambertini to come in and destroy his familial harmony, when he doesn't even understand how, at fifty-five years old, he got to be culture commissioner for the province of Catania, with both a wife and a mistress, so that when he goes down to the bar, his friends just about have their tongues falling in their coffee.

Let's hope Pirrotta does something to make Paino look bad tonight.

Falsaperla looks around for Pirrotta.

He's sitting down, all beatific, sending text messages with his cell phone. His wife has a horrible expression and she's right, because at least when you're in public, you have to let everyone see you show respect for your wife.

Hey, Falsaperla is certain Pirrotta must have a plan, because it's not possible he could be so calm otherwise.

And at the party he had been categorical. "I don't believe you have *changed your mind*, have you?"

God only knows what Pirrotta has organized for this evening.

"Everything okay, dear?"

"What the fuck do you want?" replies his wife, who's still pissed off at the Contessa for giving her the cold shoulder. These fucking countesses. They come here and play the aristocrat with the commissioner's wife. Hey, gorgeous, I'm sitting in the first tier, and you, asshole with a fan, are sitting in the second. Falsaperla's wife settles herself on the concrete step, she makes a wiggling motion with her rear end like she's hatching an egg. *My seat is in tier one, and you, with your fucking fan, are in tier two, you parvenu,* she says with a wiggle of her behind.

"Testing . . . testing . . . one two three, testing. Can you hear me?" says Paino into the microphone.

The amphitheater quiets down.

"Testing . . . can you hear me?"

The amphitheater signals yes.

Paino looks for something in his inside jacket pocket. He finds it. The folded pages of his speech. He smiles. He taps the microphone with his index finger once more to be sure everything is working. "My fellow citizens!"

His fellow citizens, but nobody else, break out in a thunderous applause.

"There are people here who have come all the way up on the mountain from Catania."

Silence.

"From Catania."

Silence.

"From Catania! My fellow citizens, do you understand?"

Thunderous applause from his fellow citizens. (And in any case why would Paino give a shit about applause from Catania, his electorate is right here in San Giovanni la Punta.)

"Welcome to this splendid stage"—Paino looks around to make sure Tafuri is there taking notes—"of our amphitheater . . . that to-day . . . is being used to host no less than . . . Shakespeare!"

Thunderous applause from the upper tiers of the amphitheater. The lower tiers are more culturally elevated, therefore snobbish, and don't applaud.

"It's pointless for me to thank the director, the actors, and the author of the immortal comedy that we are about to present, and about which"—Paino smiles, flashing a wink—"you will have read in to-day's paper!"

Thunderous applause.

From the band, the sound of a drum falling on the gravel.

The drummer pretends nothing has happened, that it wasn't him, even as the drum rolls across the gravel and comes to rest at Paino's feet.

It's as if they do it on purpose: one time they drop an instrument, another time someone faints, another time they fight with each other hooting on their clarinets. But of course, bands are made of teenagers and old farts! He must remember to put out a memo ASAP about the band.

"It must be the excitement," says Paino, adding with a big smile, "Perfectly understandable!"

Thunderous applause.

"The San Giovanni la Punta band will now play for you *Festa paesana* by Jacob de Haan, *A Little Legend* by Lorenzo della Fonte, *Aria e scherzo* for trumpet and band by Alessandro Stradella, *Brevis historia* for a large band by Silvano Scaltritti, and by request, *Elisabetta*, symphonic march by Ippolito Nievo, in honor of a great Sicilian who is making a name for himself in the heart of London! Ladies and gentlemen, Mister Alfio Turrisi!"

The name echoes through the crowd, propelled by curiosity.

Pietro turns to Turrisi, astonished.

Turrisi is already on his feet, bending in a deferential bow toward the crowd, which breaks out in yet another applause. He sits down again. "Did you see her? Did you see her?"

Carmine turns to Betty, astounded. "But wait, is it dedicated to you?"

"What do you mean, I'm called Elisabetta?"

"You're not?"

The drummer goes to reclaim his instrument, running and holding his hat.

Cosentino, behind a curtain that serves as the wings, stage-whispers, pointing at Caporeale with his thumb, "If anybody's lost his stick, it's over here!"

Caporeale turns around in his dainty floral-patterned shoes and heads back behind the curtain. "Let me know when the concert is over."

"Just kidding, just kidding!" says Cosentino.

Lambertini comes over, adjusting a tightly laced bodice. "Where's Caporeale going? Why's he walking like that?"

They can see a disgruntled Caporeale from behind, walking toward the curtain with his legs bowed out.

"He's getting into the part," says Cosentino, "but the part doesn't fit into his shorts."

Caporeale utters a loud, "Go fuck yourself."

Cosentino yells after him, "Just kidding, just kidding."

For a moment, Lambertini stops fiddling with her tits.

She looks at Cosentino.

Then she returns to the tits.

"No one told me about the band!" Cagnotto yells in Paino's ear.

"What do you mean, it's in the program."

"What program?"

Paino reaches for his inside pocket and hands a program to Cagnotto.

ROMEO AND JULIET

BY

SALVATORE CAGNOTTO

*Before the play there will be a concert by
the municipal band of San Giovanni la Punta.*

Based on an idea by Arturo Paino and William Shakespeare

*Sponsored by
the Commissioner for Culture of San Giovanni la Punta*

"No, nice idea the band, uh, I wish I had known about it before," says Cagnotto to Paino, putting the program in his pocket.

"You see that?" says Wanda to her husband, "Turrisi has dedicated a song to our daughter."

"What do you mean? Your daughter's called Elisabetta?"

"No, her name is Betty, but maybe Turrisi thinks it's her nick-name."

Pirrotta flashes a smile as big as the amphitheater. "Maybe Turrisi thinks I'm a dickhead," he says, returning to his cell phone cheerfully whistling *Aria e scherzo*.

When the band is approaching the grand finale, playing the introduction to *Elisabetta*, Betty blows Turrisi a kiss.

"Is that her?" says Pietro to Turrisi, who's still looking around.

"Who? Which one? Where?"

"That one."

"It's her!"

"She just sent you a kiss."

"A kiss? How?"

Pietro blows Turrisi a kiss.

The Contessa leans over toward the Baronessa. "So is Turrisi also one of them, like Cagnotto?"

"In what sense?"

"Oh, were you listening to the band? Did I distract you?"

"Who, me? The band?"

The Contessa nods, moving away from the Baronessa.

．　．　．

"You blew him a kiss?"

"What?"

"You blew him a kiss?"

Betty is too deeply absorbed in listening to the music to answer.

Carmine cranes his neck to see better.

Turrisi is looking at them with tears glittering in his eyes. "You blew him a kiss!"

"Shhh . . ."

Tatatah!

Thunderous applause.

The band files out.

The lights go down.

The hubbub recedes.

A little boy is crying.

A father yells, "Jennifer, leave your brother alone!"

"Shhh . . ."

Enter Chorus (Cagnotto has cut back on the Chorus. The Chorus is Alessandro Latrati, a neomelodic Neapolitan crooner from Catania. Cagnotto sees no reason why neomelodic Neapolitan crooners have to sing songs in Neapolitan dialect. "It's not like we don't have the same bullshit in Catanese," says Cagnotto.)

"Shhh . . ."

CHORUS Two households, both alike in dignity

In fair Verona, where we lay our scene

From ancient grudge break to new mutiny . . .

The audience comments.

"They got a *fair* in Verona too?"

"Sure, you think we're the only ones that have a fair?"

"But like our *'a fera 'o luni*?"

"Hey, could be."

"Shhh . . ."

The audience sits through the chorus's introduction patiently. There will be people with a *grudge* on the stage.

"Hey, just like at the fair."

"Shhh . . ."

In the audience, somebody says he wants to break another guy's neck. Another guy says he wants to get the virgins up against the wall.

"You want to shoot them?"

"Shhh . . ."

Then they begin to whack each other like at the Catania fair, until a guy comes to try to calm them down, but he doesn't succeed.

But by now all attention is focused on the entrance of the protagonists. The audience wants to see Romeo and Juliet and who gives a fuck about the others.

(Although Montague, Romeo's father, isn't bad. He's played by Carmelo Schiacchitano, who trained as a bass-baritone before moving into the theater, and who holds the stage like an opera singer.)

But under Cagnotto's direction, the performance doesn't dwell on the other actors, not one bit. He has them appear onstage in all their "stage-worn authenticity," as he puts it, which is another way of saying, get them out of the way and concentrate on Caporeale,

Cosentino, and Lambertini, actors who can grab headlines in *La Voce della Sicilia*, prime medium for funding and sponsorship.

MONTAGUE Could we but learn from whence his sorrows grow
We could as willingly give cure as know

The audience murmurs.
"Whence? Shit, what language—"
"Shhh . . . It's poetry."
"Whence, huh? Meaning *when*?"
"Ignoramus."
"Hey, he couldn't say *when*?"
"Whence doesn't mean *when*, it means *from where*."
"Where?"
"Will you shut up or shall I call the police?"
"Whence the police?"
"Shhh . . . Romeo's coming on."
"Shit, this part I want to see."

Enter Romeo. (Although it's not in the script and although Cagnotto hadn't indicated he should do so, Romeo enters with his back to the audience, scuttling backward and sideways.)

BENVOLIO Good morrow, cousin.
ROMEO (*A hand on his brow as if to make out some vague point on the horizon, still keeping his back to the audience*) Is the day so young?
BENVOLIO But new struck nine.
ROMEO (*Shrugging his shoulders*) Ay me! sad hours seem long. (*Moving his head from left to right*) Was that my father that went hence so fast?
BENVOLIO It was. What sadness lengthens Romeo's hours?

ROMEO Not having that which having makes them short.

BENVOLIO In love?

ROMEO Out—

BENVOLIO Of love?

ROMEO Out of her favor where I am in love.

BENVOLIO Alas that love, so gentle in his view,
Should be so tyrannous and rough in proof!

ROMEO (*Continuing to show the audience his back, he reaches out an arm toward* BENVOLIO *and launches into his first long speech.*) Alas that love, whose view is muffled, still . . .

ROMEO (*He lies down on his side as if on a grassy meadow and begins his second speech.*) Why, such is love's transgression.

ROMEO (*On his stomach now and resting his chin on his hands*)
Well, in that hit you miss. She'll not be hit
With Cupid's arrow.

BENVOLIO Then she hath sworn that she will still live chaste?

ROMEO (*Sitting up with some difficulty and squatting with his knees against his chest*)
She hath; and in that sparing makes huge waste.

ROMEO (*Rising, back to the audience*)
Farewell. Thou canst not teach me to forget.

Exeunt.

Cagnotto, backstage, looks at Romeo, bewildered.

"What's wrong?"

"No, I'm . . . I don't know . . . this thing of acting with your back to the audience . . ."

"I was turned toward the new day, and then toward my distant love. Then I lay down because it seemed like the kind of thing a man in love would do, to discourse on love with his chin resting on his hands."

"Yes, hmm . . . a sort of bucolic scene, yes . . ."

"That's right! That's exactly what I had in mind."

"How's the audience, Caporeale?"

"Warm, warm, it's warm."

"Oh, good, good."

Lambertini's eyes are popping out of their sockets as she looks at Caporeale's codpiece.

"They don't make them like that anymore, all we can do is pat our lips," says Cosentino to Lambertini, pretending to pat his lips with a napkin like a man for whom dinner is already over.

"Make what?"

"Actors like Caporeale. They broke the mold!"

"Hurry up, Caporeale, onstage," says Cagnotto, clapping his hands.

CAPOREALE *grabs a stunned* BENVOLIO *and comes onstage holding him tightly by the arm, walking back and forth, back and forth,* BENVOLIO *on the audience side. They're talking about the Capulet feast. When it's time to reverse direction,* CAPOREALE *is speedier than an Olympic swimmer.*

ROMEO I'll go along, no such sight to be shown,
  But to rejoice in splendor of mine own.

Exeunt.

Cagnotto looks at Caporeale. "Why so tight?"

"Tight?"

"You and Benvolio."

"Who was tight?"

"Nobody was tight. You were holding on to Benvolio tightly."

"Oh, right. That worked okay, no?"

"No idea. From here I can't tell."

"Warm, warm, the audience is warm."

Cagnotto looks at Caporeale.

Caporeale nods. "Warm."

Lambertini walks in front of Cagnotto and Caporeale, picking up speed for her first appearance onstage.

Cagnotto and Caporeale turn to look at a fast-moving Juliet.

JULIET *comes onstage running.*

JULIET How now? Who calls?

The audience breaks out in boisterous applause.

Lady Capulet tells her daughter Juliet that she would like her to marry Paris.

The feast in the Capulet household begins.

On the street, Romeo, Mercutio, Benvolio, and five or six maskers approach the house with torchbearers, servants, etc.

Mercutio, Benvolio, the five or six maskers, torchbearers, servants, etc., come onstage.

Romeo remains behind the scenes.

"Hey, Caporeale, you're on," says Cagnotto.

"Okay, just a minute, for the *suspense.*"

"Suspense?"

Caporeale nods competently. Then, still offstage, he recites his line.

The voice of ROMEO *is heard offstage.*

What, shall this speech be spoke for our excuse?

Or shall we on without apology?

Cagnotto says to Caporeale, "Caporeale, what are you up to?"

"Trust me, trust me."

BENVOLIO (*Looking around worriedly; where is* ROMEO*?*)
　The date is out of such prolixity
　We'll have no Cupid hoodwinked with a scarf,
　Bearing a Tartar's painted bow of lath,
　Scaring the ladies like a crowkeeper,
　Nor no without-book prologue, faintly spoke
　After the prompter, for our entrance
　But, let them measure us by what they will,
　We'll measure them a measure and be gone.

ROMEO (*He hurls himself onstage grabbing a torch from the hands
　of a torchbearer, and, holding it with both hands in front of his
　codpiece, exclaims*)
　Give me a torch, I am not for this ambling.
　Being but heavy, I will bear the light.

MERCUTIO Nay, gentle Romeo, we must have you dance. (MERCUTIO
　continues, although not from the script.)
　Lay down thy torch, my noble Romeo.

ROMEO Never hath the thought crossed my mind. And you,
　My trusted Mercutio, worry more about your own dances,
　Make sure they are graceful so as not to cut
　A poor figure in a house that hides a treasure. (*This too is not in
　the script, but now he picks up from Shakespeare.*)
　You have dancing shoes
　With nimble souls. I have a soul of lead
　So stakes me to the ground I cannot move. (*He adds, ad lib*)
　And so I keep the torch.

MERCUTIO . . . Put down the torch and (*He segues into the script.*)
　Borrow Cupid's wings
　And soar with them above a common bound.

ROMEO I am too sore empierced with his shaft
　To soar with his light feathers; and so bound
　I cannot bound a pitch above dull woe.
　Under love's heavy burden do I sink.

MERCUTIO And to sink in it, should you burden love—
Too great oppression for a tender thing.
ROMEO Tender is what you are, my dear Mercutio
All in our fair Verona, know your tenderness, but love (*Back to the script again*) is too rough,
Too rude, too boisterous, and it pricks like thorn.
MERCUTIO If love be rough with you, be rough with love.
Prick love for pricking, and you beat love down. (*He goes on, improvising.*)
Throw down the torch, and let us see
Your tender thing.
BENVOLIO Come, knock and enter . . .
ROMEO I'll be a candleholder and look on.

ROMEO *strides across the stage holding the torch with both hands in front of his codpiece.*

The audience is watching with great interest. They know that Romeo will see his Juliet for the first time at the Capulet feast.

ROMEO What lady's that, which doth enrich the hand
Of yonder knight?
SERVINGMAN I know not, sir.
ROMEO Oh, she doth teach the torches to burn bright!
. . . The measure done, I'll watch her place of stand
And touching hers, make blessed my rude hand.

JULIET *finishes her dance. She goes to stand near one of the tubes of the scaffolding.* ROMEO *strides toward her, torch in hand, and approaches slyly.*

ROMEO (*To* JULIET) If I profane with my unworthiest hand
This holy shrine, the gentle sin is this.

My lips, two blushing pilgrims, ready stand

To smooth that rough touch with a tender kiss. (*Off script he adds*)

I know not who thou art;

Old relic in a holy shrine thou seemst.

Hath they not told thee so?

JULIET (*Rubbing herself romantically against the scaffolding and improvising*) Thou too, good pilgrim, a relic to me seemst,

Your sister, too, though blessed with family grace. (*She segues into Shakespeare.*)

For saints have hands that pilgrims' hands do touch.

ROMEO Have not saints lips?

JULIET Ay, pilgrim, lips that they must use in prayer.

ROMEO Ah, then my fairest relic of a saint (*He segues into Shakespeare.*)

Let lips do what hands do!

They pray; grant thou, lest faith turn to despair.

JULIET Saints do not move . . .

ROMEO And therefore, my holy relic (*He segues into Shakespeare.*)

Move not while my prayer's effect I take.

Thus from my lips, by thine my sin is purged.

ROMEO *kisses* JULIET.

The audience applauds.

Act One over, Cagnotto says to Caporeale, "Nice, the ballroom scene with the torch in your hand."

Caporeale makes a gratified, modest face.

"Where you want this?" asks an Interflora deliveryman with a wisteria vine in hand.

"Oh, um, like this." Cagnotto shows him with a flip of the hand where to put the wisteria on the tubular scaffolding.

The deliveryman puts the wisteria down on the ground, gets up, looks at Cagnotto, looks at the scaffolding, and, miming the graceful gesture that Cagnotto has just made, says, "Like this?"

"Yes, that's right, like that."

"Can I take it?" asks Caporeale pointing to the wisteria.

"Be my guest," says the Interflora man, "we've got a truckful."

"Caporeale, what are you doing with that?"

"There's the garden scene and the balcony scene, no?"

The Interflora deliverymen come onstage to decorate the scaffolding with wisteria.

The audience applauds.

THE SECOND ACT BEGINS

From behind the wings, a leg appears, which we understand from the voice belongs to ROMEO.

Can I go forward when my heart is here?
Turn back, dull earth, and find thy center out.

The leg is withdrawn.

Enter BENVOLIO *and* MERCUTIO.
They are speaking of ROMEO.
From their talk we understand that ROMEO *has scaled a wall.*
The wall is that of Capulet's house.
ROMEO *is determined to meet his* JULIET.
The Capulet garden.
Enter ROMEO *with a sprig of wisteria in front of his codpiece.*

ROMEO He jests at scars that never felt a wound. (*He improvises.*)

Constrained behind a bush to spy my love!

JULIET *comes out on the balcony, stroking the wisteria.*

ROMEO But soft! What light through yonder window breaks?

It is the East, and Juliet is the sun!

. . . She speaks. Yet she says nothing. What of that?

Her eye discourses. I will answer it.

JULIET Ay me!

ROMEO She speaks. (*He improvises.*)

Behind this bush

I'll hear my love.

JULIET O Romeo, Romeo!—wherefore art thou, Romeo?

Now, ROMEO *may be in love, but* CAPOREALE *is a cynical cocksucker, so he begins to play a double who makes faces at the audience, an old trick of the trade in dialect theater. What follows are his facial expressions, with translations.*

DOUBLE (*Brings his chin forward with a jerk*) *And who should I be?*

JULIET Deny thy father and refuse thy name

Or, if thou wilt not, be but sworn my love,

And I'll no longer be a Capulet.

DOUBLE (*Closes his eyelids and simultaneously raises his eyebrows as he moves his head up and to the left*) *Let's not get carried away.*

JULIET 'Tis but thy name which is my enemy.

Thou art thyself, though not a Montague.

DOUBLE (*Knits his brows, looks up and to the right*) *I would not be me if I were not a Montague? I would be a Montague if I were not an enemy? I would be . . . what the fuck's she talking about?*

JULIET What's Montague?

DOUBLE (*Arches his eyebrows and at the same time pulls the corners of his mouth down*) What the fuck do you think it is? It's my name.

JULIET It is not hand nor foot

Nor arm nor face nor any other part

Belonging to a man.

DOUBLE (CAPOREALE *looks at his body worriedly. His arms, his feet, his back.*)

JULIET O be some other name!

What's in a name?

DOUBLE (*He clenches his teeth and widens his mouth, stretching his neck muscles.*) Shit, JULIET *is really pathetic tonight.*

JULIET That which we call a rose

By any other word would smell as sweet.

So Romeo would, were he not Romeo called,

Retain that dear perfection which he owes

Without that title.

DOUBLE (*He writes an M with his head, as if he were following a complicated argument or the flight of a butterfly.*)

JULIET Romeo, doff thy name;

And for thy name, which is no part of thee,

Take all myself.

Briskly, CAPOREALE *lets go of the bush and turns toward the balcony.*

ROMEO Call me but love (*and, he ad libs*), get it over with!

JULIET What man art thou?

ROMEO (*Ad libs*) No idea, you've messed up my mind.

Signora Spampinato, wife of Commissioner Spampinato, rushes away from her seat because she has pissed in her pants.

The courtship over, a light goes on inside the structure of tubular scaffolding. It is FRIAR LAWRENCE'*s cell.* FRIAR LAWRENCE *is already sitting down.* ROMEO, *his back as always to the audience, enters the cell and sits down.*

FRIAR LAWRENCE *has taken* ROMEO's *case to heart. He hopes that a wedding will end the historic rivalry between the two houses.*

The lights in his cell go out and the piazza lights up. BENVOLIO *and* MERCUTIO *come on, wondering what has become of Romeo.* CAPOREALE *comes out of* FRIAR LAWRENCE's *dark cell, walking backward.*

BENVOLIO Here comes Romeo, here comes Romeo!

MERCUTIO Without his roe (COSENTINO *shapes his hands in an oval, like a shad roe.*), like a dried herring. (COSENTINO *raises the little finger of his right hand.*) O flesh, flesh, how art thou fishified. Now is he for the numbers that Petrarch flowed in. Laura, to his lady, was a kitchen wench—marry, she had a better love to berhyme her—Dido a dowdy, Cleopatra a gypsy, Helen and Hero hildings and harlots, Thisbe a gray eye or so, but not to the purpose. Signor Romeo, *bonjour.* There's a French salutation (COSENTINO *touches an ear.*) to your French slop. You gave us the counterfeit fairly last night.

ROMEO Good morrow to you both. What counterfeit did I give you?

MERCUTIO The slip, sir, the slip. (*He ad libs.*) Know what I mean?

ROMEO Pardon, good Mercutio. My business was great, and in such a case as mine a man may strain courtesy.

MERCUTIO That's as much as to say, such a case as yours constrains a man to bow in the hams.

ROMEO (*His back to the audience, he bows, making a respectful gesture with his hand.*) Meaning, to curtsy.

MERCUTIO Thou hast most kindly hit it.

ROMEO (*Still bent over, still with his back to the audience, tucking* *his kidneys in to accentuate his rear end*) A most courteous exposition.

MERCUTIO (COSENTINO *is staring at* CAPOREALE's *rear end.*) Nay, I am the very pink of courtesy. (COSENTINO *makes a fist and raises his arm.*)

ROMEO Pink for flower? (CAPOREALE *closes one fist, brings it up to his ear, and opens it like a rose in the flowering dawn, caressing ever so suavely the flesh of his ear.*)

MERCUTIO (*With a quick wave of his hand, as if he were chasing off an unwelcome suitor*) Right!

CAPOREALE *bends his knees, bounces like a sumo wrestler, jumps up, pirouettes to finish with his face finally in the direction of the audience, continues to bounce on his knees for a few seconds, waiting, like the craftsman he is, until all the various tiers have become aware of what he's got in his undershorts: an outburst of creation, a delightful monstrosity, a gift of nature so extreme as to be supernatural, an explosion of love, a roar of magniloquence, a bang of surprise and joy . . .*

ROMEO (*Adjusting his codpiece*) Why, then is my pump well-flower'd!

Stuf-f-f is the sound of a bullet coming out of a gun with a silencer. Usually the only one who can hear it is the gunman, because the gun is too far away from where the bullet hits.

Sg-nack, that's what it sounds like when a bullet hits the frontal bone of the human cranium. It's as if the bony substance wasn't aware of being perforated like that all of a sudden, and didn't manage to make an appropriate sound. You would expect, just a few milliseconds later, to hear a more significant, more impressive sound, when the bullet, now flattened and misshapen from the entry point, emerges from the occipital bone in a cornucopia of cerebral matter.

Here, you're likely to be twice disappointed; for whatever reason, all that comes out is a ridiculous *Sber-equeck*.

The visual effects, however, are something else, and deliver great satisfaction. The minuscule dark dot that opens on Commissioner Falsaperla's brow (it's not red because the blood has not yet had time to seep out) corresponds, behind him, with a genuine fountain of bone, brain, and blood, a bucketful of Commissioner Falsaperla sprayed on the Contessa, the Baronessa, and assorted lady aristocrats nearby. Their summer dresses and faces suddenly covered with irregular polka dots. Clots of brain stuck in the decorations of their fans.

The Contessa, who's still contemplating the dimensions of Caporeale's member and wondering if it is a stage member or a real one, feels something damp hit her face.

She looks up to see if it's starting to rain.

Paino, not knowing what to do, orders the band to resume playing.

The band, not knowing what to do, starts off at the beginning of the program.

While Signora Falsaperla's screams die down (louder than if she had found Gnazia giving her husband a blow job) the amphitheater of San Giovanni la Punta hears the opening notes of *Festa paesana*.

Curtain.

ACT THREE

The End
of Tragedy

CHAPTER ONE

The Black Silk Sheets of Cagnotto's Bed Are Unruffled

The black silk sheets of Cagnotto's bed are unruffled, as if he hadn't come home that night. In the deserted room, a moan, a groan, perhaps a cry, can be heard.

The alarm clock continues to ring.

An arm snakes out from under the bed, gropes for the clock on the bedside table, and carries it under the bed.

The alarm stops ringing.

The moan, the groan, perhaps the cry, resumes.

Bobo has left him.

He left him while Falsaperla was still going from warm to cold, just like that, while a bunch of people were hightailing it out of there and a whole lot of others were sticking around to watch.

Falsaperla had been sitting there perfectly composed, his legs crossed at the ankle, his shiny black loafers with the tassels, the white socks, the cuffs of his trousers too wide, his hands that were still fiddling nervously with the hem of his jacket. (Probably he was ticked off at Gnazia. Or his wife. Or both.) There was just his head that was bent back, the streaks of blood (which now, yes, were coming down his forehead), and behind, the gaping hole in the occipital bone that continued to drip.

Barone Carpinelli, who had rushed over to assist Baronessa Ferla, who had fainted, had gazed into Falsaperla's cranium and fainted himself.

The Contessa had continued to fan herself. Falsaperla's exploding skull brought back happy memories of her childhood.

The Contessa had been through the war, she had. One morning, when she was six years old and still lived at Rosolini, she had come back home from the bomb shelter after a raid and found a dead man in the kitchen, inside the stone oven with his legs in rigor mortis sticking out of the mouth of the oven. When they pulled him out, he didn't have a face or one arm. In village lore and in their imaginative reconstructions, the man had been mortally wounded when a bomb exploded, had dragged himself into the Contessa's oven because the door of Casa Salieri was missing, and expired therein. Her father the count had said, "Either we get used to the idea or we have to rebuild the oven." It was wartime and they got used to the idea. After all, the oven, all you had to do was light it and it was disinfected.

An American airplane had also crashed, there in the Contessa's house, even though no one had shot it down. It just fell—an engine problem, a suicide attempt, who knew? The pilot, flung out of the cockpit on impact, had landed, decapitated, in the blue parlor while her father the count was saying the rosary. Her father the count had asked the mayor of Rosolini, who was always invited for the saying of the rosary, if he thought that AMGOT (the Allied Military Government of Occupied Territory) or, as her father the count called it, "Ammicot," would pay for the damage now that Sicily was occupied and could thus be considered an ally. Her mother the countess had

yelled at him that this wasn't the moment to think about such matters. And her father the count had replied, "You want to call the doctor? Call the doctor, so everyone in town can laugh at us. How's he
going to inspect his tongue to see if he's ill? He'll go look for it in the
garden?"

"Contessa, move back," Timpanaro had shouted at her in alarm.

"Timpanaro was thrilled to be alarmed," the Contessa had said.

Timpanaro is a theatrical impresario, very thin and very tall,
somewhat looked down upon because in Sicily today theater is
funded by the government, and so what is the point of someone being
an impresario?

"Timpanaro," said the Contessa, "what's the matter, are you
afraid? You think they'll come and *finish off* Falsaperla?"

Timpanaro had looked at her dumbfounded.

"Yes, yes, I'm coming, Timpanaro, thanks for the warning, I'll get
people moving so we don't all block the exits."

Cagnotto, backstage, had understood fuck-all. He had heard a fero-
cious scream and then the band had started up with *Festa paesana*.

Cosentino and Benvolio had come backstage without saying anything. Cagnotto was so taken aback that he didn't even think to ask
what was happening.

Caporeale had left the stage very cool and calm. With his legs
bowed, because the codpiece kept him from moving too fast.

"What happened?" Cagnotto had asked him.

"Falsaperla's not feeling well."

Cagnotto's mouth fell open. "Even here! Even here he has to
come and bust our balls."

"It's not his fault," Caporeale had added, moving slowly toward
the tent to take off his codpiece.

"Where are you going, Caporeale? We're starting up again!" Cagnotto had clapped his hands together to stir the troops.

Caporeale, without turning around, had said, "You go have a look, and then if you think we should start up again, you go right ahead and call me."

A Caporeale so well disposed, Cagnotto had never seen before, but still there was no doubt that this was as good a way as any to say, *get stuffed.*

And why is he telling me to get stuffed, now?

Cagnotto had leaned out from the wings and seen the pandemonium.

There were people climbing on other people's heads, there were people who had thrown themselves face down on the gravel, there was panic that unfurled like a victory cheer in the stadium, starting with Commissioner Falsaperla and rising up, up, and all around to the very top rungs of the amphitheater.

The band had stopped playing because even the musicians were curious. (*Screw Paino, I want to see.*)

And while Cagnotto was moving toward Falsaperla, Bobo was moving toward Cagnotto in the company of a ceramic tile exporter from Caltagirone who was famous in gay circles. (He was famous because when he came down to Catania from Caltagirone and wanted to have a good time, he never worried about spending money.)

"Crazy!" Bobo had said.

Cagnotto had looked at him in a state of shock.

"Incredible," the ceramic tile exporter from Caltagirone had said.

The ceramic tile exporter from Caltagirone looked exactly like Don Johnson in *Miami Vice*, he wore the same improbable, very eighties clothes (big wide shoulders, the sleeves of his shirt rolled up *over* the sleeves of his jacket), and he even had hair like Don Johnson (that part in the middle that made him look like a real dickhead), only he was about four feet eight and very cool with being shorter than average.

"Okay, so I'm going, Tino," Bobo had announced.

"Yeah, we're off," Don Johnson had said.

"Where are you going?" Cagnotto, still in shock about Falsaperla, had asked.

"Don't know . . . you've . . . got your hands full . . . here." Bobo had pointed at Falsaperla with his chin.

"Me?"

"Anyway, congratulations," Don Johnson had said. "Bobo?"

"Yeah, let's go. Maybe we'll be in touch in the next few days, Tino. Ciao. Thanks for the invitation."

Maybe we'll be in touch in the next few days? Thanks for the invitation?

The police had asked Cagnotto whether he'd heard the shot, and where it might have come from. Cagnotto hadn't heard any shot. Then he had answered questions he now couldn't remember.

He couldn't remember because he was in shock. The shock of Falsaperla had passed and been replaced by the shock of Bobo.

Sitting on the sofa in his own apartment, in front of the leopard skin, Cagnotto, his mouth open and his tongue out (the doctor had told him not to mix the tranquilizer and the antidepressant), had continued to call Bobo's cell phone all evening.

And then all night.

Ciao, you've reached Bobo's voice mail, if you want to, you can leave a message after the beep, but even if you don't want to, hey, leave one anyway, because I'm curious. Beep.

At dawn he had decided to go into the bedroom and get under

the bed, and stay there until he died of heartbreak (perhaps confounding heartbreak and heartburn).

An arm reaches out once again from under the bed. Cagnotto gropes for the switch of the bedside lamp. He turns it off.

Then, in the dark, he loses track of time passing.

The doorbell rings.

In the dark he hears a fuss.

The light comes on as Cagnotto is fiddling with the bedside lamp. If he has to die, at least he's wearing his pajamas.

He takes a rapid look at the bedroom to see if everything is in place.

He runs out of the bedroom and realizes that everything *shouldn't* be in place.

He races back to the bedroom and messes up the sheet and pillow on his side of the bed.

He races out.

He races back in and messes up the sheet and pillow on the other side of the bed (so Bobo can see that he, for sure, didn't sleep by himself last night).

Downstairs, Cagnotto's intercom (with a piece of balled-up chewing gum stuck on the corner by his name) squawls, "[Yawn] Yes?"

Timpanaro bends over. "Hello, it's Timpanaro, am I getting you at a bad time?"

"Who?"

"Timpanaro. Signor Cagnotto, do you remember me?"

Silence.

"Hello?"

"Yes . . ."

Timpanaro looks at the front door. He bangs it to see if it's open. He goes back to the intercom.

"It didn't open."

"No, yes, I mean, what's up?"

"I need to speak to you, Signor Cagnotto."

"Can we do it over the intercom?"

Timpanaro goes *no* with his head even though he's speaking over the intercom and Cagnotto can't see him.

Cagnotto hears no reply.

A lady with shopping bags stares at Timpanaro. Then she opens the door with a key.

Timpanaro looks at the door, looks at the lady, and pushes the door open with great gallantry.

The lady looks at Timpanaro suspiciously.

"Hello . . . hello?" says Cagnotto to the intercom.

"Yes, Tino, I'm coming up, yes, yes, it's open."

In the elevator, the lady stares at Timpanaro.

So tall, so thin, his suit hanging on his frame.

"Cagnotto is on what floor?" asks Timpanaro.

"Are you from the police?"

Timpanaro looks at the lady.

She's wearing a flannel skirt, even though the heat is ruinous, flesh-colored tights, slippers, uncombed hair, and a faded top. Somebody's wife or a cleaning lady who has gone out to do the shopping. In either case, someone who doesn't mind her own fucking business.

Timpanaro nods.

"Top floor. But why, is he involved?"

"No, no, *signora*, it's just routine business. You know, a statement."

The lady stares at Timpanaro with, if possible, even more suspicion. "I always said he was strange—too many parties, too much enthusiasm, too polite—and look how it turns out."

Timpanaro makes a face like, *Yes,* signora, *I know, but what can you do?*

• • •

Timpanaro arrives at the top floor and finds Cagnotto with his head resting on the doorframe.

"Cagnotto!"

Cagnotto looks up.

"Cagnotto, you have no idea what's going on."

All he'd needed was Timpanaro.

Right, it was Timpanaro that had been missing!

CHAPTER TWO

Betty Is in a Bad Mood

Betty is in a bad mood.

Carmine, meanwhile, is in pieces.

They are taking the sun by the sea at Acitrezza, on a platform built over the rocky volcanic seafront facing the Faraglioni, big hunks of rock that according to legend the blinded Polyphemus threw down at Ulysses.

Betty, you can see she's nervous because she's applying the tan-multiplier too vigorously.

Carmine, dressed in a caftan, is meditating while he reads *La Voce della Sicilia.*

"Will you stop reading, you're making me nervous," says Betty, her left hand stuck in the crook of her right elbow.

Carmine looks at her.

"You don't get it. Put down that paper."

Carmine puts down the paper, continuing to stare at Betty. "They killed Falsaperla."

"Yeah, I know, I was there," says Betty, starting up again to apply the tan-multiplier, "and you were there too."

"I didn't really believe it until I read it in the newspaper."

Betty nods swiftly, as if all this were *boring*.

Carmine stares at her flip-flops.

Betty lies down, careful to align herself with the sun's rays. "Take off that bathrobe, have a swim, cool down, and take some sun, because you're all white."

Carmine, who has a full-spectrum sunlamp at home, is as dark as an immigrant.

"In the newspaper, they have the last photos of Falsaperla in action, he's arm in arm with your father."

Betty nods rapidly again. "Yeah, I saw it. They published it yesterday in the article about the party at the home of that director."

"And you're having a sunbath."

"Yeah, but just for a while, then I'll put on my mourning."

Carmine puts his little finger in his ear and wiggles it vigorously. Betty, sometimes she makes his blood pressure go up and his ears get blocked. "Betty, my father's doing life in prison, my mother's in the Antilles spending whatever the judge couldn't confiscate, and I'm not—"

Betty leaps up, throws her sunglasses on the deck chair, and walks off, her ass moving back and forth, pursued by the eyes of several young men.

She hops down the steps, looks at the Faraglioni, sticks in a toe to see if the water is cold, and dives in.

She swims out to the raft, about ten yards from the sundeck, jumps up with one thrust of her arms, and lies down in the sun.

Carmine takes off the caftan, revealing a gym-toned body, and sits back down on the deck chair with a serious face.

Sometimes Carmine—he thinks of himself in the third person— gets an attack of this gay thing, tenderness, he usually gets it when his nerves are shot or when something goes wrong, like he gets a flat tire on his scooter. When that happens, he gets into a *thoughtful* thing where he stays there and meditates about stuff. Maybe it's just depression. Right now he's thinking that if Betty is Betty, it's not Betty's fault, because you too, if you were born the child of Riddu the Cement-Mixer and his wife, Wanda, would be a little bit Betty.

Betty, on the raft, snorts.

She gets up again, throws herself in the water, swims to the stairs, comes out like Venus, shedding water all over a lady who's about to go in complete with her straw hat. She takes a nervous shower to wash the salt off, walks quickly over to the deck chair, and stops, standing over Carmine.

Carmine looks back at her.

Betty nods.

She lies down.

She's edgy.

She picks up the sunglasses, which had gotten stuck under her ass.

Putting them on, she says, "You want to talk? Talk."

"I think it was Turrisi."

"Oh, leave me alone. Why the fuck do you think he would kill a commissioner for culture? It's out of the question."

Carmine's about to say something, but stops. He starts up again. "But Betty, they did kill him."

"Yeah, I know, I know. I was there too."

"But," says Carmine, all serious, "is it about that thing, the oil?"

"Who are you, the Anti-Mafia Commission? What the fuck does a culture commissioner for the province of Catania have to do with oil in the province of Siracusa?"

"Exactly."

"Exactly," says Betty, nodding.

"Unless, I don't know, they did it to spite him?"

"The commissioner? Shit, that's spite, all right. If they wanted to spite him they certainly succeeded."

"No, to spite your father."

"The commissioner wanted to spite my father?"

"No, Turrisi."

"The commissioner had himself shot to spite Turrisi?"

Fuck if a person could become Betty just by being born to Riddu the Cement-Mixer and Wanda, thinks Carmine. Maybe Riddu the Cement-Mixer and Wanda had become that way *as a result of* bringing Betty into the world.

"Go fuck yourself." Carmine lies down and picks up the paper to signal that the friendship is cold.

He turns the pages noisily.

"Carmine . . ."

"What's up? It's bothering you that I'm reading the paper? The sound of my thoughts irritates you? What do you want?"

Betty, very serious, says, "You think he did it for me?"

CHAPTER THREE

But Have You Read
the Paper?

"But have you read the paper?" shouts Timpanaro.

Why is Timpanaro shouting? thinks Cagnotto.

They're in the kitchen and Cagnotto is making coffee.

Why am I making him coffee? thinks Cagnotto.

Oh, right, because I'm gay and like all depressed gay guys I get attacks of compassion. Making coffee for Timpanaro must have unconsciously appealed to me as an activity both useful and appropriately mortifying. "Better to make coffee than to sell my body in Piazza Grenoble," says Cagnotto to Timpanaro.

"Huh?"

Cagnotto bites his tongue. The tranquilizer mixed with the antidepressant, mixed with alcohol, mixed with sleep deprivation, makes it hard for him to distinguish what he's thinking from what he's saying, Cagnotto thinks.

"Look, look at this," says Timpanaro, all excited and luckily deep in his own thoughts. Timpanaro, when mixed with Timpanaro, has trouble distinguishing what he's listening to from what he's saying, thinks Cagnotto.

Cagnotto turns around.

Timpanaro has a copy of *La Voce della Sicilia* in two hands, the entire front page a photo of Falsaperla sitting in the amphitheater, his head tipped back, his eyes toward the heavens. Pirronello must have worked on that photo from top to bottom, the reinforced concrete amphitheater that spreads out behind Commissioner Falsaperla like a peacock's tail. All that was left to do was a digital tweaking of the cloudy sky, to get a nice pinky-blue with clouds like balls of cotton. Ever since Pirronello had published, in the weekly magazine of a national daily, a photo of a film producer from Enna become a cadaver flung out on a cocktail table at a party at the Taormina film festival between little umbrellas of colored paper and stuffed olives stuck with flags from around the world because the festival was supposed to be international (the bartender, next to the ear of the dead man, had positioned a shaker with the logo of a famous rum), ever since then Pirronello had been a tiny bit fixated on these artistic photos.

Above the photo, a six-column headline reads:

SNUFFED OUT BY A SNIPER

Cagnotto moans.

He bends over.

He moans again.

"Cagnotto, are you all right?"

Cagnotto goes *no* with his head.

Cagnotto yelps.

"Just a minute."

Cagnotto goes *no, no* with his head, as if to say, *Get rid of that newspaper.*

Timpanaro opens the paper to page two and says, "You see here, on page two, are the various hypotheses about the bullet's trajectory."

"Ow!" Cagnotto puts a hand to his kidneys.

". . . Falsaperla had no enemies . . ."

"My . . . stomach." Cagnotto grabs his stomach with both hands.

". . . then there's a brief account of the commissioner's career . . . Cagnotto, are you all right?"

"No, um, my head!" Cagnotto poses a hand on his brow.

"You probably got a chill yesterday . . . wait . . . page three, the diagram . . . see what nice graphics they have?"

Cagnotto leans on the washbasin, opens the faucet, and sticks his head under.

"Good, good, get your head wet . . . fuck, there's a *beautiful* diagram of the amphitheater with a dotted line that shows the trajectory of the bullet and the place they think the killer . . ."

"Oh, help . . ."

". . . where the killer was, and there's a blowup of the weapon, you see it here in the circle? A precision rifle, shit, beautiful . . . and the killer with his mirror glasses . . . where do they get these graphic artists? And then, wait"—Timpanaro turns the page—"here it is, page four."

Cagnotto rises from the washbasin, looks for something to dry off with, finds a floor rag, and dries his forehead and his neck.

"Cagnotto's Shakespeare!"

Cagnotto stops patting his forehead with the rag.

"What does the subhead say?"

Cagnotto doesn't move a muscle.

"The drama within the drama."

Cagnotto swings around, heads for the refrigerator, opens it, gets some ice, puts it in the rag, and holds it over his wrists first, and then his brow.

"Shall I read you the pull-quote?"

Cagnotto goes *no, no* with his head.

Timpanaro goes *yes, yes.* "A hit in the making, felled before it could come to life."

Cagnotto leans toward the washbasin and vomits.

"What, did you eat shellfish? It's too hot for shellfish. And that's not all! There's a box about Caporeale, a box about Cosentino, and a box about Lambertini, the box about Lambertini is the biggest one, that's good, that's what we want. But the best part is the think piece."

Cagnotto stares with disgust at the little fragments of vomit in the sink.

"Thoughts by Giuseppe Zerbino! The biggest byline in *La Voce della Sicilia*. Shall I read you the whole thing or just the highlights?"

"Ghlights."

"'What can we expect from a Sicily that has forgotten its roots, its love for the theater, from the ancient Greeks to Pirandello to the latest generation of artists who perpetuate these very Sicilian traditions? The possible outcomes are three. Sicily will throw itself into an analysis of the Mafia, of the kind which so often has made it impossible to identify the real villains, and will abandon Cagnotto's Shakespeare to its sad destiny. A director marked forever by this tragedy . . .'"

"I got it, Timpanaro, thank you, that's enough. Please, have a coffee."

"There are two other possible outcomes."

"That's fine, never mind."

"Are you nuts? Listen to this: 'Or will Sicily reflect on the actors, the jobs, the financial resources that every year the region invests in theatrical productions, which in turn generate additional jobs? Will we be able to distinguish, as is to be hoped, the inquest for homicide from the stage play, so that this work so dramatically interrupted can return to the stage?' "

Cagnotto moves toward Timpanaro and takes a peek at the newspaper.

"What, so is Lambertini also going to bed with Zerbino?"

"Understand, Cagnotto? This thing is gold. You need an impresario! Forget about the commissioners, forget about sponsorship, with this article you'll have no trouble getting theater space. Zerbino says so in the newspaper."

"And what's the third possible outcome?"

Timpanaro looks at the paper, folds it, and puts it in his jacket pocket.

"That was the third."

"And the second?"

"Right, the second was that they would lose all the jobs."

"And the first?"

Timpanaro looks at a basket of fruit.

"Timpanaro, give me the newspaper."

"Forget the fine distinctions, Cagnotto. Leave this to me, I know the business."

"Timpanaro, give me the newspaper."

Timpanaro pulls the paper out of his pocket and hands it to Cagnotto without taking his eyes off the basket of fruit.

Cagnotto sees once more the front-page photo of the commissioner and bites his lip, feeling a sharp stab in his gallbladder.

He pages through the paper rapidly, looking for Zerbino's article.

"'The third possible outcome is that which no one can hope for. A commitment from the region not to abandon one of its cultural projects would be ill repaid if, as it is reasonable to fear, the terrible episode should be repeated.'"

CHAPTER FOUR

Pietroburger Is Crowded with Female Salesclerks

Pietroburger is crowded with female salesclerks.

The salesclerks, Pietro gives them a salesclerk discount, because they're working girls, he says.

The truth is that the salesclerks serve as poster girls for Pietroburger, but this he doesn't let them know, because he'd have to pay them as poster girls and that would be expensive.

Pietroburger is parked in Piazza Europa, next to San Giovanni li Cuti. Between Pietroburger and the sea there are only a few volcanic rocks on which, in the summertime, they put up a sundeck for the use of the citizens. (This one in Piazza Europa is free and doesn't have any palm trees or wicker chairs under umbrellas.)

Pietroburger is a van customized as a sandwich shop that brought the first historic hamburgers and hot dogs to Catania. Pietro had parked it there back in the days when, if you wanted a sandwich, you had to go into the likes of the *salumeria* owned by Signorina Quattrocchi.

The salesclerks in the shops on Corso Italia, at lunchtime, go sit in the sun at San Giovanni li Cuti and get a tan so that by night, in the discotheque, you can't see that they have a job. (In Sicily even today in some places, women who work are talked about behind their backs and nobody wants to marry them because working girls keep bad company.)

If you go to Pietroburger at two in the afternoon, when you'd expect a crowd of salesclerks, you won't find anyone. The salesclerks go down to sit in the sun and diet, so they will not only tan, but lose weight. However, at 3:45, before returning to work, they pass by Pietroburger on their scooters and catch the scent of the hot dogs, the piping-hot eggplant parmigiana, the fried peppers, the caponata, the mushrooms with mayonnaise and peperoncino, the onion frittata, the tuna with onions, and they park their scooters and put off their diets until tomorrow.

At 3:45 it's party time at Pietroburger: along with groups of brothers' cousins, sons-in-law's boyfriends, godfathers' daughters-in-law, and assorted godmothers, there are groups of salesclerks, dirty dancers married to killers, muggers on the arms of future actresses, ex-PR agents turned cocaine dealers, owners of convertibles acquired in auto leasing because they are sales representatives of mysterious clothing firms, bartenders on their day off, and fences for stolen property on parole.

On the day Pietroburger was inaugurated in the faraway 1980s, Pietro, keeping in mind that his was an American novelty, something you had just begun to see in the soap operas, had decided to dress up like Elvis Presley. At first it was just a whim, because people in kitchens wore white and to Pietro, the white, late-model Elvis costume seemed perfect for the type of American cuisine he wanted to propose to the public. Later, he really got into it. The inauguration day had been a huge success; a police car drove by twice, there was so much pushing and shoving. Pietro was happy because people were having fun. He decided that the Elvis suit brought good luck, and so he dedicated himself to the look, with a new pair of sideburns and a forelock, and he tossed out the old black loafers in favor of white boots with mirror studs, and the word PIETROBURGER spelled out in Broadway-style flashing lights.

Mister Turrisi's Aston Martin appears, laying rubber as it navigates the roundabout, the squeal of the wheels, as ever, wafting down a deserted Corso Italia.

Pietro looks up, cocks an ear, and goes back to looking at his magazine. Par for the course. Mister Turrisi always lays rubber when he gets to the roundabout; he's fixated, Turrisi, with his right-hand drive.

Now Turrisi heads up the far side of the street, at the end of which there's another roundabout. Turrisi has to go around the second roundabout so that he can drive back down and park in front of Pietroburger.

Squeal.

Sound of echo.

At the second squeal Pietro, as always, gets up from the cash register and goes to meet Turrisi, bounding down the three metal stairs and causing Pietroburger to tremble all over.

Turrisi's Aston Martin flies right past him, continuing down the street at high speed.

Pietro's Elvis-head follows the car, bewildered: Why didn't Turrisi stop? At the least, when he's in a hurry, he'll say something from the window without getting out of the car (and of course he has the wheel on the sidewalk side).

Turrisi takes the first roundabout once again.

This time the car's back end skids and Pietro thinks he even sees Turrisi turn the wheel into the skid.

Then he comes up the far side of the street once again, faster than ever, spins around the second roundabout, and finally stops in front of Pietroburger, slamming on the brakes without the least regard for his tires.

Mister Turrisi gets calmly out of the car, adjusting his hair.

"Who was it? What happened?" says Pietro in alarm, looking around to see if maybe someone is plotting a fistfight or, who knows, a murder attempt or a chase scene, it wouldn't be the first time something like that happened at Pietroburger.

Turrisi looks in the same direction that Pietro is looking. There's the statue in Piazza Europa, a mermaid, topless, with a slithery fish tail and her face turned up toward the sky in a spastic pose.

Pietro looks at Turrisi.

He looks calm, as if nothing has happened.

"Nothing. Why, what's up?" Turrisi asks Pietro.

"Um . . ."

Turrisi turns around. Piazza Europa is empty.

Lunchtime silence.

The only noise you can hear is the heat.

Pietro goes *who knows?* with his face. He asks, "Do you want to sit down?"

"Certainly!"

Pietro steps back to let Turrisi go ahead, indicating *after you* with his head, while with one eye he inspects the Aston Martin, parked a little bit crooked.

Hey.

Turrisi walks stiffly toward the VIP corner, a metal table with metal chairs positioned under an umbrella and surrounded by a plastic chain like they set up when they do roadwork. Inside the area protected by the chain is a patch of Astroturf, and on the Astroturf are some plastic flowers. From time to time Pietro sprays them with water to get a dewy effect. At night, hidden among the flowers, colored disco lights glitter.

Pietro hurries forward to unhitch the chain.

Turrisi enters the VIP zone, drags a chair out of the shadow under the umbrella, and inspects it carefully in the sunlight to see if it's dirty. He nods, replaces the seat under the umbrella, and sits down. Pietro, those chairs in the VIP zone, he polishes them with Windex every day.

Pietro closes the chain, even though there's not a soul around. He sits down next to Turrisi with a conspiratorial air. Last night, after Commissioner Falsaperla had been snuffed out, Turrisi had been dead silent. Pietro had tried to ask him something and Turrisi had indicated he'd better stay dead silent himself. Now Pietro is really curious to know what the fuck is going on.

"Something to eat or drink?"

"No, thanks, I'm in a foul mood."

"I could tell by the way you were driving."

"Why, how was I driving?"

Pietro raises the index finger of his right hand and he screws it around in the air imitating the double circuit of the Aston Martin, fast like they couldn't even come close at Imola with the Grand Prix.

Turrisi looks at Pietro's index finger but doesn't understand, and makes the annoyed face of a guy who doesn't understand. Turrisi doesn't like it when he doesn't understand.

Pietro puts his index finger on the table and lowers his eyes.

"They killed Falsaperla," says Turrisi, shifting on his chair. Turrisi likes these three-piece suits but the fucking waistcoats give him problems with chairs.

Pietro sits on the edge of his seat. Mother of God, how Pietro loves it when Turrisi gives him his high-toned thoughts about the Mafia.

"And what the fuck does Falsaperla have to do with anything?" says Turrisi, stretching out his legs and folding his hands in his lap as if he were relaxing.

"What does Falsaperla have to do with anything?" asks Pietro, ever more curious. He knows very well what Falsaperla has to do with it, Falsaperla is Pirrotta's man, everyone had seen the photo of Falsaperla arm in arm with Pirrotta, and Turrisi, it seems, has blown

Falsaperla away because he couldn't blow Pirrotta away directly. It's called a . . . wait, what do they call it? . . . oh, yeah, a *vendetta trasversale*, an indirect hit. It's hard to explain because Pietro has never really understood the *vendetta trasversale*, however, lately it's very much in vogue and he can't wait for Turrisi to explain it to him. (When somebody gets killed and nobody knows who the fuck did it, all the folks at Pietroburger say it was a *vendetta trasversale*, even when you can see they are ignorant and only open their mouths to say something smart and put their moves on the salesclerks.)

Turrisi sits up suddenly, makes a little jump in his chair, and gives the metal table a whack, which for some reason (perhaps because of Turrisi's signet ring) emits a loud *gong* sound.

Pietro jumps back.

"I have no idea what Falsaperla has to do with anything," shouts Turrisi.

"What do you mean, you have no idea?"

CHAPTER FIVE

Timpanaro Is Wearing an Earpiece

Timpanaro is wearing an earpiece so he can pace back and forth more easily in his office on Via Pacini.

Now and then he goes to the window and takes a look at the market in Piazza Carlo Alberto, the so-called *'a fera 'o luni* market, that some say means *la fiera del lunedì*, or the Monday Fair, even though they hold it every day, while according to others (those weird types who hold festivals timed to the solstices, the equinoxes, and other esoteric-type things) means *la fiera della luna*, or the Moon Fair, in honor of some Egyptian thing that got transferred to Sicily and which has an elephant with an obelisk as a symbol. These people dance at night in the countryside wearing a long white bathrobe that looks like a slip. Looked at from above, *'a fera 'o luni* is a vast spread, as far as the eye can see, of colored umbrellas.

Timpanaro likes to look at *'a fera 'o luni* because he's fond of the market. Timpanaro has introduced the commissioners to the concept of market bidding.

After Zerbino's article, all the culture commissioners in Sicily (and even a couple from Calabria and the Aeolian Islands) will do anything to get Cagnotto's production for their home city.

Since Falsaperla was taken out, all the culture commissioners want everyone to see (1) they have not forgotten that theater which in Sicily runs from the ancient Greeks through Pirandello, and (2) that they are sensitive to the workforce, the actors, Lambertini, and the new generation of directors who are perpetuating a genuine Sicilian tradition.

Timpanaro has intuition; he knew that, post-Falsaperla, the theater was going to be bigger this summer than some food festival for sausages made with Bronte pistachios.

His cell phone rings while he stands admiring the colored umbrellas of the market with a *he who laughs last laughs best* smile stamped on his face.

"Timpanaro here, what can I do for you?"

"It's Commissioner Treuzzi."

"Commissioner! What's up at San Vito lo Capo? Are they filming *Ocean's Thirteen?*"

"Forget about those Americans, Timpanaro. What we want to do here is to recover our tradition of Greco-Sicilian theater."

"And Greco-Roman wrestling," says Timpanaro nastily.

The commissioners have been mocking him for years because he likes to operate in the private sector, while they like to operate in the public sector, which is better for them. But now that he's got this contract as Cagnotto's agent in hand . . .

"Wrestling?"

"No, no, sorry, Commissioner, I was talking to my secretary. Bring me a coffee and *please*, shake it!"

Silence.

"You see, Commissioner, coffee, I like it shaken, not stirred with a spoon, otherwise it gets too sweet. So I get them to put in a lot of sugar, and then I ask them to shake it.

"Oh, yes, of course, I like it that way myself."

"You take it shaken? First you shake it and then you drink it?"

"Right, just like you."

"No, I get my secretary to shake it."

"Timpanaro, you're in good form today."

"Pardon me, Commissioner, I have a call on the other line. I must say goodbye. If I can, I'll call you back."

This dickhead Treuzzi had busted his balls for a year about the fact they were making *Ocean's Twelve* at San Vito lo Capo, like he was the one who was doing a favor to George Clooney.

Obviously Timpanaro has already made his decision, and obviously he's not yet talking about it because he likes it when the commissioners call him up and kiss his ass a little.

The setting couldn't be better: the Greek theater of Palazzolo Acreide, in ancient times Akrai, built in 663 BC by the Corinthians of Syracuse, seventy years after the founding of Syracuse, and bastion of Greek expansionism in Sicilian territory. The Greek theater, a little jewel on the summit of Mt. Akre, 2,500 feet above sea level on the heights above a valley called Scala Ragusa, brought to light in the first thirty years of the nineteenth century by the explorations of Barone Judica, a baron who didn't have fuck-all to do and who devoted himself to archaeology.

The town had been placed on the UNESCO World Heritage List because of its architecture: Palazzo Judica-Cafici, Palazzo Zocco, Palazzo Ferla, Palazzo Cappellani (this last acquired by the region and set aside to house Barone Judica's archaeological collection), and then the churches, l'Annunziata, San Paolo, San Sebastiano. ("St. Sebastian?" Cagnotto had asked, "I'm a devotee." "Sure, sure, Cagnotto, but let's not talk about it yet, let's allow interest to grow.")

Palazzolo Acreide was the perfect place in which to perpetuate an ancient tradition that ran from the Greeks through Pirandello to modern times. The tradition of murd—of the theater!

And just think that the commissioner for Palazzolo Acreide, it was Timpanaro himself who had to propose this thing to him. Half of the commissioners of Sicily were having a heart attack to get their hands on it, and the commissioner for Palazzolo Acreide was down on the beach with his wife and kids and hadn't even read the paper that day.

Timpanaro's cell phone rings.

"Timpanaro! This is Commissioner Attardi from Buscemi."

"And I don't give a shit."

"Sorry?"

"I was saying: so early in the day!"

"But, um . . . were you sleeping? It's two in the afternoon. I called Cagnotto and he told me to get in touch with you."

"Who's Cagnotto?"

Mother of God, what a ball Timpanaro is having.

CHAPTER SIX

La Voce della Sicilia Is Making His Brioche Go Down the Wrong Way

La Voce della Sicilia is making his brioche go down the wrong way. Bobo is having a granita and brioche at the foot of the steps of Caltagirone, the famous steps with the majolica risers.

It has to be said that places like Caltagirone are unbearable. Everybody knows everybody else and there's none of that city air you get in the metropolis.

Don Johnson's name is Gianni, and this morning he had taken him all around town to show off his new conquest from Catania.

Bobo feels like he's suffocating.

Cagnotto's theater?

That's *my* theater, *I'm* Cagnotto's inspiration, without *me* Cagnotto would have just continued on doing that experimental stuff and would never have discovered those stage traditions that endure from century to century, renewing themselves thanks to the inspiration gleaned from casual encounters.

"Is it good, the granita?" asks Gianni, leaning over Bobo's brioche.

Hey, keep your distance, your hair's going to fall on my plate.

Cagnotto's theater, my ass.

How's it *supposed* to taste, my granita? It's just a fucking granita like any other granita. You think I'm a tourist, I'm going to fall in love and dance the tarantella because an almond granita tastes of almond?

Gianni's in a great mood.

And here's *La Voce della Sicilia* that practically gives more prominence to Cagnotto than to the dead commissioner.

This morning in Caltagirone, everybody's talking about Shakespeare.

It's a disgrace, thinks Bobo, they murder a commissioner and people are talking about Shakespeare. He's outraged! Sicilians are brutes. Faced with a death, a murder, what are they talking about this morning as they read *La Voce della Sicilia*?

About Shakespeare.

And about Cagnotto.

The whole town is up in arms because the jobs, the actors, and the tradition could all come to nothing because of a homicide.

No wonder Sicily is in such bad shape, with these ignoramuses who don't give a fuck about a homicide.

And anyway, Cagnotto's Shakespeare is *his*. What's Cagnotto got to do with it?

That dickhead the culture commissioner for Caltagirone had even walked by, and he had bowed to Gianni like he was getting ready to take it from behind, and then he had asked whether, seeing as how Gianni often went to Catania, whether maybe he had Tino Cagnotto's phone number because he wanted to show his support and offer him the venue of Caltagirone with its famous steps.

He was asking Gianni for Tino's phone number?

"Want another?"

Bobo looks at Gianni.

He looks at his granita.

He puts the spoon down on the plate, disgusted.

"No. When are we going to Catania?"

"But we just got here! Summer in Caltagirone is great, Bobo. And I wanted to take you around to meet the craftsmen who make the ceramics."

"Is there a bus?"

CHAPTER SEVEN

Cagnotto Has Had to Turn Off His Cell Phone and Unplug His Landline

Cagnotto has had to turn off his cell phone and unplug his land-line.

La Voce della Sicilia is insisting, they want an interview.

He had a call from the reporter reminding him that she was the author of the article that had so grandly illustrated his work. She had also said, "Do give my very best regards to Bobo, he's so wonderful."

Timpanaro had been categorical: no interviews, no public appearances. It was an image question, they had to create an aura—the artist victim of Sicily's dramatic daily crime blotter, rereading Shakespeare in the pensive silence of his little room, he had said, pointing at Cagnotto's expansive apartment.

"But what are people supposed to think about what I do in the pensive silence of my little room?"

"Cagnotto, you know nothing about people: people imagine, people surmise, people think."

"They think?"

"Really." Timpanaro had looked disgusted.

Then Paino had called begging him to grant an interview to *La Voce della Sicilia.*

"Cagnotto, the editor called me, they begged me to intercede with you to get an interview. Cagnotto, they went so far as to black-mail me, they'll only do an article about San Giovanni la Punta if I get you to give them an interview. Cagnotto, you owe it to me."

Timpanaro had told him he didn't owe anybody anything, and that now, if they wanted Cagnotto's Shakespeare, they would have to pay, and then some.

"Look, Paino, you only gave me the piazza, the rest I had to pay myself."

"Listen Cagnotto, I wouldn't use that tone of voice, because I, you know, don't talk to me like that because now that Falsaperla is no longer with us, now I become . . . Cagnotto? . . . Cagnotto?

Cagnotto has hung up.

"You filthy cocksucking bastard of a director. You owe me every-thing, you half-wit, and I'm going to make you pay."

Cagnotto is off to wash his hair.

The Contessa has been on the phone all morning. Following Zerbino's article, the Contessa was very keen to see the whole of Cagnotto's play, to see how things worked out.

Baronessa Ferla has spent the whole morning on the phone telling her friends that the Contessa likes it when they kill people, she had learned this from Farina, who had learned it from Cosenza.

Gnazia has spent the whole morning making and receiving phone calls in relation to her new status as a widow. She complained that Falsaperla's wife hadn't called her, "after everything I've done for her." Then she had asked Quattrocchi how she should behave at the funeral—what to wear, where to sit. "You know about these things, you always read the society magazines. And finally, when they come to pay their condolences, where should I be?"

"You're the mistress, not the wife; it's the wife who gets condolences."

"What's the wife got to do with it? Doesn't she already get the inheritance?"

The managing editor of *La Voce della Sicilia* is going seriously crazy. He has dedicated twelve pages to the Falsaperla homicide and he can't begin to slot all the advertising that's pouring in. The commissioners all want it to be known that they would be delighted to host Cagnotto's *Romeo and Juliet* in their hometowns, and are keen to make a declaration, give an interview, leave a quote, or post a statement on the state of the theater in Sicily, in Europe, and in the world. The managing editor is playing hard to get: the paper is full of news and it's full of ads. The commissioners know how to get around the problem. They call the advertising department and order page upon page of specials, backgrounders, and advertorials: a ricotta festival and a *caciotta* festival, a couscous contest, a seafood happy hour, a Latin American dance congress. Then they call the managing editor back, and this time, he's more obliging.

Commendatore Fragalà, arms merchant and opera singer, has bought four ad pages showing summer specials, from treadmills and exercycles to Smith & Wesson .357 Magnums and precision compressed air rifles, earning himself an editorial column on page sixteen in which he can express his opinions on the Sicilian theater, *bel canto*, and the latest-model precision weapons for big game.

It's amazing what a kick Falsaperla has given to the market, getting blown away.

CHAPTER EIGHT

Dawn Comes at Dusk

DAWN COMES AT DUSK

is the headline of the page-one comment in *La Voce della Sicilia,* under the byline of Giuseppe Zerbino. "In the glorious setting of the Greek theater of Palazzolo Acreide, two hours before sunset as tradition would have it, the celebrated and tormented *Romeo and Juliet* of the young Tino Cagnotto will return to the stage. Our compliments to Commissioner Ronsisvalle, who with courage and drive has revived the work of the celebrated director, over which a pall of gloom was cast, as we know, by events we shall not dwell on here. With no fear of contradiction, we can say that today at nightfall we will applaud not merely an historic interpretation of the Bard's immortal verses, but, above all, the dawn of a new era for theater in Sicily, the latest in a long legitimate line of ancient Greek theater, that theater which has shaped our world."

Cagnotto is unable to continue reading. He has tears in his eyes, Zerbino had called him "young."

"Did you see that, Cagnotto?"

Timpanaro looks less emaciated somehow, his shoulders broader, his skin tanned.

Cagnotto nods, moved.

"Take it easy, Cagnotto, take it easy. You deserve it! And, you put yourself in good hands." Timpanaro gives Cagnotto a pat on his left shoulder.

Cagnotto sighs happily, showing his gratitude with a languid look.

"Right, Cagnotto, to work, your actors are waiting."

The actors couldn't give a shit about Cagnotto.

They're in the necropolis next to the Greek theater of Palazzolo Acreide, having their photos taken. There are even a couple of reporters from the national newspapers. Caporeale is walking around the site with his codpiece prominently on display, being interviewed. For the photos, consummate actor that he is, he even tilts his pelvis forward a little bit. "Let's do one in profile," he says to *La Repubblica*'s photographer, standing sideways in front of the door to one of the tombs.

Cosentino, somewhat envious of Caporeale's codpiece and the photographer from *La Repubblica*—a national newspaper, not a local one like the one whose journalist he is talking to—rushes over, saying, "Yes, yes, in profile."

Cosentino gets in front of Caporeale and bends down in Mercutio's famous bow.

Caporeale and Cosentino both turn their heads to smile at the camera.

The photographer lowers his camera and looks at them, puzzled.

Cosentino and Caporeale freeze like that, smiles stamped on their faces, one with his codpiece thrust forward, the other bent over at a right angle, not understanding why the photographer doesn't proceed.

The photographer doesn't want to say anything, because they're in a Greek theater and these two are not only old—no, senior citizens—but also actors working on the stage in a Greek theater.

Caporeale and Cosentino still don't understand what's wrong with the photographer, who instead of snapping is staring at them.

Cosentino twists his head around looking for Caporeale to ask him with his eyes what the fuck is going on.

Caporeale too looks toward Cosentino and sees, for the first time, his rear end, and then his face, peering behind it.

He notices with horror that between the codpiece and Cosentino's rear end, there is at most three to four inches.

Caporeale makes an instant pirouette, turning the other way, while Cosentino leaps upright.

Click: *Cosentino and Caporeale, two pillars of Catania dialect theater, upright and proud in Shakespearean costume, shoulder to shoulder with the ruins of ancient Akrai in the background.*

Half of Catania, half of Messina, and of course half of Siracusa are arriving in Palazzolo Acreide. The ladies are in evening dress although it's afternoon, but it's as if this were evening because in ancient Greece the evening took place in the late afternoon. The only concession to afternoon are the hats, as with the races at Ascot.

Betty is wearing a simple veil.

Black.

It's held in front of her face with a diamond tiara.

Her hair is swept up with a coral comb.

Her black linen dress rises high in the neck.

Behind, the neckline plunges to her hips, on which are dancing a string of pearls hanging like a plumb line that follows the sinuous action of her spine.

Carmine's eyes are popping out, if he weren't a gay guy he would screw her himself.

"Where is he?" asks Betty, looking straight ahead.

"Who?" asks Carmine, who, although not reneging on his gay status, cannot help but follow that ass and the hypnotic effect of those pearls on the tanned back.

"Th-isi," says Betty without opening her mouth.

"Huh?"

Betty stops cold on the path leading to the theater. She looks at Carmine. She looks around at her back as if to say, *Why are you looking at my ass, have you turned into a moron?*

"Okay, I'll look for him myself. You continue to meditate."

Betty walks off under the gaze of the police force, which is armed and deployed in the park.

Paino in his blue linen suit that's fashionably rumpled, his Persol sunglasses, and his Dolce & Gabbana patent leather loafers, is sitting all alone and solitary on the steps of the theater. Even the Contessa has snubbed him, she had acknowledged him swiftly with the words, "You did well to come, Paino. Certainly *your* theater is in better shape than this one. Why don't you get Intelisano to come and put down a nice coat of asphalt here too?"

And to think that the credit was all his. But now that Falsaperla is no more, just wait a little, and then we'll see what Paino can do. In any case, when he got there, the traffic squad had been very polite to him, and they let him park his convertible right in front of the entrance, while they sent the others around to the parking lot.

"Hey, are they following us?" asks Pietro, who's sitting on the passenger side while Turrisi struggles with the curves along the road from Noto to Palazzolo Acreide.

"Certainly they're following us," says Turrisi, furious.

Pietro smiles as he looks in the rearview mirror. There's a red

Fiat Panda that hasn't let them out of its sight since they left Catania. The two guys in the car, you don't need binoculars to see they're cops.

"What the fuck you got to smile about?"

"They're following us."

Turrisi, ever more furious, slams on the brake because a sheep, frozen in the middle of the road, is staring bewildered at the Aston Martin. Probably the sheep has never seen an automobile with right-hand drive before.

The red Fiat Panda, in a genius move, brakes too, keeping a distance of about a hundred yards.

"And they say they don't know how to fight the Mafia in Sicily."

"Huh?" says Pietro, mesmerized by the sheep.

"Nothing, nothing. Hey, Pietro, do me a favor, move that sheep."

"Huh?"

Turrisi looks at him.

"Okay, sure."

Pietro gets out of the car.

Turrisi is thinking about that scum Pirrotta, who arranged that own-goal with Falsaperla just so he could put the blame on Turrisi.

Mother of God, what a scumbag.

And now Turrisi is going to score an own-goal by hitting Paino, so they will be fair and square and can start all over again. Is it possible to be more of a scum than Pirrotta?

Betty sits down on a riser and crosses her legs, showing off a perfect little foot in a sandal so delicate it is almost nonexistent except for the five-inch heel. Betty's wearing transparent toenail polish.

Carmine sits down next to her, continuing to stare at her.

"Hey, is something going on with you?" asks Betty.

"What do you mean, going on?"

"Um, okay, we don't need to worry?"

"Betty, what the fuck are you talking about?"

"Nothing, nothing. I don't see him. Maybe he's absconded."

"Absconded?"

"Yeah, after what happened."

Carmine spreads his hands and throws Betty a questioning look.

Betty stares at her feet, rocking back and forth. Then she looks at Carmine and says, "Carmine, you're weird today."

Lambertini, it's like she scored a goal in the World Cup. The commissioners from halfway across Sicily are thronging around her to express joy and congratulations. Her interpretation of Juliet is a milestone, one fellow has offered her a recital, another, upping the stakes, is offering her the director's job at the City Theater.

Gnazia and Signora Falsaperla are battling it out on the widow front.

Gnazia, not to be outdone, bursts into tears.

Signora Falsaperla passes out under a carob tree.

Gnazia lets it be known that she's ready to say farewell to this cruel world.

Signora Falsaperla asks for some sugar water.

Gnazia maintains that Signora Falsaperla shouldn't have come to the theater so soon after her loss.

Signora Falsaperla insists that this is what her husband would have wanted, that she is sacrificing herself on behalf of the culture her husband so dearly loved.

Gnazia spreads the word that Signora Falsaperla only finished elementary school.

Signora Falsaperla spreads the word that her husband had a mistress, he knew how to choose a mistress, and the mistress was the type who knew her place in the world, and who wasn't here tonight.

"What do you mean, she's not here?" yells Gnazia with a shout that echoes down the valley.

"Yes, no, thank you, I feel so much better already," says Signora Falsaperla with a strange smile on her face, as she refuses a glass of tamarind syrup.

Commissioner Ronsisvalle is about to pass out between two members of the traffic squad. He's been standing there for an hour in front of the police barricades, waiting for Turrisi. Turrisi is late and if he doesn't show up soon the sun's going to go down and the commissioner doesn't know how he's going to put on the show, because he doesn't have the right kind of artificial light. Finally he sees him. "The barricades! Move the barricades."

Pirrotta is radiant. Betty is wearing a tiara with a veil, and all the princesses, the baronesses, the countesses, all the fucking coats of arms can suck his daughter's dick, his daughter who, God willing, is forgetting about Turrisi. Today he saw she had a new sparkle in her eyes and his father's heart melted. Luckily she's young, and young people, as we know, soon forget love's hurts.

Wanda, lately her husband has been stirring her up like she can't fathom. He's, I don't know, more erect, he's got the charisma, he walks the way he did when he was way up high at the wheel of his cement-mixer, his hands on the great big wheel, so that when he would come by to pick her up and he made sure that everybody saw, Wanda would make him the big eyes and Turi would say, "You like the way I handle the wheel, don't you, Wanda? Take a look at what I can do." And then Turi would push a button while Wanda began to tremble all over with excitement, and then she would watch the cement-mixer that slowly, slowly pushed upright toward the sky, and then begin to whirl around with a whirl that whirled even inside Wanda's head, and finally Turi would even let her see the gush of cement pouring out, and Wanda's eyes would be shining.

Bobo, standing in line at the box office to pay for his ticket, is waiting for Cagnotto to catch sight of him.

So Cagnotto comes along, sees him standing there humbly in a queue at the box office to pay for his ticket out of pure love for Art, and calls out to him, shouting, "Bobo, what are you doing? You're paying for a ticket? You! You, the inspiration, the alpha and omega, the source of my genius, you, to whom Shakespeare owes everything! Come, come here under my protective wing."

Fat chance. No sight of Cagnotto.

Bobo looks around. He can't stand these peasants from Palazzolo Acreide, all waiting in line to see Shakespeare. What do they know about Shakespeare, peasants!

Quattrocchi, you'd think it was *her* lover who had been blown away, she's so involved in Gnazia's widowhood; you should see how she pats her, how she hands her a Kleenex, how she strokes her arm.

Caporeale, his legs bowed, approaches Gnazia and Quattrocchi, thrusting out his chest and his codpiece. Because Quattrocchi is one of his fans, and everybody knows fans have to be cultivated, that you have to be modest with your fans, because fans are, yes, fans, but woe to him who abuses them, because fans abused, shit, they say they are more terrible than a wife.

"Signorina Quattrocchi!"

Signorina Quattrocchi gives him a dirty look.

Can't you see we're in mourning?

"My dear Signorina Gnazia!"

Signorina? Gnazia? Is that any way to address a freshly widowed widow?

Gnazia and Quattrocchi stare at Caporeale with contempt.

Caporeale thrusts out his chest and his codpiece.

"It's the wrong moment, Caporeale," says Quattrocchi, deep into Gnazia's sorrow.

"Okay, right, sorry." Caporeale whips his codpiece around and goes off, thinking that it's true, they're right, it's absolutely the case, that you can't be successful for more than a minute before the fans go and act superior. And then they'll say you're snubbing them, these parvenu fans.

Commissioner Ronsisvalle walks Turrisi respectfully to his seat.

Turrisi sees Paino. He stops.

"Mister Turrisi, please, you know, there's the sunset, we have to hurry."

Turrisi looks at Pietro.

Pietro looks at Commissioner Ronsisvalle.

Commissioner Ronsisvalle says, "You ought to see what a sunset we have here at Palazzolo Acreide. It's really spectacular."

Turrisi's not even listening. He's walking toward Paino with a huge, white smile.

Pirrotta can't help but see him. "And what the fuck's he doing here?"

"Huh?" says Wanda, who was thinking about the days when he used to show her how to whip up a cement-mixer.

Pirrotta's already on the cell phone, punching in a number.

. . .

Betty gets up. She smooths her skirt. She fiddles with the nipped-in waistline that allows the plunging neckline over her back to ease slightly and show off the curve of her breasts.

Betty takes the stairs as if she has never done anything else in her life besides walk on high heels out-of-doors.

The spectators who see first Betty, then Carmine, are asking themselves why that beautiful piece of ass should be going out with that guy who looks like a faggot.

But then everybody knows that girls like that marry rich faggots, daddy's boys.

Carmine notices the looks of contempt.

He returns them.

Pirrotta stops, cell phone in hand.

What the fuck is Betty doing?

"Commissioner, my friend!"

Paino jumps to his feet as the crowd settles down on the stairs. Jumping to your feet in the theater, especially if you're in one of the front rows and the whole audience is watching, is mandatory. Obviously, if you jump to your feet you have to let it be seen you're talking to someone. If you jump to your feet and stand there all alone, they'll think you're nuts. Paino couldn't wait to jump to his feet.

"Mister Turrisi!"

Pietro bows in Commissioner Paino's direction.

Turrisi looks around. The police have not stopped keeping him under surveillance.

"Do you know Commissioner Ronsisvalle?"

Paino looks at Ronsisvalle with a smile that opens up while his eyes close to a tiny slit. Paino's very pleased with this expression. He has practiced it at length before the mirror: the affectionate smile, the eyes closed to a slit, it looks a little bit like a snake (although Caporeale says it looks more like a Simeto eel, the ones that were caught a couple of days ago and which nobody in the market wants to get stuck with).

Fuck if he doesn't know Ronsisvalle, this asshole who's getting all the benefit from the murder of Falsaperla, with his asshole original Greek theater. "*Dawn Comes at Dusk*," Zerbino had written in *La Voce della Sicilia*, as if we were talking about that asshole film with the naked vampires. "Certainly I know him!"

Paino and Ronsisvalle shake hands.

Ronsisvalle's looking around because he's worried that the sun's going to go down on him. He had told the mayor they needed to put in lighting. They made beautiful lighting today, like the stuff they use at the stadium when they do the night games or the Champion's League. Fat chance. The mayor said it clashed. What the fuck was it supposed to clash with? At the Greek theater in Taormina they had put them in, those fucking lights like they use in the stadium. "And in fact, they don't do classical theater in Taormina," the mayor had said.

Paino thinks Ronsisvalle is looking around so he won't have to look him in the eyes and snub him.

"We need to speak," Turrisi is saying to him.

Paino lets go of that moron Ronsisvalle's hand. "At your service!"

"Sure, okay, but not now. I'll call you."

Paino, without meaning to, practically jumps to attention.

Unexpectedly, Turrisi kisses him on both cheeks. And while Paino is still recovering from the surprise, he gets two kisses from Pietro too.

Turrisi turns around to find his seat and sees Betty, with the heel of her left shoe pivoted in the dirt, revolving her little foot in a circle, her chin down, her gaze, behind the veil, pointed up, as if she were just waiting for Turrisi to stop talking.

Turrisi, instinctively, looks up the stairs to see if Pirrotta is there.

He doesn't have time to find him before Betty is saying to him, "Mister Turrisi, I was waiting for you. What's wrong? You're not going to say hello?"

Turrisi looks at Pietro.

Pietro doesn't know what to say.

Turrisi bows.

Betty holds out her hand. "I very much appreciated what you did for me."

Turrisi, his lips near her hand, looks puzzled, then in a flash, all is clear to him.

He looks around for Pietro, terrorized.

Pietro is smiling romantically.

Pirrotta is watching the scene with his mouth open.

With her mouth open, Wanda too is watching.

Pirrotta turns slowly toward his wife Wanda, his open mouth transmuting into a smile.

His wife Wanda doesn't understand.

"I got to say, he's smart, that dickhead Turrisi," says Pirrotta.

Wanda still has her mouth open. She doesn't understand.

Pirrotta makes a strange move with his head, he inclines it to the left and points a few times with his chin to the right, as if he were congratulating himself. "Did you see how it's good with him that they killed Falsaperla?"

His wife Wanda, it's like she's being carried off by Turks, as they say. "But wasn't Falsaperla your man?"

"Woman! Shut up, and your husband, if you behave and don't bust his balls, will maybe explain everything to you later."

Holy Mary! Was there a cement-mixer at Palazzolo Acreide? One they could rent and then make the road home a parking lot, and so forth and so on?

"Woman, behave like a female and even if you don't understand, obey your husband and be polite to that dickhead Turrisi."

Sure she'll obey. As if she wouldn't.

"Mister Turrisi, pardon, the play must begin."

Turrisi looks at Ronsisvalle with surprise mixed with pique.

Pietro takes Ronsisvalle by the arm and walks off with him.

"But—" Ronsisvalle begins.

"Commissioner, come with me because I want to tell you something," says Pietro.

"But . . . the sunset . . ."

"That's what we must talk about, Commissioner, about the sunset. Come with me, come with me."

"Signorina," says Turrisi, who doesn't know what the fuck to say.

"You don't mind if I sit next to you, do you?" Betty asks.

Turrisi looks at Pietro, who's walking off with the commissioner.

"No, not at all, it's Pietro's seat, but—"

"Oh, no, if it's a problem, never mind."

"No!" shouts Turrisi. "It's not a problem, it's only that Pietro . . . Pietro!"

Pietro doesn't hear him. He's walking toward the stage with the commissioner.

Turrisi looks at Betty.

"Yes or no?" says Betty.

"Yes, of course."

Pietro is pushing the commissioner onto the stage.

Ronsisvalle looks at Pietro. Pietro nods.

Ronsisvalle approaches the microphone.

He's still looking at Pietro.

Pietro nods again.

Ronsisvalle pulls out his glasses and a sheet of paper.

"The show's beginning," says Betty, who's getting impatient.

"Be my guest," says Turrisi, showing the way with his hand and pointing at the seats in the front row.

Turrisi notices that Betty, from behind, is practically naked.

"My fellow citizens," says Ronsisvalle at the microphone.

A sudden silence falls on the Greek theater of Palazzolo Acreide.

Then there's an equally sudden burst of applause.

Turrisi is waiting impatiently for Betty to sit down. He sits down next to her, and, trying not to let it be seen he is nervous, struggles to extract his cell phone from his pin-striped jacket. These fucking English tailors don't seem to know that people might have to sit down, they make a suit like a straitjacket.

While the applause in the Greek theater dies down, Turrisi feels Betty's hand run swiftly up the inside of his thigh. Then she takes his arm, putting on an interested face, while her dress gaps right to the hip.

Turrisi freezes.

With his cell phone in hand.

The echo of an ancient, distant call can be heard.

"I am Lambertini-i-i-i."

The audience looks around.

Ronsisvalle clears his throat and continues. "Welcome to this splendid setting."

Applause.

Lambertini has a hoe in hand and is whacking the camper that Timpanaro has provided for a dressing room.

Caporeale, Cosentino, Cagnotto, and the codpiece walk by without a glance in her direction.

"If it's all right with you, I have a thought about how I might update my interpretation tonight," Caporeale is saying to Cagnotto.

"Rosanna . . ." says Cagnotto.

Lambertini stops, hoe in hand.

Cagnotto points to his watch. "It's late, the reporters are already sitting down, you should have thought about this before. You still aren't changed?"

Lambertini looks contemptuously at the three men and climbs into the camper, slamming the door.

"No, go right ahead, Caporeale, I have complete faith in you, you know."

Two police officers approach, hands on their holsters.

"What was that? Who was yelling?"

"Oh, nothing," says Cosentino, "it was Lambertini, who couldn't get the door of the camper open and thought it was locked. You know, it's late, and she still hadn't changed."

The police officers look at the camper suspiciously.

Enter Chorus.

Turrisi is trying to phone Pietro.

Do you know who I am
Have you any idea who I am
Yes it's been quite a while
And it's so good to see you again

Fucking Pietro with his fucking voice-mail message with the Elvis songs!

"Darling, what's wrong?" Betty whispers in his ear, stroking his thigh once again.

The first act is all like that, with Betty running her hand up his thigh and that shithead Elvis Presley singing on Pietro's cell phone.

You will know who I am
When the time comes you'll know who I am

This is precisely Turrisi's problem: he got his calculations wrong and now he really doesn't want that time to come.

JULIET My only love, sprung from my only hate!
Too early seen unknown,

Have you any idea who I am . . .

And known too late!

You will know who I am . . .

Betty's hand goes past all frontiers, known and unknown.

The first act ends.
Turrisi jumps up. "I'm sorry, signorina."
"Don't be sorry," says Betty with a smile, studying Turrisi's fly.
Turrisi looks down.
He looks up, alarmed.
He sees Pirrotta, a few tiers up, rise with a satisfied smile and bow in his direction.
Beside him his wife, mother of Betty, mother-in-law Wanda, sends him a cordial smile, her head tipped elegantly to one side, her eyes lit up.
Turrisi's eyes widen.
He sits down rapidly.
"Problems?" asks Betty.
Turrisi, his face flushed, says, "No . . . yes . . . Pietro, I must find Pietro."

Betty nods. "It's that important?"

The audience begins to file out for the interval, people want to have a look at the necropolis, the archaeological dig, take a couple of pictures, grab an ice cream and brioche.

Pietro, hands in his pockets, walks coolly in front of Turrisi, sending him a smile of complicity.

Turrisi shoots out an arm to stop him. "Pietro!" he shouts.

"Ladies and gentlemen, we're sorry, but on account of the sunset, we will not be observing the interval. Please don't leave your seats, the show will resume immediately," says Ronsisvalle to the microphone.

Pietro shrugs his shoulders. He sends Turrisi another smile, turns on the white heels of his boots, and looks for his seat.

Turrisi looks around.

Betty is staring at him, curious.

Turrisi doesn't give a shit about Ronsisvalle, he gets up and moves toward Pietro. He grabs him. "Why the fuck is your phone turned off? Why the fuck?"

"But we're at the theater."

"I'm at the theater, you're on the job. The fuck you turn off your phone, the fuck you do."

The audience stares at Turrisi raving.

Pirrotta rests his right elbow on his right knee and puts his forehead on his hands.

"What's the matter, baby?" says Wanda, caressing her husband's thigh.

Pirrotta looks at her with disdain.

Wanda removes her hand.

Pirrotta says, "You want to bet that Turrisi is more of a dickhead than the departed Falsaperla?"

"I don't understand."

Pirrotta looks at his wife with a face that says, *and what's new about that?*

"Stop him . . . stop him . . . stop him . . ." Turrisi is shaking Pietro by the shoulders.

"But Mister Turrisi, how?"

"How? What do you mean, how? You call him up and stop him."

Pietro looks around. He wishes Turrisi would at least stop shouting. Pietro tries to get close to Turrisi's ear.

Turrisi backs off, disgusted.

Pietro signals that he has to tell him something and that something, he has to tell it to him in his ear.

Turrisi looks around.

All eyes are on them.

Including those of the police, just in case anybody doubted it.

Turrisi puts his ear up next to Pietro's mouth.

"Do you really think that Giacomo, who's already in position with his precision rifle, has his cell phone on, so they can go and pick him up right there where he's standing?"

Turrisi claps his hands together. He wants to scream. Instead he signals to Pietro to come closer.

Pietro comes closer.

Turrisi says in his ear, "And he doesn't have a vibration option?"

Turrisi puts his ear up to Pietro's mouth. "No, it's turned off, he can't have the phone vibrating while he's taking aim. Anyway, Giacomo, he probably doesn't even have the phone on him. He was in the SAS. He's a strange guy."

"Try, damn it, try. I'm going to move Paino."

"What are you doing?"

"What the fuck should I do? I'm moving him."

"Mister Turrisi, please sit down," the voice of Ronsisvalle, amplified by the microphone, booms over the Greek theater.

Turrisi's flesh is crawling.

He looks at Pietro, desperate.

Pirrotta pushes his face forward as if to say, *Don't bother explaining anything, you're a dickhead like all sons-in-law.*

Turrisi runs over to Paino.

"Commissioner, come with me."

"Me?" says Paino.

"Come, Commissioner, I'll explain, come."

Paino, sitting in row two, struggles to step over Signora Falsaperla, who gives him a disgusted face. Is this how people think they're supposed to behave in a Greek theater?

Turrisi grabs Paino's arm and takes him toward the path that leads to the exit.

Enter Chorus.

"Halt! Where are you going?" A carabiniere stops Paino and Turrisi.

"Um . . . I . . . have to go to the car."

"You can't go out."

"What do you mean, we can't go out?"

"It's a question of public safety. No one can leave the theater before the end of the play."

Turrisi looks at Paino.

Paino says, "I'm Commissioner Paino."

"Sorry, Commissioner."

Turrisi intervenes. "I absolutely must get to my car."

"I'm sorry."

"We'll just be a minute and then we'll be right back."

"I'm sorry."

Piano interrupts. "But this is a holdup!"

"Sorry, Commissioner. Public safety. We warned people about it at the box office."

"But we didn't go through the box office. We're guests."

"Right, that must be the reason," says the carabiniere. "Anyway, you still can't go out."

MERCUTIO If love be blind, love cannot hit the mark . . .

"Paino, listen, get behind me."

"What am I supposed to do?"

Turrisi looks at him. He's about to burst into tears. He looks at the carabiniere. "And what am I supposed to do?"

"Nothing, just stand there. When the second act is over you can resume your seats."

"Call your commanding officer," orders Paino.

"Okay, I'll call him. But you two stay here."

"Hurry up. I'm Commissioner Paino."

The carabiniere says something into his walkie-talkie.

Paino whispers to Turrisi, "What's going on?"

Turrisi looks at Paino.

He looks around at the limestone ridges, the necropolis, the trees, the walls, the hills, the valleys, the doors to the tombs . . .

ROMEO Pardon, good Mercutio. My business was great and in such
a case as mine a man may strain courtesy.

MERCUTIO That's as much as to say, such a case as yours constrains
a man to bow in the hams.

ROMEO (*Bowing gracefully*) Meaning, to curtsy?

MERCUTIO (*Looking at* ROMEO's *backside*) Thou hast most kindly hit it.

ROMEO (*Pushing his backside forward*) A most courteous exposition.

MERCUTIO Nay, I am the very pink of courtesy.

ROMEO Pink for flower?

MERCUTIO Right!

Turrisi looks at Paino.

ROMEO (*Outlining a wide circle in the air with his arm, he boldly clutches his codpiece, leaps up, and lands on his feet, bouncing on his knees.*) Why, then is my *prick* well-flower'd!

Paino falls like a tree in the forest.
Chaos breaks out.

CHAPTER NINE

Cagnotto Is Terrorized

Cagnotto is terrorized, Caporeale and Cosentino don't understand fuck-all, Lambertini says that everyone is against her, she's complaining that they don't want her to die. "They don't want me to die! Me, who in *Romeo and Juliet* dies not once but twice."

Timpanaro, all professional, is trying to reassure them.

He has invited them to lunch at Don Mimmo in Piazza Borgo, tables outside, amid some eighteenth century Baroque, a palazzo in reinforced concrete from the sixties, and a gas station.

Catania is deserted at lunchtime because everyone goes to the beach, so you can get a table at Don Mimmo. A bus that passes now and then, the roar of a scooter with a souped-up engine. Silence.

"It's normal that you feel traumatized," says Timpanaro, who's waiting for the lemon juice to marinate his raw *alici*.

Lambertini must have forgotten to go to the hairdresser this morning; she has a piece of hair that doesn't have fuck-all to do with the rest sticking straight up over her right temple.

Cagnotto has spent the night throwing up, he mixed the antidepressant, the tranquilizer, alcohol, aspirin, a painkiller, and drank some mouthwash by mistake.

First he had to wait in line because the police wanted to question him, then Bobo had reappeared.

Traumatized?

Cagnotto has lost track of the things to be traumatized about, if only he could figure out what was traumatizing him maybe the doctor could get him on the right medication. "We're going to fine-tune it for you," the doctor had told him.

"Let's not play the moralists now, however," continues Timpanaro, looking at his *alici* with interest, "we're grown up, a little homicide, sooner or later, happens to the best of us. Just think about the people who work in the emergency ward, how much of that stuff they see."

"Two little homicides," Caporeale interrupts.

Cosentino nods. "Right when Caporeale grabs his codpiece. It's like Cagnotto did it on purpose, it is."

"I *told* you that the codpiece, I didn't want to grab it."

"What are you saying, that it was me?" yells Cagnotto.

"Oh, well, that I couldn't say," says Caporeale, who's sucking out a raw sea urchin, "anyway don't worry, I didn't tell the cop who took my statement that it was you who kept insisting that I had to grab my prick."

"And why didn't you tell him?" Cagnotto is scandalized.

"Just minding my own business."

"Good work," says Cosentino. "The way things are shaping up, whatever you say is wrong."

"But what does the codpiece have to do—" Cagnotto says defensively.

"Who ordered the mussels in pepper sauce?" asks a waiter, interrupting them.

"Over here."

"*Aiola* for the lady," says the waiter, putting a plate of grilled fish under Lambertini's nose.

"What's that?"

"*Aiola, signora.*"

"Well, I ordered *bresaola.*"

The waiter looks at the fish. "And there you are!"

To Cagnotto they all seem crazy.

The doctor says the depression, he says that when you're depressed everyone seems crazy. He'd better tell the doctor to fine-tune it because Cagnotto has been taking the antidepressant for a couple of months and they all continue to seem crazy to him.

"Don Mimmo!" the waiter shouts. "We got *bresaola?*"

Don Mimmo, the proprietor, seated on a straw-backed chair watching his customers, yells back, "What's the matter? Tell the lady to grab the *aiola* because it's fresh. *Bresaola* is an Atlantic fish and we don't carry it."*

The waiter puts the plate down in front of Lambertini and walks off. He asked the boss, the boss answered, and now they can deal with it themselves.

To Cagnotto, Lambertini, that piece of hair sticking straight up over her right temple, is scary, she looks crazy.

However, he's not really sure whether she looks crazy to him because she looks crazy, or only because he's depressed and the doctor has messed up on the fine-tuning.

Cagnotto, putting a hand to his right temple, signals to Lambertini to fix that piece of hair.

Lambertini figures that Cagnotto is signaling that the waiter and Don Mimmo are crazy, and so she nods and says, "Totally."

Cagnotto puts his elbow on the table and holds his forehead.

"Fine," says Timpanaro, finally taking a bite of his *alici*, the

---

Aiola, a Mediterranean fish. *Bresaola*, cured beef, a popular dish from Northern Italy.

marinade of oil and lemon running down his chin. "So what difference is there between one little homicide and two? It's normal for
there to be a first homicide, and then, usually, they commit another
one. Zerbino even said so in the newspaper, don't you remember,
Cagnotto? It's normal. They call it a *vendetta trasversale* for that very
reason! It's not like we have to make a tragedy out of it, a *vendetta
trasversale*. Let's concentrate on business. I had a call from the
prefect."

"Who?" says Cagnotto, who hasn't ordered anything because his
stomach is upset.

"The prefect."

"And what did he want?"

"He wanted to talk about Noto."

"The prefect wanted to talk about Noto?" says Lambertini.

"Precisely," says Timpanaro, nodding and chewing.

Cagnotto feels slightly dizzy.

CHAPTER TEN

On the Terrace of the Top Floor of the Una Palace Hotel

On the terrace of the top floor of the Una Palace Hotel, Pirrotta has asked to be seated in the breeziest corner where the drapes are flapping around him.

The terrace on the top floor of the Una Palace Hotel is decorated in oriental-chic.

The bar is deserted.

There are no waiters and no bartender.

In front of Pirrotta, there's a huge glass of Campari with a slice of orange impaled on the edge of the glass.

Mister Turrisi's Aston Martin, laying rubber, takes the curve that leads from Via Passo Gravina down to Piazza Stesicoro and boldly slams into a garbage bin.

The Aston Martin backs up coolly, disengages, and looks for a parking space.

Mister Turrisi leaps out of the car like a demon, slams the door, takes a quick look at the headlight that's hanging down like a gouged-out eyeball, and heads down Via Etnea with a stride that echoes down the Baroque corridors.

Pirrotta had said he wanted some *privacy*.

His boys, in front of the elevator, are stopping the hotel's clients and sending them away, telling them the bar is closed for cleaning.

From the windows you can see the roofs of Catania.

Pirrotta is wearing his sunglasses.

He's immobile.

The only things in motion are the voluminous, pure-white drapes flapping in the breeze.

The elevator door opens and there's Mister Turrisi combing his hair in the mirror.

He looks distractedly at Pirrotta's boys.

He finishes combing his hair.

Even though his heart is in turmoil, even though he knows he's responsible for a fucking mess, even though he hasn't the slightest idea how to resolve the matter, even though an hour ago he had showed up at Pietroburger and Pietro had told him that Pirrotta wanted to see him at the Una Palace Hotel, at the bar on the top floor, even though he had practically had a panic attack because Pietro had specified, "They said you should come alone. You can't even take me," even though he had messed up the Aston Martin and there was a headlight hanging down, you must never let the boys see you are nervous, and above all, not your enemy's boys. "Reserve is the basis of all elegance," they had explained to him in London back in the days when he would begin to shriek like a washerwoman at the first obstacle.

The elevator doors close under the contemptuous gaze of Pirrotta's boys.

Mister Turrisi, comb in hand, is terribly annoyed.

Pirrotta takes a slow sip of his Campari.

He puts down the glass and meticulously adjusts the orange slice to keep it nice and upright.

He sits back in his chair and is once again immobile.

Turrisi comes in, out of breath and buttoning his jacket.

Pirrotta doesn't even look at him.

Turrisi looks around.

He looks at a chair.

He unbuttons his jacket and sits down.

He stares at Pirrotta.

Pirrotta is silent.

The truth is that Pirrotta too has no idea what to say.

He might have a glimmer, but he's awaiting confirmation.

After a few seconds, Turrisi turns his head to look for a waiter.

He realizes that the bar is deserted.

He looks at Pirrotta's Campari.

With the orange slice.

Pirrotta did this specially to show who's boss. I have a glass of Campari and you have fuck-all.

Turrisi nods.

He nods because he's caught his drift, because he's a diplomatic whiz, because he knows that in these cases you have to nod, particularly when you've been responsible for a fuckup like that with Paino.

Paino! Turrisi had better not start thinking about him or he's going to start chewing his fingers.

He settles himself in his chair.

When Turrisi is nervous, there's this thing that he can never get comfortable in his chair, and he blames those English tailors.

Now it's Pirrotta's turn to nod.

Pirrotta picks up the glass, takes a slow and noisy suck letting the ice rattle against his dentures, puts the glass down, nods again, looks at Turrisi, and says, "So what did you have to say to me?"

Turrisi sighs.

Pirrotta had summoned *him*, he was sucking his Campari, and he's even asking him what he had to say to him.

Betty in beach attire, with a sarong that opens to her armpit so as to offer a glimpse of her nipple, thong sandals with a sado-masochistic heel, walks through the living room in front of her mother, who's flipping through a magazine.

"Is Papa here?"

Wanda, who doesn't look up from her magazine, signals *no* with her head.

"Oh, all right, if you see him would you give him a message that he's an asshole?"

Wanda, her eyes glued to the magazine, nods.

Betty goes off *tick-tack-ticking* nervously on her heels. "I'm going to the beach to do some blow jobs. That'll teach all of you."

Wanda raises her eyes from the magazine, shakes her head as if in admiration, and says, "So you've just come up with the vindictive slut? Shit, before you got there, nobody had ever thought of it!" and turns her gaze back to her reading.

"Go fuck yourself."

• • •

"I . . ." says Turrisi, and finds himself wordless.

Pirrotta nods as if to invite him to continue.

"Can I speak frankly, Signor . . . Mister Pirrotta?"

Pirrotta jerks up his right hand, brings it toward his sunglasses, and—so it appears—studies the nail of his little finger to see if the manicurist has filed it correctly. "Be my guest."

"I sent you a *pizzino* . . ."

Pirrotta turns stiff as a board.

"And you, with all due respect before the blessed Virgin, consented to let me go out with the highly esteemed Signorina Betty. No?"

Pirrotta abandons his fingernail.

Sure, he consented.

Shit, you propose to get Betty off my balls, you propose a remedial matrimony for the Ispica business, and what do I do, I don't consent? "And who told you I didn't consent?"

"What do you mean, who told me? Signorina Elisabetta."

Luckily Pirrotta's wearing sunglasses, otherwise his eyeballs would have popped out and fallen into the glass with the Campari. "Shit, just like her mother!" says Pirrotta, giving himself a slap on the knee.

Holy Mary, a slut in the great tradition of her mother!

Turi remembers it well, how he used to drive by in the cement-mixer and that super-slut Wanda didn't even look up at him. Until the day, however, when certain rumors began to circulate about what Turi did, or did not, do with the cement-mixer.

Down in Civita, praise God, people never minded their own fucking business, and when someone disappeared (either because he got drunk, or went whoring in Messina, or because he really disappeared and they never found him again), you could bet that in Civita they would say, "Well, maybe that one ended up in Riddu's cement-mixer."

And that's when Wanda began to look at him in a different way! Wanda, that slut, and her daughter too.

One morning at the bar, it was about seven, and Riddu had been working all night and was just downing a Fernet-Branca before turning in, well, along comes Wanda with a flowered miniskirt and her legs making an X, and she says, without Riddu having to ask her fuck-all, "You're that guy that shows off outside my house? My name is Wanda and if you want to know why I'm called that you need to know I have the same name as Wanda Osiris."

Then she walked off like she was offended, worse than if he'd given her a little pat on the ass. (In Civita, that's how the females act when they're in love: they go and get offended, I don't know how they do with you.)

And who the fuck was this stupid Wanda Osiris? Riddu, who worked from morning to night, it's not like he had time to watch variety shows. Osiris, he later learned, was a TV starlet and she must have been famous, if they had named Wanda after her.

And then they say you *learn* to be a whore.

Anyway, after that encounter, Riddu had really started showing off in front of Wanda's house.

"But what does the respected Lady Mother have to do with any of this?" asks Turrisi.

Pirrotta looks at Turrisi.

Turrisi, to tell the truth, has too dumb a face for you to be able to explain to him the intimate female soul of a woman who's in the grip of a hysteric pussy fit.

Fuck, you can really see that Turrisi, he's never been married in his life!

What the fuck does the mother have to do with it, he asks.

And how the fuck could you explain to him that Betty is even more of a slut than her mother?

"My daughter is as pure as the driven snow. Just like her mother," says Pirrotta, to be on the safe side.

CHAPTER ELEVEN

Will You Please Tell Me What the Fuck Is Going On?

"Will you please tell me what the fuck is going on?"

In his villa deep in the lemon groves of the Trapani countryside (acquired for practically nothing from Barone Gibuado, who had some problems, he had, the baron), on the other side of the island from Catania, Melo Vaccalluzzo, wearing an ample California-style cotton shirt printed with palms and surfers, a pair of pants cut off at the calf and held to his legs with elastic, Nike basketball shoes, and a chain with the medal of the Palermo soccer team, is studying the healing process of his latest tattoo—a Chinese dragon on his left forearm that the tattoo artist had sold him as a symbol of the Samurai power of the Japanese Yakuza gangs.

Melo Vaccalluzzo is having some problems with the healing process because he's seventy-three years old and if Viagra is shrinking the skin of his prick (his wife Saretta says that Viagra has damaged his gray matter), the skin on his forearm continues to be loose, thin and bony as he is.

"Pirrotta and Turrisi have started playing the dickheads," says Paolino, who's instead wearing the regulation blue suit the boys wear.

"What's happening, those little jerks want to step on my dick?"

Melo Vaccalluzzo, son of the Camorra boss Gennaro Russo, had been adopted by Salvatore Vaccalluzzo when Gennaro, they found him on ice with the tuna fish in the port of Naples. Salvatore Vaccalluzzo, who at the time was just getting into the cocaine coming from America, decided to take the little boy and make him his son, he raised him as a Sicilian, he gave him his surname, and before he died he had regretted it all, although it was too late.

Melo, who has inherited the income, status, and privileges of his adoptive father, still breaks out in Neapolitan, even though he struggles without much success to speak Sicilian.

"It's *'o petrolio*," says Paolino, who because he talks to Vaccalluzzo all the time has begun to take on Camorra inflections.

"*'O petrolio?* What the fuck are they doing with oil if we're still discussing it in the regional assembly?"

"They're moving ahead with the job."

"What oil are we talking about? When we still don't know whether this business is going ahead or whether we should keep on cultivating carob trees in Ispica. And what do they think, that Virtude is the same guy he once was? These jerks from Catania had better take it easy. In this *petrolio* business we first have to hear what the Americans have to say, and secondly, even if these guys pick up all the land, we still get ninety percent. And they're blowing people away for ten percent?"

"Don Melo, these guys from Catania are, they think they are . . . who knows what they think? And excuse me, but ten percent of *'o petrolio* isn't exactly the same as ten percent of fake Dolce & Gabbana T-shirts."

"Right. So what's the point?"

"They've opened an investigation."

"Who?"

"Who, who, Don Melo, the magistrates."

Vaccalluzzo spits out the seed of a grape he is eating. "What, they gone crazy?"

"They got two dead there."

"Yeah, I know how many there are. Think I don't know how to count?"

Paolino looks down.

This thing that it always has to be him to go and talk with Vaccalluzzo is getting really fucking annoying.

"I mean *them*. They gone nuts? They don't know that we don't *do* homicide anymore? They think we're muggers?"

Paolino doesn't know what the fuck to say, he merely raises his shoulders. This fuckhead Vaccalluzzo, who has to stay on the terrace because he wants to get a tan on his dick-face, and *he's* wearing a dark suit and sweltering in the heat.

"Right. So we have to take a trip to Catania. Did they close San Berillo?"

"Yes, Don Melo. There's nothing left but the transvestites."

"And what am I supposed to do with drag queens?"

"No, sorry, what I meant to say is that there are the clubs."

"The what?"

"The clubs."

"Okay, so we go to the clubs. When we put on the funeral for those two little jerks, we want everyone to know that Carmelo Vaccalluzzo is in Catania. We're in favor of law and order. Everyone needs to know that, both the families and the magistrates."

Vaccalluzzo stands up and scratches his ass in such a satisfying way that the elastic on his pants rides up from his calf to his knee.

"That way the magistrates will go back to giving interviews on the nightly news and stop busting our balls," says Paolino with the smirk of a man who thinks he's clever.

Vaccalluzzo freezes, interrupting his ass-scratching in midair. He gives him a dirty look and says, "You, show some respect for the magistrates."

CHAPTER TWELVE

No One Would Ever Dare to Question Signorina Betty's Virtue and Good Name

"No one would ever dare to question Signorina Betty's virtue and good name."

"Oh, yeah, right," says Pirrotta, who doesn't know where to look. His daughter, that great big slut!

"And anyone who dares to," says Turrisi, swelling out his chest, "I can swear before the Queen, will have to deal with me first."

"Who? Marina Doria?"

"No, sir! Before Queen Elizabeth in person, who has the same name as your daughter."

"No, actually, she's just called Bet—Yes, Turrisi! Well said! I thank you as her father. But as Pirrotta, no. What's going on here? You want to even the odds? I take out Falsaperla and you take out Paino?

Turrisi looks around, freaked.

"Don't worry, there aren't any bugs."

Turrisi looks at Pirrotta, then lowers his eyes. "And what was I supposed to do? Shut up and swallow it that you took out one of yours so the blame would fall on me?"

Pirrotta goes *no* with his head.

Even this sad bastard Turrisi has his own logic.

Then he thinks about it. "Right, absolutely!" he says, giving himself another slap on the knee.

"Huh?"

Pirrotta improvises. He can't decide whether he should use the *tu* or the *Lei* with Turrisi. "See, I could have put your loyalty to the family to the test. It's called a duty hit. Just like that."

"Huh?"

"Yeah, a duty hit! I show you disrespect and you drop your horns down and drag them in the dirt as an act of devotion to the family. You want to join the family, no?"

Turrisi joins his two hands together. "God willing!"

"Well, then why, you dumb fool, didn't you just shut up?"

"But first Signorina Elisabetta told me that you, sir, didn't consent to the engagement, and then you, sir, blew Falsaperla away to make me look bad not only with the prosecutors, bless them, but also with the people from Palermo, who, as you know, would like us to keep quiet. But why, sir, did you first consent and then say no? What did I do wrong?"

And now what the fuck was he supposed to tell him?

"Never! I never consented." Pirrotta stares at Turrisi.

Then, so as to seem more credible, he gives himself another slap on the knee.

"But one of your boys came to Pietroburger and gave me an appointment with Betty at Trinacria in Bocca."

"Turrisi. My wife and my daughter, they got together. And the boys, these days at my house, obey my wife more than they do me."

"But your boy didn't tell you that your wife had sent him out?"

Fuck, what a nitpicker this fuckhead Turrisi is.

What the fuck business does he have, meddling in Pirrotta's home affairs?

Fuck, he starts behaving like this as a son-in-law and he'll end up taking a ride in the cement-mixer.

"Of course he told me, but it was too late."

Turrisi nods.

"And then of course Betty was crazy about you," adds Pirrotta. "You saw, no, how she greeted you so affectionately at Palazzolo Acreide, and even sat down next to you, defying my fatherly paternal authority?"

Turrisi thinks about how Betty had stroked his leg and about how, if he hadn't tried to save Paino, who knows what she might have got up to stroking.

"Think about it. Betty, who always obeyed me, defied my fatherly paternal authority to go and sit next to you." Pirrotta makes a disgusted face.

Turrisi nods, devastated, repentant, touched, his face a mask of regret.

"And just because she thought that Falsaperla, you had blown him away. To spite me," says Pirrotta.

"Don't twist the knife in the wound!"

"Certainly I'm going to twist it. Betty may be naive but she's not stupid. You started to do that dance at Palazzolo Acreide and suddenly Betty understood everything. That I took down Falsaperla to put the blame on you, and that you took down Paino to put the blame on me."

"But can't we try to fix it, this problem? In the end, by evening the score, I challenged you with a public demonstration of my love for Betty."

"Turrisi, can I tell you something?"

"Please, it would be an honor."

"Okay, Turrisi, get this through your head. You, about females, understand fuck-all."

CHAPTER THIRTEEN

You Understand?

"You understand? Those scumbags, those shitheads. I'm going to turn into a lesbian. First a whore, however, and then a lesbian."

Betty is flipping out on the beach, leaning over the table at an Afro-bar on the sand, yelling directly into Carmine's ear.

"You understand? I don't count for anything! The only fucking thing they had on their minds was oil. Turrisi's love . . ."

Betty takes a champagne flute and hurls it toward the sand. The flute hits the beach without breaking.

"That's where all that love was going. That's where it was. Oil! Oil! Oil! That's what interests those two shithead faggot males, who can screw each other as much as they want, bastards who fool around with the feelings and the lives of others . . ."

Carmine is massaging his forehead, his head down because he's embarrassed.

"And . . . and . . ." Betty has used up all her insults. She crosses her arms and sits back in her chair, spreading her legs.

Carmine lifts an eye to see whether, by venting, she has calmed down.

"Oh, yes . . ." Betty leans forward again. "But now I'm going to show them what I'm capable of, you think I'm going to let it pass like that, they thought I was going to ruin my life, at my age, for oil, money . . . You understand, Carmine, how disgusting? For money! But me, what a slut, I go and give it gratis, understand, Carmine, because if my father wanted me to sell my body to Turrisi, you understand, Carmine, my *body*"—Betty puts her hand on her shoulder and takes the fabric of her white linen caftan between thumb and index finger and gives it a little lift—"my body for money, well, then I"—a little lift to the caftan—"my body, I'll give it away gratis, gratis, gratis."

Betty freezes like that, immobile, her fingers pinching the linen.

Her body, my big fucking gay prick.

"Hey, Betty, you said yourself that you didn't like Turrisi, you told Turrisi that your father didn't want—"

Betty jumps up.

She looks at Carmine with loathing, contempt, disdain, and outraged dignity.

Betty's extremely loud *"Gofuckyourself!"* makes almost a mile of beach turn toward the Afro-bar.

Beyond the mile, thank heavens, people hear something like the shriek of a seagull.

CHAPTER FOURTEEN

And So the Prefect Wants to Resolve the Situation and He's Asking Me the Favor

"And so the prefect wants to resolve the situation and he's asking me the favor." In front of a huge slice of watermelon Timpanaro is explaining the prefect's plan. "He says he'll even put in air-conditioning," he goes on happily.

"Ah," yells Cagnotto suddenly, frightening the whole table.

"What's that? What happened?" says Caporeale.

Cagnotto looks around with wide eyes. "I don't know. I thought I was falling."

"Falling?" says Timpanaro, interested.

"Must be vertigo," says Lambertini.

Cagnotto looks at them as if he's never seen them before.

"Cagnotto, cheer up!" says Timpanaro. "They're giving us air-conditioning! We'll be performing indoors, to enhance police surveillance! They'll have law and order in Noto! There will be journalists from outside Sicily, from outside Italy! It looks to me like the regional

commissioner for sport, tourism, and entertainment is also getting involved. Cagnotto, maybe this means nothing to you, but here, a *situation* creates business opportunities. Think about it, Cagnotto. What
do you want to do? You want to say no to such an opportunity?"

"I want to die," says Lambertini. "The show must go on."

Cagnotto looks at Lambertini.

He had heard her say "I want to die" but probably he had heard
her wrong.

"Why are you looking at me like that, Cagnotto?"

"No, it's, um . . ."

"All right, are we all in agreement?"

Cosentino looks at Caporeale, gives him a wink, and says, "What
do you think?"

"No, no, I agree, Lambertini must die."

Lambertini nods her head, satisfied. At least somebody understands her.

CHAPTER FIFTEEN

Look, Don't Even Let Me Think About What Betty's Thinking About Right Now!

"Look, don't even let me think about what Betty's thinking about right now!"

Pirrotta has moved on to the diplomatic *Lei*, he's dropped the *tu* charged with intimate contempt.

"In this moment Betty feels wounded, cheated, bitter." Pirrotta makes a face with a bitter smirk. "She's a woman who believes in feelings, know what I mean, Turrisi?"

Turrisi nods compassionately.

"She thinks we're at war for oil, for business, that we're insensible to the call of love."

"No, no. I'd do anything for Elisabetta!"

"No, she's called Bet— Call her Betty! Turrisi, just call her Betty! I can see, I can see your intentions are serious. Only now the problem is not just my daughter. Now we got two homicides."

Turrisi gestures with his chin, as if to say, *I know how many there are.*

"But Turrisi, how did it ever cross your mind to take down Paino?"

"As I told you—"

"No, do me a favor. Don't talk. Did you know that the magistrates have opened an inquest? Yeah? The prefect has put his nose in. They're organizing something in Noto . . ."

"Okay, but what can those fuckers—"

"No, look, I asked you to shut up."

Turrisi nods, saying *sorry* with his eyes.

"The national newspapers are even talking about it, they say *La Voce della Sicilia* got a call from a paper in London wanting to know if it was all true."

"From London?"

"Turrisi, don't start up with London now!"

Turrisi nods, saying *sorry* once again with his eyes.

"And that's not the only problem. They're getting nervous in Palermo."

"Scum," says Turrisi.

Pirrotta looks at him.

Hadn't he told him to shut up?

Okay, but he was right, the guys from Palermo are scum, it's true. "If it weren't for Jacobbo Maretta, Virtude's man of honor who's got the situation in hand, things in Sicily would be worse than a mess right now. In Palermo, with Virtude in Ucciardone Prison, this bunch of jack-offs are out there fooling around. But hey, where did you ever get the idea of blowing away Paino?" Pirrotta can't stop thinking about it.

"But if I hadn't done it, in Palermo they would have thought it was me who took down Falsaperla, and they would have gone after me for starting a gang war."

"Ah, yes, and now that they're pissed off at both of us, things are much better, aren't they?"

Turrisi looks at Pirrotta.

Pirrotta looks away. "And where did you get the idea of doing it that way, so theatrical? During the same play, during the same line! No wonder the newspapers in London are talking about it."

"Hey, what about that magistrate they blew up with the whole newsstand where he went to get his papers?"

"Well, in that case it means they didn't have any other way to get him," says Pirrotta. Sounding none too sure of himself, to tell the truth.

"I," says Turrisi, "I had to show who Turrisi is. If it had to be war, it had to be war."

Pirrotta raises his eyes to the heavens.

He sighs.

Best to remain calm. "Okay, trivialities. Don't worry."

"But how are we going to resolve the situation?" says Turrisi in a low voice.

Pirrotta nods, removing his sunglasses.

You never conclude a deal with sunglasses.

Pirrotta looks around. "You still got Giacomo in hand?" he asks.

"How do you know about Giacomo?"

"Paino, like that—only Giacomo could do that. He was in the SAS, no?"

"And when he turns on his cell phone, that dickhead, yes, sure, I've got him in hand."

Pirrotta insists on walking him to his car.

"It was that garbage bin over there, see?"

Pirrotta looks at the garbage bin as if it were slime. "They got to go and put these things in the middle of the street," he says indignantly.

"I was coming down that way, and what was I supposed to do?"

"Madness. Not to mention extremely dangerous for anyone on a motorbike. Hey, it's really a beautiful car, however," says Pirrotta, turning to admire the Aston Martin.

"I can't look at it with the broken headlight, Signor Pirrotta."

Pirrotta looks at Turrisi.

He nods.

He lowers his head.

He stares at his shoe.

"Turi, call me Turi. You're a good kid. Call me Turi."

Turrisi lifts a hand to his mouth.

Then, not to let him see the emotion that's gripping his throat, he embraces Pirrotta and whispers in his ear, "Papa, Papa!"

Pirrotta raises his eyes to the heavens.

Mother of God, how good it used to be in the days when he drove the cement-mixer, drank Fernet at the bar, and nobody busted his balls.

CHAPTER SIXTEEN

SS Really Exists, Nobody Knows About It, Even Though Everybody Knows

SS really exists, nobody knows about it, even though everybody knows. Swim Shoot, it's called in the business. Once upon a time they specialized in swimming pool deaths.

It's something nobody is supposed to know about.

And in fact nobody does.

Even though everybody knows.

The swimming pool deaths were an invention of Don Vincenzino in New York, when the Cosa Nostra, between the sixties and the seventies, decided to take advantage of the crisis the studios were in and invest in the movies in order to launder some money—those were the days when indie film was born.

The stars, the directors, and the producers all went around with bodyguards, everybody knew everybody, everybody was sleeping with everybody, and if you had something to do you couldn't do it in the old-fashioned way because the FBI would get you immediately.

It's not like you could send a killer into a pool party full of movie stars. How would he even get in without an invitation?

So Don Vincenzino began to get bit parts for his assistants, or he made them the dummy heads of the independent film companies, officially the producers, or sometimes he made them directors—in those days so much bullshit was being made that one more, one less, nobody noticed.

The best of them all was —— (redacted), his brain so worm-eaten that he became really famous as a director of super-violent movies. (Not a fucking bad idea, he knew how certain details worked.)

Anyway, if you have ever asked yourself how it is that there are so many pool deaths in Hollywood, now you know why and who.

Ottone and Ernst are part of this tradition.

Twin brothers, they are independent film producers with offices in New York, London, and Berlin. They make police procedurals that they sell to cable TV, and every year they rescue tons of ex-models who have hit age thirty (nobody wants models who have hit age thirty) and as a side business they've opened a plastic surgery clinic in Hamburg, and like so many businesses born as fronts, this has become a big moneymaker.

Ottone and Ernst have just arrived in Catania.

They've taken a suite at the Una Palace.

They're getting ready to immerse themselves in the Sicilian Baroque.

They have an appointment with the film commissioner.

It seems you can make movies cheap in Catania.

They also have an appointment with a local handler, Rattalina. A guy who knows how to deal with the bureaucracy.

• • •

"And fireworks, no?" the mayor of Noto asks the city council.

The culture commissioner, Chartered Accountant Intelisano, gets to his feet. "Your Honor, my fellow commissioners, I think it's a bad idea."

The mayor looks at the council.

The councillors are looking at Intelisano the way they always look at him, as if he's a total moron.

"And why do you think it's a bad idea?" asks the mayor.

"Let's not forget that this tragedy has been stalked by tragedy. There will be newspapers, TV, this is Noto, capital of the Sicilian Baroque. It doesn't seem serious."

"No, we must have fireworks," says the mayor.

Intelisano sits down, looks around, and says, "No. Yes, I agree."

The commissioners and the mayor stand up. Average length of a special city council meeting in August, five minutes.

The commissioner for city planning—highly respected in Noto because in the middle of the capital of the Baroque they have built two skycrapers and the commissioner still hasn't had them demolished—approaches the mayor. "While they're putting in the air-conditioning in the theater, couldn't we get them to put air-conditioning in here too? The old system doesn't work very well."

"I'll ask, Commissioner, I'll ask, but I can't guarantee anything."

The bell is ringing in the Villa Wanda living room.

"Mister ring?"

"Bring me a glass of whiskey, a double gin, a vodka, and a Campari. And bring me a bucket of ice."

"Are you crazy?" yells Wanda.

"Shhh, it's not for me to drink. I'll explain."

"Explain what? You're driving me nuts!"

"Listen, woman, I told you to zip it up!"

"But—"

"Zip it!"

Oh, Holy Mary, when he says "zip it." Sure, sure, I'll zip it, I'll shut up. Oh, Riddu! Oh, God.

"Wanda."

"Yes?"

"Why are you looking at me like that?"

"Me?"

The maid comes in with the tray full of drinks. She puts it down carefully in front of Pirrotta.

"Wait," says Pirrotta.

He takes the glass of whiskey and pours it in the bucket of ice. He does the same with the vodka and the Campari.

The double gin, first he looks at Wanda, then he downs it as if it were tap water.

Zipped up, yes, I'm zipped up.

"Wanda."

"Yes?"

Pirrotta holds out the fingers of his right hand and waves them up and down, up and down. "Okay, now get out of here."

Wanda gets up and smooths her skirt. "I'll wait for you . . . in the bedroom?"

"Wanda, what's the matter with you, the menopause? Get out of here and go wherever you want. Leave me alone because your daughter is on the way."

Betty is coming in the huge front door.

She looks at the door.

She puts her mini-bag on the floor and takes off the thong sandals with the heels.

She grabs the door handle and slams it as hard as she can.

• • •

Pirrotta hears the bang and nods.

He takes off his jacket, loosens the knot of his tie, unbuttons his top shirt button, and lies back in the chair trying to look troubled.

It isn't that hard.

Holy Mary, how sweet it was in the days of the cement-mixer. No worries, no responsibilities, once in a while a little poke with Wanda, and all was well.

Betty puts her sandals back on because the nervous walk doesn't work when she's barefoot, picks up her mini-bag, and moves toward the living room.

She stops when she sees her father.

Her father is slumped in the chair with all those glasses lined up in front of him like he's drowned himself in drink.

He's looking at her with lifeless eyes.

"Asshole."

Her father doesn't react.

"I'm not a virgin anymore."

Nothing.

Pirrotta mumbles, his voice blurred, "He's a monster looking for blood and revenge."

What the fuck is her father trying to say?

"What?"

"A man of untold violence."

"What, your diabetes is acting up?"

"A ruthless assassin capable of unbelievable cruelty."

"Papa, what the fuck is wrong?"

"Your Turrisi."

"*Your* Turrisi." Betty tosses her mini-bag against a chair.

"I saw him . . ."

"What the fuck did you do?"

"He asked to see me. And he threatened me."

"Who?"

"Turrisi."

"And why the fuck are you telling me?"

"He's . . . he's . . . I don't even know *what* he is. A kind of Orlando Furioso who's lost touch with reality. He swore revenge against me and all my descendants down the centuries."

"Fine. Do what the fuck you want but don't bust my balls."

Pirrotta, flailing around in the chair, sits up on the edge. "Okay, you really don't get it, do you? You drove that guy *insane*. You got him to where he's capable of who knows what shit."

"And what the fuck do I have to do with it?"

"He's out of his mind in love with you, he says he's going to start blowing people away left and right." Pirrotta begins to make agitated gestures with his hands. "His eyes were hanging out, his tongue was yellow, his hair was standing straight up, his ears were red, and his nose was enormous. He says he's going to start a bloodbath."

"That's your problem, I don't have fuck-all to do with it."

"Oh, no. Yes, you do. Because I told him I was getting out of this business in Ispica. I said I could see he was merciless, that he didn't even give a fuck about the *cupola* . . . about our friends the big bosses in Palermo."

"You told him you were getting out?"

"I'm too old for this stuff. These young people are hotheads. I've got a family, I've got you, I've got Wanda, that guy is single and he's crazy."

Betty crosses her arms. "And what did he say?"

"He said he's going to start a bloodbath anyway."

"Sure. I bet." Betty twirls on her sandals and goes off toward her room.

Pirrotta follows her with his gaze.

He picks up the bell.

Now he's going to sit down with another nice big double gin, and let's see if he can get two birds with one stone.

Pirrotta smiles.

"Mister ring?"

Vaccalluzzo, in a nightclub at Acicastello that's open all afternoon, a pair of mirror sunglasses on his face, is wiggling around the pole with a Romanian lap dancer while the boys keep time with their hands.

CHAPTER SEVENTEEN

Giacomo Smiles, Looking Curiously at the Mortars

Giacomo smiles, looking curiously at the mortars.

He's wearing the uniform of the firm that installs air-conditioning.

The workers from Imposimato Brothers, the most famous fireworks artists in all of Sicily, are unloading their van.

A worker comes over, says hello to Giacomo, opens the rear doors of the Fiat Ducato van, and asks, "Got a wheelbarrow?"

Giacomo nods *yes*, pointing with his chin toward a brand-new wheelbarrow.

"Fuck, it's heavy. We made it like you said. Where you got to put this fucking mortar?"

"Huh?"

The worker is pulling out a cardboard box. "If you don't help me, I can't do this by myself. Hey, if it wasn't for this van, fuck if there was a way to get explosives into Noto today. They have the town surrounded and they're checking every car."

Giacomo nods. "Where do you live?"

"Catania."

"Which part?"

"Via Messina, luckily, with this heat at least I'm right next to the sea," says the worker, smiling.

"Via Messina," says Giacomo, who doesn't like people who talk too much, especially when they talk too much about his business. And he doesn't like people who call him *tu*.

The Baroque historic center of Noto is behind police lines.

Beyond the lines the crowd is piling up worse than if they were at the World Cup final.

Carabinieri, police, commanders, prefects, park rangers—all the available agents are spread out along the Corso and the cross streets. Nobody gets in unless they have been patted down and have gone through the metal detector under Porta Reale where the Corso begins.

Giacomo, with his wheelbarrow, heads toward the van of the company that's installing the air-conditioning, opens the doors, puts the mortar inside, gets up inside himself, puts the mortar inside an empty air conditioner, puts the air conditioner in a box marked POLAR BEAR AIR CONDITIONERS, gets down from the van, puts the box in the wheelbarrow, turns on his iPod, and makes for the theater, keeping time with the music.

"That club was fucking awful," says Vaccalluzzo, getting out of the car. They had to park in the lot in front of the villa.

Fine, that way he would walk all the way down the Corso and everyone would see that he had arrived in Noto.

"Tonight we'll try a different one, Don Melo."

Vaccalluzzo's wearing torn Dolce & Gabbana jeans, gold sneakers with Velcro straps, a lacy shirt, and the jacket of a tux.

As he walks down the street, the metallized fuchsia-pink sunset flashes off him, sparkling on the KISS ME spelled out in rhinestones on his rear end.

Maybe she was right, Signora Saretta, when she said that Viagra was having a strange effect on her husband. ("When he had that crisis at fifty, he had a thing for German girls, but it never got this bad.")

Giacomo has finished fiddling with a screwdriver on the underside of a red velvet seat in the front row.

He gets up, looks around.

Nice, this theater in Noto.

"Hey, you, what are you doing?"

Giacomo doesn't reply.

The security guards hasten over, alarmed. "What are you doing here?"

Giacomo looks at them, blinking.

He takes off the earphones of the iPod.

He sighs deeply and says, "What do you think? Cool enough?"

The security guards look at each other and begin to laugh. "Shit, we're freezing to death."

"That's because the people haven't come in yet, when they do, the temperature will be fine."

"Fuck, let's hope so, it feels like a freezer."

Giacomo puts on his earphones, picks up the wheelbarrow, and walks off.

Ottone and Ernst, seated at a bar on the Corso, are watching society arrive. Ottone is eating an almond granita, Ernst a huge strawberry ice cream. They're wearing lightweight tailored blue suits over blue shirts, and the only thing that distinguishes them are the ties, one blue and one red.

Ernst looks at his watch.

He returns to his ice cream.

Timpanaro's rented limousine parks in the center of the piazza in front of the theater.

Cagnotto is happy.

The doctor has fine-tuned his medication and with this sunset, Baroque Noto looks psychedelic. Maybe it's the lights that illuminate the downtown, maybe it's the vans in the colors of Sicilian carts selling ice cream and brioches, maybe it's the sidewalk salesmen hawking balloons, maybe it's the flourescent necklaces that begin to glow as the sun goes down in a haze of metallized fuchsia-pink.

Cagnotto gets out of the limousine and is hit by a breeze smelling of salt and lemon, of hair spray and shoe polish, of deodorant and shampoo, the smell of a small-town street festival.

A group of security agents surrounds the limousine to check them out.

Cagnotto spreads his arms while a cop pats his hips.

He takes a deep breath.

Then they escort them into the dressing rooms.

Turrisi and Pietro appear at the bar in the piazza.

Commissioner Intelisano, sitting in the bar, gets up and begins to leap around, making signs with his hands.

Turrisi looks at Pietro.

Pietro nods.

They hurry over to sit down with the commissioner.

"Mister Turrisi! What an honor. Sit down, sit down. I got box seats for you, are you happy? Yeah? Happy?"

Intelisano pulls the tickets and the invitation out of his bag.

Pirrotta and Wanda arrive at the same bar.

Pirrotta takes a look at the tables.

There's Turrisi and Pietro with that sad-sack Commissioner Intelisano.

And there's Rattalina, bending over the newspaper, not talking to anyone.

"Rattalina!" shouts Pirrotta.

From a van with megaphones on top comes an announcement. "Guests with invitations can begin to go in. Guests with invitations can begin to go in. Guests with tickets will be able to enter the theater in twenty minutes. Please wait your turn. We repeat, please wait your turn."

Pirrotta gives Turrisi a reproachful look as if to say, *See what a mess you made?*

Turrisi pretends not to see him.

The ambulance parked in front of the theater is under siege. There's a long line of commissioners, consultants, mayors, MPs, and a couple of senators with low blood pressure and panic attacks.

They're all trying to be ill enough to be hospitalized.

Despite all the security forces deployed, word has gone around that Pirrotta's men and Turrisi's men are at risk, all of them.

And Pirrotta's men and Turrisi's men in Noto—just over ten miles from Ispica—are numerous.

Pirrotta and Turrisi have let it be known that not to show up for the performance would be considered an insult and a slight, considering the protection the family is capable of providing. And if Falsaperla and Paino ended up the way they ended up, people shouldn't worry because it was none of their business.

But as they say, "He who looks out, lives long."

The commissioner for education for Ispica, planted in the job by Turrisi although he had barely finished elementary school, broke his little toe, dropping a crystal vase given to him by the best man at his wedding.

Turrisi had sent someone to get him at the Avola hospital and brought him over to Noto with his foot in plaster.

One of them tries to fake a heart attack, another pretends to talk strange as if he's had a stroke.

The nurses in the ambulance don't fall for it.

They have been hired at the Noto hospital thanks, needless to say, to Pirrotta and Turrisi.

Vaccalluzzo, invitation in hand, turns out to be the first to be security-checked at the entrance to the theater.

They've put him in the box next to the Royal Box.

He's also the first to be photographed by the paparazzi.

Then it's Turrisi's turn, arm in arm with Intelisano.

Then comes Pirrotta with Rattalina.

Cagnotto, behind the curtain, peers out.

It can't be that something strange will happen again tonight.

They're indoors, everyone who comes in is checked, there are plainclothes police all over the place, there's no way anybody can do anything.

Tonight will be the night of his success.

Finally, the attention will turn to his production, his rereading of Shakespeare, to theatrical neorealism using actors from the dialect stage, the "street actors" of the theater.

He looks around.

The empty stage.

Juliet's balcony, the exact reproduction of a Baroque balcony of the eighteenth century, gargoyles and all. The mayor of Noto had insisted on having the Baroque onstage.

Cagnotto looks around again.

He wants to savor this moment.

He alone, in his solitude.

He and himself, the author of all this.

The eyes of all Sicily on his art.

He, who has combined classical Shakespeare with a bold new interpretation of the text.

He, who as *La Voce della Sicilia* says, combines Greek theater, Pirandello, and Shakespeare!

He's about to cry.

God, how he misses Bobo.

Obviously the kid had been traumatized by the death of Falsaperla.

Of course he had wanted to run away with a ceramic tile exporter from Caltagirone, someone who could promise him a normal provincial life far from murder's violence.

Of course that's why Bobo did it.

Bobo just wanted a normal life.

Bobo, so sensitive and so enthusiastic about life!

Bobo, who had put him on Art's right path. Bobo . . . Bobo . . .

Cagnotto looks for his cell phone.

He calls him.

Ciao, you've reached Bobo's voice mail, if you want to, you can leave a message after the beep, but even if you don't want to, hey, leave one anyway, because I'm curious. Beep.

Cagnotto bites his lip.

Bobo, in that very moment, is passing through the metal detector.

Caporeale, bowlegged on account of the codpiece, walks across the stage.

He sees Cagnotto.

"I was looking for you."

"What's up?"

"Look at this." Caporeale turns around. "I've got a run in my tights."

"Oh, God, come on, let's get Lambertini to loan us some nail polish."

"Nail polish?"

"Yeah, we'll put nail polish on it so it won't run more."

"Okay, nail polish."

Cagnotto looks at Caporeale. "Hey, Caporeale, this codpiece is bigger than the one you had before."

Caporeale looks down. "Is it obvious?"

The prefects of Catania and Siracusa appear. "Okay, let's get going, they're almost all seated. Everybody's nervous inside."

The first call sounds.

Little knots of people break up and sit down.

The police are muttering into their walkie-talkies.

Ottone and Ernst knock at box number two, last row, open the door, and go in. Rattalina, who is already sitting down, jumps to his feet. "Thompson brothers?"

"Signor Rattalina?"

"Pleased to meet you!"

"The pleasure is ours! You were right, Noto is magnificent!"

Rattalina's face lights up and he spreads his arms as if to say, *And what did I tell you?*

The prefects order the second call to be sounded.

The lights go down.

Betty whispers into Carmine's ear, "And now I want to see what the fuck they do, those two faggots Turrisi and my father."

The curtain opens, silence falls in the theater.

Enter Chorus.

CHORUS Two households, both alike in dignity
　　In fair Verona where we lay our scene
　　From ancient grudge break to new mutiny
　　Where civil blood makes civil hands unclean.

　　Vaccalluzzo says to Paolino, "How long does it last?"

Then Lady Capulet explains to Juliet that she must marry Paris, Romeo changes his mind about Rosalina and decides to go for Juliet. He stakes out the balcony and discovers that Juliet is a Capulet, daughter of that slimeball Capulet.

•　•　•

"See?" says Betty at the end of the first act. "Nothing happened. Let's go to the bar, I'm nervous."

Carmine gets up, adjusts his cuff links, looks at Betty with contempt.

"Where's Turrisi sitting?"

Carmine doesn't reply, he's heading for the foyer.

"And this is the foyer. Okay? Here we can do whatever we want. You see an angle you like? At your service. You want us to close the Corso? We'll close it. Oh, and obviously the same thing all over Sicily. Everybody's working with us, the mayors, the commissioners, the caterers. Oh, and in addition to locations, we can also do casting, obviously, which is a good deal, by the way. Sicilian actors will work for nothing just to have a job, if you get my drift." Rattalina is telling the Thompson brothers why it's advantageous to make films in Sicily. "And if you decide you want to make a series, I can get you further discounts on the prices."

Avvocato Coco passes out at the feet of the Thompson brothers.

Rattalina, embarrassed, steps over Coco while a group of police officers come running.

Vaccalluzzo on the other hand, has remained in his box, looking down.

Like Pirrotta.

Who's looking at him from a box not far away.

Vaccalluzzo stares back and nods.

Pirrotta stands up and bows toward Vaccalluzzo.

Vaccalluzzo turns toward Paolino. "What the fuck does Pirrotta have in mind?"

Paolino looks toward Pirrotta.

"What's he supposed to have in mind? His funeral, no?"

Vaccalluzzo looks at Paolino. Then he hurries to the door of the box and opens it. His boys are on guard.

"Everything under control here?"

His boys nod.

Behind the scenes, everybody's pretending nothing is up, except for Lambertini, who's replaying the death of Juliet in two versions, the fake and the real one.

A British TV crew wants to get a close-up of Caporeale's codpiece. "Could you lie back on that divan, please? You know, like in the famous painting, *The Origin of the World*?"

The second call sounds.

The audience take their seats for the beginning of Act Two.

The police are tense, ready to jump.

The lights go down.

CHORUS But passion lends them power, time means, to meet
Tempering extremities with extreme sweet.

Turrisi squeezes the velvet border on the balcony of his box.

Enter Romeo.

BENVOLIO Here comes Romeo! Here comes Romeo!
MERCUTIO (*Looking toward the public, half squatting, with a screwing motion thrusts up his arm and then follows through with his whole body, rising off the stage in a little hop.*)
Nay, I am the very *pink* of courtesy.
ROMEO (*Covering his crotch with both hands, then spreading them out slowly as if something were swelling in his undershorts*)
Pink in the sense of something that flowers? That explodes with the joy of springtime? Or pink like something that pricks? That

swells and stands up? Stands up like a turret? Pointed like a mountaintop? (*He joins the five fingers of his right hand and thrusts it upward.*) Or are you not speaking of an uphill struggle through nettlesome bushes?

Pause.

MERCUTIO (*Bouncing on his knees while he moves his arm back and forward like a pendulum, a pendulum that culminates in a finger pointing toward* ROMEO)
Thou hast most kindly hit it.
ROMEO (*Brief pause while he appears, although no one can be sure, to wink at the audience, then moves his arms in a circle and positions his hands once again on his crotch, which he clutches meaningfully*)
You want to hear my reply? It's this great, big, pointed, sweet-smelling, flowering explosion of my great, big, hotheaded, crazy dick.

Caporeale and Cosentino turn toward the audience while the mortar under Chartered Accountant Intelisano's rear end begins to ignite.

It all happens in an instant.

Chartered Accountant Intelisano lifts off from the pit while Caporeale and Cosentino follow him with their eyes.

Backstage, Lambertini is listening,
She's waiting for the next line.
She's looking at Cagnotto.
The pause goes on longer than necessary.
Lambertini yells, "Fuck, no—not again!"

•   •   •

Special Agent Cavallaro runs up onstage to prevent panic. "Stay in your seats! Lights up! Lights up!"

No need for Cavallaro to say so, the lights are already coming up.

The hall sits immobile, gazing up.

Down at the feet of Special Agent Cavallaro, with a sound of bones crunching, falls Rattalina's body.

The audience looks down toward the stage.

Chartered Accountant Intelisano descends from the plaster angels on the ceiling and comes down on top of Commendatore Calì, president of the local Rotary Club.

CHAPTER EIGHTEEN

It's a Beautiful Day and Villa Wanda Is Full of Cops

It's a beautiful day and Villa Wanda is full of cops.

Turi Pirrotta is very nervous.

Wanda even more so.

Cops coming out of every room, walking all over the place, hustling around.

To say that Vaccalluzzo was pissed off was to seriously understate the matter.

First he had leaned over to see if he had seen right.

He had seen right.

Then, with his boys deployed around him, he had tried to leave, but they had stopped him and identified him. "But if you know very well who I am . . ." he had said to the police commissioner of Siracusa.

The police commissioner had no desire to play the fool.

Vaccalluzzo had raced down the Corso talking on his secure cell phone. "They've all gone nuts here. Face it, they're going to send in the army again."

He got to his car and that dickhead Corrado, his driver, wasn't there.

The boys had pulled their guns.

Corrado appeared, running. "Sorry, Don Melo, there was a tourist who collapsed because of the heat."

"Heat! Let's get out of here!"

They got in the car, Corrado turned on the engine, and Don Melo's Lexus went *ka-pow.*

The crime scene investigation squad said that the car blew up in that unusual way because it was armored. The armored parts remained more or less whole, and the Lexus—so said the crime scene investigation squad without the least sense of humor (and without any respect for Chartered Accountant Intelisano)—had "acted like a mortar." Vaccalluzzo's gold left sneaker with his foot inside was found in a tree three hundred yards away, by a man whose kid had been frightened by the bang and had let go of his balloon, which got stuck in the branches.

Nobody could understand why Rattalina had chosen that particular moment to commit suicide. Zerbino had written that probably a man of the theater like Rattalina had been devastated by the havoc wrought on Shakespeare. Half of Sicily, the half that knew Rattalina, thought that was hilarious.

He had been in the box with the Thompson brothers, he had been taking them around Sicily because they wanted to shoot some movies on the island with the support of the Film Commission, and all of a sudden, said the Thompson brothers, he had looked at them with a crazy look and leaped onto the stage. Ernst, who was telling the reporters, didn't mention that Ottone, just to be sure, had dislocated his neck before he tossed him over.

And he did well, because you can never be too sure in these matters. Intelisano, despite the theatrical nature of his farewell, had broken just about everything there was to break, but he hadn't croaked. While Commendatore Calì, the shock alone had finished him off.

Giacomo had said that the Imposimato brothers were to blame, that he had been specific about the diameter of the mortar and the quantity of explosive. The Imposimato brothers had blamed Giacomo, who had done his calculations on the computer, and with this fucking technology they were all going crazy, and if next time they wanted a job well done they had better rely on artisanal expertise.

Giacomo wanted to be paid in full for the job because in any case someone had been taken out, Commendatore Calì, even if—so he told Turrisi, who was haggling over the price—"on the rebound."

The prefects had resigned, officially because they hadn't been able to keep order, unofficially because they had started to get really freaked.

The police and the carabinieri had held a joint press conference, very mysterious, in which they had hinted that the secret services were involved.

Obviously, all eyes were on Pirrotta and Turrisi.

Today, Betty is genuinely freaked.

She's crawled under the bed and doesn't want to come out, although Carmine is there trying to persuade her. "Not in prison, no!" she screams while Carmine tries to reassure a carabinieri sergeant with his eyes.

In the garden, two officers are trailing Turrisi.

One of them says to him, "Don't get any ideas, now, if you try to escape we'll catch you and bring you back."

The two officers start laughing.

Turrisi gives them a dirty look.

Pietro, wearing his loudest Elvis outfit, silvery fringe on the jacket sleeves and his white boots with the mirror studs, is crying behind his Ray·Bans, tears are rolling down the teardrop lenses.

Pirrotta, dressed to the hilt, sitting on the bed, stares at his shoes.

Wanda, biting her lip, approaches him and pats his head.

Pirrotta looks at her with teary eyes. "I'm going."

"Yes."

The Contessa, seated in the front row, is fanning herself.

Gnazia and Quattrocchi too are already seated. Gnazia's still wearing mourning.

Quattrocchi warns her, "Gnazia, you know you're my best friend, but don't get any funny ideas. When Betty throws the bouquet, see, I'm going to snatch it like I was a rugby champion, and I'm not afraid of anyone, friend or foe."

The Contessa turns and, continuing to fan, says, "Think it's so easy, my dear?"

Carmine, on his knees, is smiling as he tries to get Betty to come out from under the bed. "Darling, marriage is not *prison*."

The officer says to Turrisi, "Making you wait, huh? My advice to you, however, is don't try to escape."

Pietro puts a hand to his mouth.

Betty had wanted a *garden* wedding, like they do in American movies.

The priest wouldn't hear of it, and so Pirrotta and Turrisi had to set up a fund for Mafia widows, and Pirrotta had to hustle to build a little chapel in the garden and have it consecrated.

Caporeale is already dressed in tights and codpiece.

Pirrotta and Turrisi have decided to offer the guests a private performance of *Romeo and Juliet.*

That's why there are so many cops.

They wanted to send a signal that the gang war was over. A trouble-free performance of *Romeo and Juliet* seemed like the best thing.

The officer says to Turrisi, "I'm sure nothing's going to happen today, I'm sure your wedding won't be spoiled, but tell me, how is it that you thought of a theatrical show on this occasion?"

Turrisi looks at the officer. He's about to say something, then he turns to Pietro and asks, "Did you take care of the rings?"

Pirrotta hurries by, signaling to Turrisi.

"I'll be right back," he says.

An Arab-style tent mounted in the garden flaps lightly in the breeze. Individuals wearing earpieces and total black Armani stand around it, their legs apart.

Pirrotta and Turrisi go in, buttoning their jackets.

Inside, in a little sitting area with wicker furniture, is Jacobbo Maretta. Virtude's main man. The Scarlet Pimpernel. The fugitive from justice that nobody knows if he really exists.

He exists and he's wearing white linen. Gold eyeglass frames, dark brown lenses, hair dyed dead black, like his mustache. They make him feel like Charles Bronson.

Next to the furniture, a brazier exudes a smell of incense.

The air-conditioning is turned up to the max.

Pirrotta and Turrisi sit down in the wicker chairs.

On the table, everything a man could want to eat or drink.

"I thank you for the honor you have paid me, inviting me on this day when you celebrate old-fashioned family values," says Maretta.

Pirrotta and Turrisi look at each other.

"Because you know, don't you," adds Maretta, pouring himself a J&B, "that peace in the family is all-important. You know how it is, no? The neighbors talk, people don't mind their own fucking business, and so when you have to disagree in the family, you have to disagree discreetly. That's how my grandmother Michela used to say, discreetly." Maretta looks at Pirrotta and Turrisi.

Pirrotta and Turrisi nod.

"Because if not, then it's better to get divorced. Am I right?"

"Right you are!" says Pirrotta.

Turrisi merely nods.

"Exactly. My grandmother was a true Catholic. However, for her, silence was golden. Shit, she was like the thing, the Indian chief, what was his name? Saskatchewan? No, no, Sitting Bull. "If there has to be nastiness in the family, divorce is better."

"Let's not speak of divorce on this happy day. We couldn't agree more."

Maretta looks at his whiskey. "You must apologize on my behalf to the police outside if I don't go out, but you know how it is, no? What a life I lead! It's got to the point where the sunlight gets to me. I've become, how do you say, *photophobic*. So I can't go out."

"Please don't worry," exclaims Pirrotta.

Maretta looks at him. "I'm not worrying, I'm saying it to be polite. Alfio!" Maretta turns toward Turrisi. "What the fuck happened in Noto?"

Turrisi looks at Pirrotta.

Pirrotta nods.

Maretta has turned to the younger of the two to get an explanation. That's a good sign.

Turrisi lowers his eyes. "Your Honor must excuse us if we didn't contact you sooner, but we didn't think they would go so far."

Maretta nods. He takes a cube of ice from the bucket, puts it in his glass, and moves his head, indicating he should continue.

"We didn't think that Vaccalluzzo, after having taken out Falsaperla on my side and Paino from my future father-in-law, would go and get involved in this fuckup in Noto. We thought he'd remain silent, follow orders, and that we could come to an agreement."

Maretta raises his voice. "What are you talking about? I don't understand fuck-all!"

Turrisi looks at Pirrotta.

Pirrotta makes a sign with his head that he shouldn't worry.

Turrisi understands. Maybe he shouldn't speak so explicitly.

"We're becoming a family," says Turrisi, "me with Signor Pirrotta and Signor Pirrotta with me."

Maretta makes a face that says, *Wow, how interesting, this is a wedding, so what do you expect?*

"And in the family, it's right that one person should give a hand to another."

Maretta is forced to nod agreement.

"So when we saw that what was happening was happening, we thought we should do something about it immediately. Do you like the Lexus as a car? I have to say I don't care much for that car. There was a guy I knew who had an armored one, but I didn't care for it."

"The Lexus," says Pirrotta.

Turrisi nods.

Maretta takes off his sunglasses. "Now, to me, I always thought the Lexus was a nice, quiet car."

"No, sir!" exclaims Turrisi. "Actually, it's extremely noisy."

Maretta scratches behind one ear. He nods to himself. "And who was he, this fellow you knew who had the Lexus?"

Turrisi looks at Pirrotta.

Pirrotta nods.

"He was called Vaccalluzzo," says Turrisi.

Maretta looks at Turrisi, then he looks at Pirrotta. He thinks, swirling the ice in his glass. Then finally he says, "Fine. This Vaccalluzzo, I don't know him. If you tell me the Lexus is a noisy car, that's fine. By the way, how is this fellow with the Lexus?"

"Not so good," says Pirrotta.

"Very sorry to hear that," says Maretta. "But what can I do? Can I do anything? Any way I can be of help?"

Pirrotta goes *no* with his head.

Maretta's face is pained. "Everyone suffers his own setbacks, what can I say? As the saying goes, when the Pope dies, they elect a new one. You two are becoming part of the same family, right?"

Pirrotta and Turrisi nod.

"And you're not people who go out and besmirch the family, right?"

"You can bet on that," says Pirrotta.

Maretta smiles. "What, now I'm not going to trust Riddu?"

Pirrotta lowers his eyes.

"May this marriage be blessed by the Lord," says Maretta. "By the way, I brought a little something for the families." Maretta twists around on the wicker sofa, trying to grab his wallet.

He pulls two *santini* out of the wallet. Two little pictures of Jesus' Sacred Heart. "It's only a little something. I hope I don't offend you, but you know how it is, it's all that I can do with the taxes, the internal revenue."

Pirrotta and Turrisi join hands.

"One for the Pirrotta family, one for the Turrisi family."

Pirrotta unhooks the band of his Rolex and cuts a finger with the buckle.

"Shit, I cut myself," says Pirrotta.

"Let me see," says Turrisi, "Ow, I cut myself too."

"Do take care," says Maretta.

Pirrotta gets to his feet and walks over to the brazier. What's that, the smell of lemon?

Maretta, pretending not to watch, smiles.

Pirrotta leans over to smell and tosses the *santini* into the brazier.

Maretta gets up. "So what else do I have to say to you? Peace and prosperity."

Pirrotta and Turrisi exit the tent.

"I'm going to see what the bride has to say," says Pirrotta.

"Will you look at that codpiece?" says Quattrocchi to Gnazia, elbowing her.

Gnazia nods, making a face of congratulations.

"If I get that bouquet . . ."—Quattrocchi joins the fingertips of her right hand and brings the hand to her mouth—"I'm going to gobble it all up."

Wanda, a hand on her breast, runs out in the garden to spread the word. "She's decided, she's decided, hurry, take your places before she reconsiders, hurry."

Pirrotta looks at himself in the mirror.

Fuck, he's getting old.

That white, white hair, the dentures, and this daughter of his who's getting married.

Pirrotta grabs the bottle of cologne and sprays it all around, around, to keep himself from being overcome with emotion.

Then he goes to his daughter's room.

He knocks on the door.

Betty opens, her eyes downcast.

Six little pageboys are twisted up in a six-yard-long veil of genuine nineteenth century lace, snatched up at a bargain price from the Contessa.

Betty adjusts her dress, bustier in ecru-colored Sicilian tulle, embroidered with Sciacca coral.

"Let's go, Pietro," says Turrisi. And then, on a lighter note, "Take it easy, this is the only time I'll ever want you to be a witness to anything!"

Carmine races to sit beside Cagnotto.

He elbows him.

He smiles.

"Hey, you did it!" says Cagnotto.

Carmine crosses his legs, puts an elbow on his knee, his chin in hand, raises an eyebrow, and gives Cagnotto a look that, hey, we really can't tell you what he was thinking.

"Yes," says Carmine. "Yes."

EPILOGUE

Enter Chorus.

CHORUS Isn't there always something strange about the interval between the acts, whether it's at a play or an opera, isn't there always a distance, a gap, between what's happening on the stage and in the foyer? Can it be that these people are really improved by going to the theater? What's the problem? *Is* there a problem?

In any case, the actors bow and pay their respects, they have put blood and sweat into it, and fiction and falsehoods and tricks and codpieces, to represent life and make it sound true.

Or false, as only life can be.

The curtain falls.

In the distance, music.

CHORUS The chorus doesn't care about what's center stage, but what surpasses. Isn't there always a distance, a gap between what's happening on the stage and in the foyer? We are such stuff as dreams are made on, and not one hair was plucked from those you heard scream, from those you saw shipwrecked.

Do you think for that, the story we have told is any less true?

As tradition would have it, you are invited to the last ball, it's up to you to decide whether, limping like us, you want to take part, or head for the foyer. Here we are paid to dance, the dead and the living together, as once they did in the days of Elizabeth. *God save the Queen.*

One moment, please.

ROMEO Pardon, good Mercutio, my business was great and in such a case as mine a man may strain courtesy.

MERCUTIO That's as much as to say, such a case as yours constrains a man to bow in the hams.

ROMEO (*Bending over at the waist*) Meaning, to curtsy.

MERCUTIO (*Looking at* ROMEO'*s backside*) Thou hast most kindly hit it.

ROMEO (*Arching his kidneys*) A most courteous exposition.

MERCUTIO Nay, I am the very *pink* of courtesy.

ROMEO Pink for flower.

MERCUTIO (*Miming with his hands something that swells*) Right.

Pause.

Caporeale and Cosentino look at the audience.
They turn toward the bride and groom.
Both bend in a courteous bow, as if to dedicate the line.
Then they resume their places.
Caporeale bounces on his knees, rocking the codpiece back and forth.
He waves his elbows as if he wants to take off.
He jumps up.
He lands, flapping the codpiece with both hands.

ROMEO Why, then is my pump well-flower'd!

Pause.

Lambertini is listening.

It's silent in the garden.

The priest coughs.

Caporeale looks at Cosentino.
    Cosentino goes no *with his head.*
    Caporeale goes yes, yes *with his head.*

Cagnotto clasps his hands.
    He looks at Carmine.
    He smiles, content.

Cosentino makes a face that says, Oh, all right.
    Cosentino turns around.
    He bends over at the waist.
    Caporeale comes forward with the codpiece and smiles at the audience.

MERCUTIO (*Bent over at the waist*) Sure wit, follow me this jest now
    till thou hast worn out thy pump!

· · ·

The audience applauds.

Carmine smiles.

Cagnotto, putting his clasped hands under his chin, makes a face as if to say, *Isn't this great?*

Carmine lays an arm around his shoulder, puts his mouth up close to his ear, and whispers, "Bravo. Bravo."

And then?

Well, then the speakers begin to blast out a crescendo of techno with "Push the Button," and, to the dance beat of the Chemical Brothers, we see Falsaperla begin to do the tarantella with Gnazia and his wife, a bopping Paino bring the Contessa onto the floor, Intelisano throwing off his plaster as Commedatore Calì looks on smiling, Lambertini getting down with Vaccalluzzo and Rattalina, Caporeale throwing himself into a belly dance around a preening Quattrocchi, Bobo at work with the Baronessa, and yes, Betty, a tender look on her face, patting the head of one of her pages.

CHORUS Do you think for that, the story we have told is any less
    true?

THE END